The

GREAT

& the SMALL

Written and Illustrated by

A. T BALSARA

The
GREAT
& the SMALL

CDP

Published by Common Deer Press.

Copyright © 2017 A. T. Balsara

Published in 2017 by Common Deer Press
London, Ontario, Canada
ellie@commondeerpress.com

This book is a work of fiction. Names, characters, places, and incidents are either the product of the author's imagination or are used fictitiously.

Library and Archives Canada Cataloguing in Publication
Balsara, A. T.—First edition.
The Great & the Small / A. T. Balsara
ISBN: 978-1-988761-10-7 (paperback)
ISBN: 978-1-988761-12-1 (hardcover)
ISBN: 978-1-988761-11-4 (e-book)

Cover Image and all Illustrations: © A. T. Balsara with the exception of those found on pages 105, 118, and 192. More information on these images can be found on page 287.

Book Design: Ellie Sipila www.movetothewrite.com

Printed in the United States of America

www.commondeerpress.com

To those who whispered in my ear, on that day so long ago, whose lives planted the seed for this story...

I hope I have kept my promise.

A. T. B.

PART ONE

PROLOGUE

"And now disaster is at hand…"

Gabriele de' Mussis, lawyer, Italy, 1348

The rat dug a burrow in the most remote area of the Lower Tunnels that she could find. She dug feverishly, using tooth and claw, feeling as she did that eyes watched her from behind. Her baby was curled up, asleep—a blessing. Expecting at every moment to feel long, curved teeth sink into her shoulder, she shuddered, making her fur ripple up and down her back. Finally done, she climbed inside with her wisp-thin pup, pulling him close. Her tooth marks grooved the damp earthen chamber; dirt clung to her claws and trembled on the ends of her whiskers. The ever-present stink of the Lowers hovered in the air like a brown fog, but she didn't care. Maybe here, at the end of nowhere, she and her baby could be safe.

The mother's name was Nia.

She let out a breath that she hadn't realized she'd been holding. Pulling her pup tight, Nia licked his head, his ears, his tiny pink paws.

The Great & the Small

"Pip," she murmured. She'd named him Pip because he was as tiny as a seed. Seeds can grow into strong trees. "My sweet Pip," she whispered in his ear.

Directly over her head, through thirty feet of dirt and rusting pipes, in the weak December sun, the harbour city's popular market was bustling with people looking for last minute presents. Middle-Gate Market was festive with its potted evergreen trees and strands of blinking coloured lights. Shiny red balls trembled on the boughs of the tinsel-dressed pines as salt air gusted up the hill from the sea below and rattled the lights against the rafters where they were strung.

Watching over all of this, under the faux Gothic clock, stood Middle-Gate's most famous tourist attraction: a brass statue modeled after the gargoyles of Paris's Notre Dame cathedral. The monster stood on guard, a five-foot winged beast that stood meekly by while tourists thronged around it, snapped selfies, and rubbed the creature's flared nostrils for luck.

That was the side of the market the tourists saw and the locals loved. They had no idea of the other side, the one that lay below. A distinct world, with its own ways, its own rules: a colony of rats.

Tunnels wound underneath the hill, tooth-carved thoroughfares, veiled from the eyes of humans. There were tunnels high up and tunnels below that snaked deep into the hill's belly.

The Uppers were dug alongside the city's swanky cafés and eateries, and food was never far away. But lower down the hill, below the heart of the market, it was different. Tangles of narrow tunnels limped through broken pipes, leaking sewers, and sodden earth, connecting scores of foul smelling, crumbling burrows.

No rat lived in the Lowers by choice. Except one, that is.

Nia had been staring, listening, for many beats of her heart. Nothing. Her son lay in the warm crook of her belly, snoring softly.

Nia's eyelids drifted closed. She shook them open. But the warmth of Pip against her, his sweet, newborn smell, made her sleepy. Her eyelids wavered. So sleepy…

Shhooosh.

Her eyes flew open.

A brush of sound came from the outside tunnel. Nia pushed her pup down and stood over him, scanning the air with her nose. Pip squirmed under her with a squeak of protest.

"Shh!" Nia lowered herself and pulled him close, hardly daring to breathe. Her abandoned burrow in the Uppers still held the bodies of her other pups. They lay scattered around like dried leaves. On each of their necks a single bite mark, a red half-moon. She had not been able to save them, but here, now, there was still hope.

She kept her eyes on Pip.

"Nia?" A voice broke the stillness.

She gasped and fumbled to hide Pip beneath her. "Go away!" she cried. Tears bunched behind her eyes, threatening to spring.

A shadow filled the entrance hole. "You're not still angry, are you? I had no choice!"

"No choice?" Nia laughed bitterly. "Yes, poor you. Poor *helpless* you!"

As she spoke, Pip wriggled out from under her. He sniffed the air like a wobbly snake. She grabbed him and pushed him back down. But it was too late.

The shadow hissed. "You hid one from me? You deceitful, conniving—"

"You can't have Pip!" said Nia through gritted teeth. Tears dripped onto Pip's head and darkened his fur like a bloom of blood. "I will not let you!"

The voice roared with laughter. "You won't *let* me? *You* have no choice."

"No!" she screamed. Nia coiled her back legs and leaped, claws extended, teeth bared. The figure met her mid-air. She dug her claws into his back and tore at his thick, ropy neck with her teeth but was flung against the wall. Pain shot through her. "Run, Pip!" she screamed, even though her pup was too young to understand.

The voice laughed. "Yes, Pip. Run."

They rolled over and over, ripping, scratching, biting. Shrieks echoed off the wall. There was scuffling, a squeal.

And then…silence.

Pip sniffed the air, his small, shell-like ears turning toward the sound. He was cold. Where was she, the one who was warm and smelled like milk? He nosed impatiently through the nesting and plopped out onto the dirt. He found her, and nuzzled against her paw, but it flopped back down. Warm, sticky fluid flowed from her and he wrinkled his nose and sneezed. He poked her again. *Wake up! Wake up!*

"Pip." The voice behind him made him jerk his head around. Sharp teeth gripped his hind paw, yanked him across the floor. Pip squealed and scratched, but the cruel teeth bit through.

His tiny paw burst with pain, and he fell into darkness.

CHAPTER·ONE

"A staggering number of people died…
In many towns only two people out of twenty survived."

Jean de Venette, Carmelite friar, 1359–60

"This way!" shouted Fin, as he scuttled up the column. Even with his bad paw he could outrun Scratch. He popped out on a rooftop that overlooked the market.

Scratch laboured up, panting. "Not…fair…Fin! Daylight… no good…can't see! You know I can't see!" Reaching the top, he stepped into the sun next to Fin. Scratch squinted at Fin accusingly. His blood-red eyes, almost blind in the daylight, watered in the hot sun, streaming down his wisp-white fur. Scratch was the only rat Fin had seen besides himself who wasn't brown or black, but he was different even from Scratch. Fin had a ridiculous cape of grey fur that started on his head and continued down his back, and two large ears that stuck out. To make matters worse, he was as scrawny as a pup.

Scratch sniffed the air and froze mid-sniff. "We're at the market? I said I didn't want to go! It's not allowed, Fin! Not allowed!"

The Great & the Small

"Stop worrying," said Fin. "Come on!" He ran headlong down the column.

The market was busy, swarming with two-legs. Their noisy machines inched along the roadway next to the fruit stands, mixing exhaust with the smell of ripe cherries, strawberries, apricots, and other two-leg things.

Fin plunged through the sea of legs, which parted before him, shrieks ripping the air. Skirting around the bronze statue that looked like a giant rat with wings, he whooped and hollered. "Yeah! You run! You'd better run from *Mister* Fin!"

Ahead, an old two-leg sat on a bench, its withered claws resting on a curved stick. Fin veered for it and sprang onto its lap. It screamed, flapping its claws at Fin until it teetered sideways and fell off the bench.

Fin streaked under a market stall. Peering from under the overhang of a plastic tablecloth, he smiled, panting as he watched two-legs gather around the wrinkly old one.

Fin had caused that trouble. He, himself. Fin. The so-called puny nephew of the Beloved Chairman. Fin had heard other Tunnel Rats murmur behind his back, "The poor Chairman! Nephew looks like a mouse!" If only he could tell his uncle about this, tell everyone, but he didn't dare.

What he was doing was against Tunnel Law.

Tunnel Law was clear: NO TUNNEL-RAT SHALL GO INTO TWO-LEG TERRITORY UNTIL COVER OF NIGHT. Fin's uncle, the Tunnel's Beloved Chairman, the one called "Papa" by every loyal Tunnel Rat, was the one who had *made* the law.

Back on the rooftop, Scratch flicked his ears and wagged his nose from side to side, his red eyes bulging with terror. Calling ultrasonically to Fin in a voice too high for the two-legs to hear, he cried, *"Come back! If Papa finds out, the ARM will collect us. No, not us. I'll be the one who's collected! Me! That's who! They won't collect the Chairman's nephew."*

Fin snorted. The ARM protected the Tunnels. Papa said so. He called to Scratch, *"I told you, there* are *no collect—"*

"Come back here right now! Right now, Fin! Fin? Do you hear me? Fiiiinnn!"

Fin shook his ears to stop their ringing. "Next time I'll come alone," he muttered. With Scratch still screeching in the background, Fin scanned the air with quivering nostrils, his nose high.

The smell of fish, old, stinking, putrid, curled up before him. Its scent-trail shimmered like a winding silver pathway, leading him further into the market. He followed it. He ducked in and out of shadows and under stalls. The silver wisp drew him forward, leading him, until it circled over one fish-laden stall. No, not over it, *under.* The fish on top were fresh; the wisp snaked underneath the table. Whatever it was waited for him below. And it was guarded by an enormous two-leg.

The two-leg patrolled the fish stall, walking back and forth, its rubber boots thudding against the pavement. Something flashed metallic in its fist. Fin knew the ugly two-leg couldn't see him where he hid, but even so his heart pounded in his ears. The silver trail danced and wove under the table, tempting him. But it was such a big two-leg.

He watched as another two-leg, this one much smaller, approached. The huge one turned, making barking, gibberish sounds with its mouth, its attention away from the ground. Fin darted from his hiding place and scooted under the table.

He slipped behind the table leg and froze, listening, sniffing. The two-leg was still jabbering.

It was dark and cool underneath the table, and the tile floor was damp. The silver scent-trail of old fish was thick here, so thick Fin could almost taste it. It hovered over a half-open box in the corner.

Fin took one hesitant step, his ears swivelling, his nose sniffing. Nothing. He took another step and then leaped, landing on one of the closed flaps of the box. It sagged under his weight, and he slid down, trying to get a claw-hold as the flap lowered. A mountain of fish heads rose up to meet him, but glinting amongst them, the gleam of metal. A trap!

Fin twisted wildly but crashed into the pile of fish heads, which toppled toward the yawning jaws of the trap. *Tchik!* The jaws crushed a fish head, squirting Fin with slime. He clawed frantically against the box flap, but it was wet and heavy. He lost his hold and fell back onto the fish.

"*Scratch!*" he screamed. "*Help me!*"

Two-leg voices shouted gibberish.

The floor shook. *THUNK-THUNK-THUNK-THUNK…* The big one was coming!

Scratch called, faint and far away. "*Fin? Oh no! Oh no! Fiiinnnn!*"

Fin hunched, quaking in the corner of the box. Fish heads cascaded onto him as the box flaps were torn back. The two-leg was monstrous. It spied Fin, and its mouth gaped open in a roar, teeth bared. Its eyes bulged, red-veined and popping. It swung its arm down hard. Fin dived to one side. A knife whooshed over his head.

Again, the knife swung down. Fin leaped out of the box, onto the two-leg's bare arm. He vaulted off, soaring through the air, and landed on the pavement. His lame paw bent under his weight. He fell, sprawling.

The two-leg stood over him. Brought its boot crashing down. Fin jumped to one side. Too late. Pain shot through Fin's curled paw. He squealed, tried to run, but his foot was smashed into the pavement. The two-leg raised its boot again. Fin curled close to the ground, waiting for the final blow, when a high-pitched scream flattened his ears. Jabberings of two-leg voices rose, shouting, screaming. Tree-trunk legs swarmed around him.

Digging in his claws, Fin yanked his glued foot off the pavement. Pain shot up his leg. He ran on three paws. Behind him, he heard—or rather, he *felt*—the thunder of boots. The two-leg was coming after him.

Fin leaped for the column. He climbed, dragging his crushed leg behind him.

Scratch screamed from the roof, "*The two-leg is close! Hurry! Hurry, Fin!*"

The Great & the Small

A boot whizzed by Fin's ear. It bounced against the column. A second boot followed. Fin kept climbing. When he reached the top where Scratch waited, he collapsed.

"Thank the Old Ones you survived!" said Scratch. "But what will our Beloved Chairman say? Oh, what *will* he say?"

Fin's eyes rolled back in his head, and he fainted.

CHAPTER TWO·

"Gratitude is a dog's disease."

Josef Stalin

The market was crazy, even for a Saturday, but it was still one of Ananda Blake's favourite places to be. She and her family had only lived in the city for four months after moving yet again for her dad's work. Despite her frustration at having been uprooted for the millionth time, there was a life to this particular place that delighted her, even its underbelly—the smell of urine in the alleys, the cigarette-strewn gutters, and the night dwellers who came out, pale and blinking into the sunshine, eyes bloodshot, hair uncombed, bristling with piercings like edgy porcupines. Middle-Gate Market: a place where anything was possible.

Ananda waited by the newsstand while her father, Tom, browsed through the magazines and papers. Leaning against the railing, she watched a group of tourists pass. They spoke in what sounded like random noises. But their smiles she could understand. And the wonder in their eyes as they looked around this new and foreign place.

The Great & the Small

Where had they come from? What were their stories? That was one good thing about moving so much. It made Ananda appreciate other cultures. It was the only good thing, though.

Her dad was still nose-deep in magazines, so Ananda passed the time by making up histories about the people who filtered by. One woman was dressed in a hot pink draping of material with a band of gold on its edges that beautifully framed her dark skin. She looked to be of Indian heritage, like Ananda's mom. Ananda took a mental snapshot. She'd try to recreate the woman with pastels on paper when she got home.

Her stomach growled. She glanced over at her dad. Tom was bent over a newspaper, his thick eyebrows drawn together.

"Dad, can we go now? Dad?"

He looked up, blinking. "Oh. Ready?"

She rolled her eyes heavenward like one of the martyred saints. "Uh, yeah. I've been waiting for you! I'm hungry."

"Okay, okay! Let's just take a quick look at the bookstore downstairs." He paid for his paper, tucked it under his arm, and veered into the stream of people. Ananda sighed, then waded after him.

"I'm gonna tell Mom that you're going to the bookstore again!" she called.

"No you're not," he called back.

They passed near a bakery stall. The irresistible aroma of baking bread made Ananda's stomach gurgle. As she trudged after her dad, her eyes lingered on the trays of cinnamon rolls slathered with icing.

They walked down a broad set of wooden stairs, grooved by the generations who'd walked down before them, and entered the shop almost as if they were entering a church. Books were stacked as high as Ananda's head. It was quiet in here, with that fusty smell particular to used bookshops. Ananda breathed in and smiled, tucking her hair behind her ear.

This was one of those little secrets between Ananda and her dad; they'd often sneak more books into the house even though Ananda's mother, Perrin, had pronounced a moratorium on buying books until they'd read the ones they already had at home, waiting to be unpacked. Boxes of books followed them from move to move like old friends. But Ananda's mother was a writer; Perrin couldn't resist a good book any more than her daughter or her husband could.

Books were one of the few things Ananda and her dad could talk about anymore. She certainly couldn't talk to him about his job—at least not without causing the start of World War III.

Humming tunelessly, Ananda slowly walked down each aisle, her fingers bumping along the book spines. In the "Art books, Used" section, her fingers stopped on *Sketch What You See*. She pulled it out of the leaning stack and read the back:

Learn to see things as they actually are, not how you think they are.

"Did you find something?" asked Tom, coming up behind her.

Ananda held out the book.

He read the back, nodded, then held out a thick paperback. "I found this."

The Great & the Small

Ananda took it. A wavy-haired man smiled out from the cover, gazing into the distance as if he were seeing heaven itself. "Who is he?"

"Josef Stalin. One of the biggest mass-murderers in history. Want to borrow it?"

Good non-fiction was irresistible to her, like candy to a child. "Of course!" she said.

"I thought so. Just don't tell your mom!"

Ananda laughed. She widened her eyes and mimed locking her lips together and pocketing the key.

Having bought the books, Tom dug in his pocket and pulled out a handwritten list. "I almost forgot why we came here in the first place! Your mother would not be impressed if I forgot the things on her list." They waded back into the sea of people and grabbed fresh cinnamon rolls from the bakery, which they ate as they wandered slowly in the direction of the main market. It was a beautiful day; the sun was shining, slanting through the clouds like a Michelangelo painting. Off to the side, a street musician sawed away at an old battered guitar while his partner played an antique washboard with thimbles on her fingers. For a moment, everything was perfect.

As they moved past the market's main entrance near the bronze gargoyle, there was some kind of disturbance. There was always a crowd there, but this was different. An old man was being pulled up from the ground, his cane handed to him. Many hands helped him onto a nearby bench.

Ananda and Tom stopped near an idling van where buckets of daisies, roses, and dahlias were being unloaded. The smell of fumes mixed with the fragrance of flowers. *Typical Middle-Gate*, thought Ananda. *Sweet with the sour.*

Tom squinted at the list. "Could your mom write any smaller? Let's see…bread, eggs, cheese—"

A loud crash boomed from the fish stalls, making them both jump.

A huge man wearing rubber boots and a plastic apron came charging down the aisle. "You filthy piece of… I'm gonna get you!" He was focused on something on the ground and didn't seem to notice that he was charging straight at them.

Ananda's father braced himself, toothpick though he was, in front of her. But the fishmonger barrelled past, following a streak of white and grey. A mouse! The man raised his boot, slammed it down on the mouse.

Ananda gasped. So did others in the crowd. The mouse squirmed in pain, its back paw crushed. A dark splotch of blood bloomed on the pavement.

The man lifted his boot again.

Everything seemed to slow down for Ananda. "Stop!" she roared. She pushed by her dad and jumped between the man and the mouse. Blood pounded in her ears and her heart thrummed. She held up her hands to block him and shouted, "Leave it the Hell alone!"

The man stumbled backward, tripping over his own enormous boot. He pulled himself up to his full height and glowered down at her. His face was as red as boiled lobster, and a sheen of sweat glistened on his fat upper lip and quivering jowls. He sneered.

"What's your problem, you stupid kid?" he snarled.

Ananda was too pumped with adrenaline to be cowed by this mastodon. She rose to her full five-foot-one-inch height and glared up at the giant. "I'm not the troublemaker here, you bloody, murderous jerk! What gives you the right to hurt an innocent animal?"

"Are you crazy?" the guy sputtered.

The Great & the Small

Ananda wanted to sink her fist into his fat ham of a face. "No, *you're* crazy! Torturing an innocent mouse who hasn't done you any harm—ouch!" She was suddenly yanked to one side.

Her skinny father, with his thick glasses and mop of dark brown hair, stepped forward, putting himself between her and the fish-selling Goliath. Tom pushed his glasses up his nose. "Let's all just calm down…"

Giant Fish-Guy began ranting, waving his meaty hands, drops of sweat flying off him like a dog shaking itself after a dip in the pond. Tom's voice began to rise.

Leaving her dad to it, Ananda swooped around and crouched on the ground before the mouse. It was white with grey markings. It looked like it had a little cape. It was still moving, its long, pink tail flickering like a groggy snake.

"Come on, little guy," whispered Ananda. "You've got to get up now."

The small creature seemed to know it had been given a reprieve. It picked itself up, slowly peeled its crushed back paw from the pavement, gave itself a small shake, and lolloped away, holding its crushed paw to its belly. It made it past the gargoyle statue. It had just leaped onto the column when Fish-Guy caught sight of it. He swore and lumbered after it.

"Leave it alone!" screamed Ananda. She went to run after him but was stopped by an iron grip on her arm. "Stop him, somebody!" she shrieked.

By now, the entire market had stopped to gawk. The mouse was halfway up the column. Cursing, Fish-Guy hopped on one foot and ripped off a boot. He threw it. The boot bounced off the column.

The mouse kept climbing.

Fish-Guy threw the other boot. Missed!

Ananda cheered as the mouse slid over the rooftop. "Yes! The mouse got away!" She jumped up and down, clapping, and swung around. Dozens of people were staring, jaws flapped open. She froze. In the crowd she saw one of the guys from her school. He looked like Ed the Hyena from *The Lion King*. His mouth was in perma-sneer mode, and his head thrust forward on his neck like someone was leading him by his pimply nostrils. He shook his head at her. "Loser," he mouthed, and laughed. She'd seen his type a million times. A coward until he smelled blood. There was no way he was going to bully her.

Although prickling sweat had broken out all over her body, Ananda thrust out her chin. She smiled—a bright, fake mask. "Good!" she called to the crowd. "The mouse is safe. All's well that ends well,

The Great & the Small

right?" She curled her mouth into a sarcastic grin and stared down the hyena.

His quarry having shown some backbone, Ed the Hyena sauntered off in search of softer targets. Ananda watched him leave then swung around. She covered her face with her hands, breathing hard, grateful that her long, dark hair helped curtain her face.

She was jarred back into the moment when she heard the rubbery tromp of the fishmonger behind her and felt his sizzle-stare on the back of her head. A few choice words were thrown her way.

"Yeah, well right back at you!" she called, dropping her hands and balling them into fists.

The everyday hum of the market slowly came back as if nothing had disturbed it. Ananda sighed. Two brutes beaten off in the space of a minute.

Her father took off his glasses and wiped the lenses with his shirt. Sweat had broken out along his forehead. He swallowed, shaking his head. "Well, that was quite a show!"

"Yeah," she breathed. "But I saved a helpless mouse from being squashed like a bug. It got away, and that's what counts."

"Ananda," said Tom, rubbing his eyes wearily. "That was a rat. A *wild* rat. Probably a descendent of an escaped pet by the looks of it, but it's feral now."

Ananda's mouth had dropped open like it was on a greased hinge. Eww. A *rat*? So that's why its tail was naked and bristly! In spite of herself, a shiver rolled down her spine. Yes, she loved animals and felt it was her duty to protect them against cruelty. But in spite of herself, rats creeped Ananda out. Their buggy eyes looked like they were going to pop out, and their tails were like fat, bleached worms.

Her father was watching her.

Shrugging, she thrust out her chin and said, "Rats have rights too, you know!"

"Wild rats spread disease, Ananda." Tom's voice rose. "And this is a market where people buy and sell *food*. We can't have vermin infesting this place, or we'll all get sick!"

Ananda raised her eyebrows and stared wide-eyed at the ground. Her dad thought what she'd done was wrong. He'd been *embarrassed* by her. And she'd only tried to do what was right.

Hot tears betrayed her, spilling down her nose and staining the front of her shirt. Anger reared up like a rogue wave. She snarled, "Of course you don't care about a poor, innocent rat. You kill rats all the time at your so-called *work*!"

The blood ran from her dad's face as he did a sharp intake of breath. He stared at her with rounded eyes.

"Really, Ananda? That's how you see my work?"

Thomas Blake was a cancer researcher. Part of his work involved experimenting on rats.

To Ananda, he purposefully infected them, cut into them, *tortured* them, all in the name of science. It was crap.

He was still staring at her, open-mouthed.

She looked down to hide the sudden burning in her cheeks. Silence mounted between father and daughter. Ananda raised her eyes and stared at him. A razor-sharp smile curved her mouth. She shrugged. "So?"

Tom closed his eyes for a moment. He said quietly, "There are a lot of people who are *alive* because of my cancer research. I don't… *enjoy* dissecting animals, and I don't let them suffer any more than I have to. But it saves human lives. That is what's important to me. It could even save your life one day."

He sighed, put a hand on her shoulder. It felt heavy. She shrugged it off.

"Okay, have it your way," he said. "I'm still getting the stuff on the list, but in the meantime you can sit here read this." He stuffed a folded newspaper under her arm, turned, and walked away. He called over his shoulder, "I'll be back to get you in thirty minutes."

Ananda watched him disappear into the crowd. She sat down on a nearby bench but took in nothing of the market moving around her. She kept seeing the mouse, the bully of a man, and the look in her father's eyes. She'd done the right thing. So why did she feel like someone had scraped out a hollow place inside of her? The paper stayed under her arm, forgotten.

The bus ride home was a grim test of endurance. Neither of them acknowledged the other, both of them suddenly fascinated with looking out the window.

In the safety of her room, Ananda collapsed on her bed. The paper her dad had given her was crumpled underneath her. Contorting herself, she pulled it out and flung it toward the garbage. It landed in a flutter, the front page facing her. Half of it was taken up by a huge photo.

Ananda frowned. She reached down and picked up the page. The photo showed rows of wrapped bodies, stacked like the sausages she'd just seen at the market. A single person stood in the middle, covered in a white suit and mask, hands outstretched as if pleading for help. The caption read, "Virulent Bubonic Plague Strain Terrorizes India and is Feared to Have Already Spread to Neighbouring Countries. Scientists Baffled by the New Strain of an Old Enemy."

Wild rats carried fleas, which carried plague bacilli. Her hand covered her mouth. Ananda knew from her history books what had happened the last time a strain of the plague "terrorized" people.

The Black Death. The Great Mortality. The Bubonic Plague.

It was back.

"Bloody hell," she said.

CHAPTER THREE

"God tests those he loves so that they may become stronger."

William Zouche, Archbishop of York, 1348

Blurred, dim shapes move around him. He noses along warm fur, following the smell of milk. He has been here before. She licks his ear, grooms his fur. But then the warmth is gone. Sharp noises bounce around him. He gropes blindly in the nest. There is a tug on his paw…

"Fin! Fin! Wake up! Oh, wake up!" Scratch whimpered. "We've got to get out of here—we've got to get out of here now!"

Fin moaned, opening his eyes a sliver.

Scratch babbled, "Oh Fin! Your foot! It's a mess! They'll find out. I know they'll find out. Can't hide it. Oh, why can't you follow the rules for once? Just once!" He burst into a flurry of weeping.

"Don't worry…my uncle…"

"The Chairman won't help *me*, Fin. I'm Mister Nobody from the Lower Tunnels. No one to help me," Scratch sobbed. "I'll be…I'll be *collected!*"

When Fin began to protest, Scratch sobbed louder. *"Collected!* I'll never see my sister again! Oh, what's she going to say? Zumi *told* me not to be friends with you…"

Fin shook his head to clear it. "What?"

"Trouble!" said Scratch. "That's what she called you. Now I know why! Now I'm going to be *collected!"* Scratch burst into fresh tears.

Fin's paw had been crushed and Scratch was crying over Collections that didn't even exist? "I *told* you that there's no such—"

Scratch nipped him hard on the ear.

"Ouch!" cried Fin. "You *bit* me?"

"Don't you—don't you *dare* tell me," spluttered Scratch, his eyes narrowed at Fin. "Mister High-and-Mighty, you have no idea—"

"Okay, okay. We'll…we'll say that I fell."

Scratch wept. "No one will believe you. Especially not…not…the Chairman! This is all your fault!" He nipped Fin on the rump.

"Ouch! Stop biting me! Papa doesn't know about this. And if you can calm down, he won't *ever* know."

The Great & the Small

Scratch sat up, blinking at Fin through his tears. "He w-won't?"

"No, but our stories need to be exactly the same. We'll say I was running along the ceiling pipe that runs over the market, doing surveillance—"

"Surv...what?"

"Sur-vei-llance." Fin wanted to scream, his crushed paw throbbed so. But he said slowly, "It means I was watching the two-legs, seeing what traps they were setting for us. So, I was *helping* the Tunnels."

Scratch looked puzzled.

"The rules said we can't go *in* the two-leg territory," explained Fin. "Two-legs don't run under the ceiling."

Hope flickered in Scratch's eyes. "That's good! That's good, Fin!" His face darkened. "But your paw..."

"Ummm...I lost my balance on the ceiling pipe!" said Fin.

Scratch brightened.

"I lost my balance on the pipe, because of my curled foot."

Scratch nodded eagerly.

"And...and then I slipped and landed wrong and some ugly two-leg stepped on it. So I won't even mention you were there."

Scratch's expression was blank for a moment as he took in what Fin had said. Then a smile spread across his face.

"Yeah?" said Fin. "It's good?"

"Yeah!" said Scratch, bobbing his head. "It's good! It's good, Fin!"

"Great," sighed Fin, slumping down, "because I'm going to sleep now. My paw is killing me."

Scratch poked him with his nose. "No you don't. Get up, get up! Can't stay here! The ugly two-legs will climb up. They'll finish you off for sure!"

"How do you know they're ugly when you're as blind as a naked mole rat?"

Scratch gave him another bite on the rump. "I just know, okay, *Mister Fin?*"

"Ouch! Okay! Okay!"

Fin's nest was in the Upper Burrows, but he could hardly walk, so Scratch steered him to his own small nest in the Lowers, tucked within the belly of the market.

Neither of them realized they were being watched.

CHAPTER FOUR

"With death all around, we are stirred to be watchful."

Thomas Brinton, Bishop of Rochester, 1375

"Why did you bring him here, Scratch?"

The voice woke Fin. It was female and sounded angry. Fin was curled up in Scratch's nest, which lay deep below the market, deeper than he'd ever been.

The burrow was tiny, located at the bottom of a tunnel so dotted with burrow holes that it looked like Swiss cheese. The bedding was damp, and the burrow smelled sour, a little like sewage. But when they had finally limped in, Scratch insisted Fin stay.

"It's not nice, like yours," Scratch had babbled, "but it's close. Closer than your nest in the Upper Tunnels, and you're hurt, so now you're going to do as Mister Scratch says!"

Fin had nodded, too tired to worry about the smell. Hobbling to the pile of rags, he'd dropped to sleep.

"This is my nest, too," Scratch now said. His voice sounded muffled. "I can bring whoever I want here, so there!"

"But he's the Chairman's nephew! You're too trusting. You think because he *says* he's your friend that he won't turn you in?"

"He won't, Zumi. He won't! Fin isn't like that, he's—"

"Like what?" said Fin, lifting himself up. A brown female rat squealed with surprise. Except for her colour Scratch's sister looked identical to Scratch. She stared at Fin, open-mouthed, her pink nose turning even pinker.

"Didn't your mother teach you not to spy?" she snapped.

"My mother is dead," said Fin. "I'm surprised you didn't know that, since you seem to know everything else about me. And I wasn't spying. I was just lying here."

Zumi frowned. "Maybe, maybe not."

"Zumi!" said Scratch. "He's Papa's nephew. His nephew! So be nice."

"Do I have a choice?" She looked away, shaking her head.

"Hey," said Fin, "I'm not here to cause trouble. I had a run-in with a two-leg and—"

"And put all of us in danger!" said Zumi. "Why couldn't you just stay where you belong? You have no business being down here."

"Scratch *helped* me," said Fin. "I'm not going to 'turn you in,' or whatever you were talking about. Just because I'm the Chairman's nephew, you act like I'm a …a *Plague Rat* or something!" At the words *Plague Rat*, Zumi gasped and Scratch's eyes went as round as red currants.

Fin's ears burned. He wasn't even sure what a Plague Rat was— something to do with the Great Dying from long ago. Nobody talked about the Great Dying except in whispers. He snapped, "You know what? I'm leaving! I hope you're happy!" He tried to walk, but his paw was so swollen he stumbled. He leaned against the dirt wall.

The Great & the Small

"No, Fin!" cried Scratch. "You can't! Don't listen to my bossy sister!"

Zumi stared at his bloody paw, her nose twitching. "You really can't walk, can you? Okay, okay, you can stay here. Just don't tell *anyone*—"

A voice interrupted her, bellowing from the outer tunnel. "Is Fin here? Nephew, are you here?"

Zumi gasped, shrinking into the shadows. Scratch hunched into a tight ball, squeaking, "Oh! Oh! Oh!"

The Chairman was coming.

CHAPTER FIVE

"The life we lead is but a sleep; whatever we do, only dreams."

Petrarch, Italian scholar and poet, 1349

Fin's uncle charged through the burrow opening. Papa was as large as a well-fed cat. His velvety black fur rippled across his back.

"Fin! Where are you?" His eyes darted over the crouched brother and sister. He spied Fin.

"Nephew!" In one bound he reached Fin. He sniffed him from tip to tail. When he found the wounded paw, he froze.

"Papa, I can explain," said Fin.

The Chairman drew himself up. "You disobeyed!"

"No, Papa! We were doing surv—"

"Every *good* Tunnel Rat follows the *rules*!"

"But I ran under the ceiling," Fin said. "Two-legs can't go under the ceil—" His uncle began to pace.

"Your antics were noted by several witnesses, as were *his*." He jerked his head toward Scratch. "Bothwell and his ARM say they saw this young fellow biting you!" Scratch flattened himself against the wall, shaking his head wildly, his eyes bulging with fear. Zumi stood like a stone.

The Great & the Small

"No, no, Papa!" cried Fin. "Scratch saved my life! It wasn't his fault, it was mine!"

"Saw him *pushing* you along," said his uncle, speaking over him, "after your little escapade."

"*Surveillance,*" said Fin. "We were doing surveillance! We were trying to help the Tunnels—"

"You expect me to believe that?" The Chairman stood on his hind legs and glared down at his nephew. His eyes burrowed into Fin.

Even though Fin's heart galloped, he held his uncle's gaze. His uncle's eyes narrowed. Still Fin did not look away.

A growl started in the Chairman's chest, but as it grew, it swelled into laughter. Papa threw back his head, guffawing. "Ah, Nephew! Trouble must run in the family! I don't like rules either!" Still chuckling, he leaned in close. "But mind it doesn't happen again, young pup. Eh?"

Fin let out his breath. "Yes, Papa! Thank you, Papa!" He grinned over at Scratch, but Scratch glowered at him, his eyes crescent-shaped slits. Fin's smile froze.

The Chairman spoke, smiling down at Scratch's sister. "And who is *this* friend of my nephew's?"

Before Zumi could answer, Fin said, "Oh, that's just Scratch's sister. *This* is my friend. Right?" He looked hopefully at Scratch.

Whatever had bothered Scratch melted away before the Beloved Chairman of the Tunnels. Scratch bobbed up and down, a smile crinkling his cheeks. "Your Majesty…I mean, your Grace. No—"

Papa laughed. "We're all equals here, friend. Equals! There is no 'king' here! I am only Council Chairman. You know our most precious Tunnel Law: 'Every rat is equal! Every nest for all!'"

Scratch bobbed. "Yes, your Majesty! I mean, your…your Lordship."

The Chairman laughed again. "*Papa* will do. Scratch, is it? Such a loyal Tunnel Rat! Such a loyal friend to my nephew! The Council values loyalty above all!"

Scratch's ears turned even pinker than usual, and his head bobbed so vigorously that it looked in danger of flying off his neck. His sister, however, stood off to one side, her face as pinched and stiff as an old cheese. She turned and caught Fin staring. He looked away.

Papa gazed around the nest.

Scratch followed the Chairman's movements, his small, pale shoulders hunched and quivering. Papa sniffed the air, murmured, "Acceptable. Clean." He sniffed again. "Close to food. Excellent. Council shall hear of your living conditions."

Scratch probably hadn't a clue what the Chairman was talking about, but his shoulders heaved with relief. "Oh, thank you! We find it quite acceptable!"

Addressing Fin, Papa went on. "Your mother, Nia, lived under the market too. Down the hill. Do you remember, Nephew?"

Fin snorted. "No. I was only a few nights old when you adopted me."

"Ahh. Nia begged me to take you. Her dream was that you would one day stand by my side as Chairman of the Tunnels."

"Why didn't she raise him herself?" asked Zumi. She hadn't

moved from the shadows. The smile froze on the Chairman's face. There was an awkward silence.

Fin glared at her. "Because she was dying, Mumi, or Fumi, or whatever your name is! And if it weren't for Papa, I'd be dead too!"

"Now, now, Nephew. I have nothing to hide." Papa bowed to Zumi, who looked more like a pinched cheese than ever. "I will answer this good Tunnel Rat's question. It is time the truth came out."

Papa began to pace. "Fin's mother was my dear sister. She chose a mate, though, who was…how to say it…dangerous." He paced faster. "I warned Nia. I told her he was an outsider, a Wrecker. An enemy of the Tunnels." His eyes flicked toward Fin. "And so cruel."

Fin frowned. "Wh-why? What did he do?"

Papa's eyes glinted with tears. "I tried to warn her…" He bowed his head. "He murdered her. That dirty Wrecker murdered your dear mother. Murdered your brothers and sisters and then—then tried to kill *you*. He dragged you out of your mother's nest by your paw."

Fin's lame foot began to throb. "No," he said.

The Chairman shook his head and said to Scratch, "That's why his foot will never be right. I called him Fin because his curled paw reminded me of a tiny fin."

Scratch nodded, his eyes huge.

A tear slid down Papa's cheek. "When my nephew was dragged away, it was only through my…my…*ah!*" He choked up and was silent.

Fin's mouth moved. He tried to speak, but no sound came. Voices babbled in his head: *My father…killed my mother…killed my brothers…my sisters…tried to kill me….* The voices buzzed around, swarming him. *He killed her… He killed my mother…*

"Fin?" Scratch nudged him. "You okay?"

"I...I'm fine..." he lied. He lurched forward and fell.

Nia's face hovers over him. He tries to snuggle into her side, but she noses him up, her eyes piercing his. Her mouth moves. She is saying something, but he is so sleepy...

Something tugs at his paw. Fire licks up his leg.

His eyes fly open. But there is only shadow.

CHAPTER SIX

"I give credit to the great Party—
it bore me and raised me in its own image."

Josef Stalin

Ananda peeked into the History room. It was a new semester and she was late getting to class; she'd sat too long in the courtyard, reading. Now she had to run the gauntlet: find a seat in a crowded classroom.

She scanned the rows of chairs, but there was only one seat left... behind Hyena-Boy from the market.

"Great. Just bloody great," she muttered, as she slid into the chair.

He swivelled and said, "Hey, it's the crazy girl! *'Stop it! Oh, stop it! You're sooo mean!'* I didn't know you went to this school, Rat-Girl."

Ananda just stared at him, smirking, the master of calm and cool. It was crap, of course. Inside, she wanted to punch him between his dumb, idiot eyes, right on his bushy unibrow.

"Shut-up, Chris," said the girl next to her, looking over her shoulder at Ananda. "I'm George." Her eyes slid to Chris. "Don't mind him. He's harmless." George looked more Greek goddess than high school student. Ananda had seen her around school, but this was the first class they'd had together. Chris scowled at them both but turned around and faced the front.

Ananda smiled at George, suddenly feeling shy and painfully aware of the pimple that was growing on her chin. In the few months she'd been attending the school, Ananda had noticed her; George who seemed effortlessly popular, lived two houses down from her, but it might as well have been in a different universe. She had long blonde hair that fell like a sheet across her back, perfect skin that had never been besmirched by a zit, and a body that didn't shop in the petite section.

The teacher was sitting on the corner of her desk looking over her notes. She stood up.

"Without further ado, I'm Mrs. Zimmer. I'm here to teach you something about the world you live in." She paused, looking at them.

"One question: why study history?"

Mrs. Zimmer's question hung in the air like a bad smell. Eyes stayed lowered, or stared out of windows. Ananda doodled in the margins of her notebook. The question was so easy.

Hyena-Boy belched. A waft drifted back to Ananda in a humid cloud. Vomit rose in her throat, which she gulped back down.

Mrs. Zimmer said dryly, "Thank you, Mr. Litko." She asked again, "Why study history?" A pencil drummed on a desk. Giggling on the far side of the room. A yawn. "Well? It's going to be a long semester, people, if you don't participate."

"To torture us," Chris muttered.

Ananda rolled her eyes. She raised her hand.

Mrs. Zimmer's eyes lit up. "Yes?"

The Great & the Small

Ananda tucked her hair behind her ear. "History is the story of humanity." She looked around. Everyone looked back at her like she'd sprouted a couple of extra heads.

Chris swivelled in his seat to stare, his unibrow raised.

Instant sweat stung Ananda's armpits, and her mouth went dry, but she plunged on, feeling the need to explain. "It's the story of *us*. When I read history, I feel connected to people who lived ages ago. I think it's because for them it *wasn't* history. It was life. Just like ours is to us."

To Ananda's surprise, some of her classmates looked thoughtful. George shrugged and nodded. "Huh. I never thought of it that way." Litko just looked puzzled, his fat lower lip drooping open. Maybe hyenas needed more processing time. Or maybe that Neanderthal unibrow was sucking up too many grey cells.

Ananda leaned forward and whispered, "Shut your mouth." His jaw snapped closed and his unibrow lowered in menace.

Mrs. Zimmer, who hadn't heard Ananda's taunt, said, "That's so true! Very insightful, umm…Miss…?"

"Ananda Blake."

"Very insightful, Ananda!" Mrs. Zimmer whipped out a folded newspaper, warming to her subject. "Ananda's comments lead beautifully to my topic today. Did any of you see this article?" She opened the paper with a flourish, like a magician who had just pulled a rabbit from a hat.

Ananda glanced at it, then bolted upright. It was the same front-page article her dad had shown her—the exact same photo. The person in the white hazmat suit surrounded by stacked sausage-bodies, wretched hands outstretched.

As Mrs. Zimmer read the article, Ananda's mind raced. Did her dad call the teacher about the article? No. Even he wouldn't stoop so low. But twice in two days?

"Now, why did I read this?" continued the teacher. "The Middle Ages is part of our first unit, and during that time the Black Death killed one-third of the population. One-third. Look around. That means out of every three of you students, one would die." A few people shifted in their seats. "Imagine, everywhere you go, whether it's to the mall, to church or mosque, to work, to the movies, or home with your family, one out of three people, gone. "

Ananda felt like something was pressing on her head. *Coincidence. That's all.* She picked up her pen and began to doodle. Thoughts swarmed like moths around a street lamp.

Mrs. Zimmer was relentless. "So how does something that happened in the 1300s relate to us today? How does this photo connect us to the plague?" A few students put up their hands.

Mrs. Zimmer's words floated in and out. Ananda's head pounded; her ears buzzed. "Those who do not study history are doomed to repeat it…"

As the rest of the class discussed the plague of the Middle Ages, Ananda drew in her notebook. *Coincidence. Definitely. Just a coincidence.*

The bell rang, bringing Ananda back into the present moment. Looking down at her notebook, she saw that she had doodled the rat at the market. She ripped the paper off and bunched it up, gathered her books and, head down, beelined out the door.

The Great & the Small

Chris was waiting for her. He bumped her arm and scattered her books. "Hey, Rat-Girl!" he said. His cronies snickered behind her.

Ananda wanted to punch him. "Very clever name, Chris." She widened her eyes and said sweetly, "And by the way, I have an extra razor if you want to shave your unibrow."

His friends guffawed and slapped him on the back.

Chris touched his eyebrows and frowned at her. She stared him down.

For a moment, Ananda wasn't sure which way it was going to go. Finally, Chris snorted and turned away. The group slouched and swaggered its way around the corner.

She breathed out and, now that no one could see it, tears sprang to her eyes. She wiped a sleeve across her face. Someone put a hand on her shoulder, and she jumped.

It was George. "Everything okay?"

Ananda laughed. "Yeah! I'm just clumsy. And my eyes won't stop watering. Must have gotten a stupid cat hair in my eye or something."

Her books were strewn across the hall. George gathered a few of them and handed them to her. "I've got to get to class, but you should get allergy testing. I did, and it helps a lot."

"Yeah, okay," Ananda said brightly. "Thanks!" She stared after George as she walked away, her perfect figure receding down the hall.

Ananda gathered the rest of her books as tears slid down her cheeks. "Bloody flipping hell," she muttered as the bell rang.

She was late for class, again.

CHAPTER SEVEN

"Loving Lord, do not condemn the just with the unjust."

Gabriele de' Mussis, 1348

After Fin collapsed, his uncle carried him by his scruff back through the sewers, drainage pipes, and crevices that led from the Lowers to the Upper Tunnels where they shared a nest.

Over the next few moonrises, Fin passed in and out of consciousness. Waking once, he realized he was back in the nest. His uncle was sitting by the burrow opening, his nose high, nostrils working as he swept his head back and forth, scanning the air.

"Papa?"

"I'm here, Nephew. Go to sleep."

Fin sank back into restless sleep.

One sunrise, Fin woke to find Papa crouching by the opening again, scanning the air. Fin sniffed, but the only thing he could smell was food. As Chairman, his uncle had first dibs from the Tunnel's night foragings. After he'd eaten his fill, there was always plenty left for Fin.

"Papa, what are you doing? And why aren't you asleep yet?"

His uncle grunted and waved for Fin to be quiet. His nose continued to sweep back and forth.

Fin shrugged. Sometimes he couldn't figure Papa out. He picked at a bit of cold scrambled egg then lay back with a sigh. A fine salty breeze riffled through the burrow's entrance and snaked back out through the bolt-hole at the back of the nest. Fin's nostrils quivered as aromas from the market wafted by. Oh, how he wanted to go outside.

Papa turned and said, "Patience, Nephew. You'll be free soon enough. You do remember what patience is?"

Fin lowered his head, snuggled into a ball, and tucked his tail around himself. "Of course, Papa. Patience is one of my strong points."

"Ha!" Papa dug into the bedding, circled until he found the perfect spot, and flopped down.

Another waft of air. Fin didn't raise his head but breathed deeply. A thought occurred to him.

"Papa?"

One of his uncle's eyelids opened a sliver. "Eh?"

"Am I…" Fin's voice trailed off.

Papa raised his head and looked at him. "Are you what?"

"A…a good Tunnel Rat?" asked Fin. "My father was a dirty Wrecker, and me? I…I look more like a mouse."

Papa chuckled. "Now, now. Of course you are a good Tunnel Rat. You are *my* nephew. No matter who your father was, you are mine now." He began to groom Fin, licking his fur the way a mama would groom her pup. "No more talk. Sleep."

Fin settled in to his bedding and closed his eyes. They sprang back open. "Papa, what's a Plague Rat? I've heard of them, but what are they?"

His uncle paused his licking, then said, "Nothing. Go to sleep."

"Will you tell me later?"

"Yes, but not now. Sleep."

"Tell me now," said Fin, fighting to stay awake.

Papa chuckled. "No."

Fin nuzzled into his uncle's side and drifted off to sleep. Below them, across the alley and down the hill, the market was waking. The fishmongers laid out rows of fresh fish, farmers stacked their choicest fruits, and at the newsstand the day's papers were arranged, their front pages blaring the news.

CHAPTER EIGHT

"From your kingdom of joy, watch over us and protect us from harm."

John Lydgate, fifteenth-century poet

The sun was high above the market when Papa nudged Fin awake. "Up! Let's go! Up! Up!"

Fin blinked. "But it's still daylight."

"Come!"

"Papa, I don't want—" The look in his uncle's eyes stopped him. Fin pulled himself up. Leaning heavily on his uncle, he limped to the alley. His paw already throbbed. "Papa, I can't!"

Without a word, the Chairman gripped Fin by his scruff, lifting him off the ground, and padded across the open alley. He squeezed into a pipe that disappeared deep into a building. The Chairman's nails pinged against metal. He trotted through a maze of pipes and ventilation ducts then climbed into a long, narrow drainage pipe. Water trickled along the bottom, heading toward a glowing circle of daylight. The circle grew larger and larger until it glimmered before them.

The Chairman set Fin down. Fin could smell the market, could hear it, even *taste* it. But all he could see was blinding light.

"Look down," ordered Papa.

Fin forced himself to peer out. The ground was dozens of tail-lengths below: a dizzying blur. He shrank back.

"You are a Tunnel Rat. Do not look away!"

Again, Fin crept forward. He allowed the market to flow over him. His ears swivelled toward sounds, deciphering them: two-legs shouting; bottles clinking; a horn blasting, another one responding; the squawk of seagulls nearby; the faint caw of crows....

Fanning his nose back and forth, Fin smelled the tang of blood. The fish stall. It was right below them. And something else—his fur prickled—the cruel two-leg. Its stench was loud and clear. Fin gagged. "Papa, I...I can't..."

"Open your ears, and keep your nostrils wide! You are a brave Tunnel Rat!"

Fin shivered. The stink pressed against his nose.

"Show me," said the Chairman. "Show me the ugly two-leg who did this to you."

"I..." croaked Fin. The blinding sky spun, smearing the market and the two-leg's stench together.

Fin swayed. The floor buckled. All went silent.

When he awoke, he was back in the nest. Papa was gone.

The squad scoured the Lowers for some time before they finally landed a good one: a solitary rat, a loner. Common enough in the Lowers and rarely missed.

"Stop resisting," hissed a rat into the struggling one's ear. "Consider this your personal contribution to the Common Good."

Laughter. A muffled yelp.

The Great & the Small

"It's strong for half-starved," puffed another rat who leaned heavily against the captive.

Out of the gloom, a huge rat appeared with a small, pale rat at his side. All fell silent. The squad shuffled out of their way.

The big rat nudged the pale one forward. *"Kill it."*

"Me?" The small one shrank back. *"I don't know..."*

"Hold it still, boys," growled the big rat. He stared down at the little pale one. *"Do it."*

The small rat faced the prisoner, silver whiskers trembling.

The prisoner's teeth chattered. *"Please, no! Have mercy!"*

The pale one stared at the prisoner, his brow furrowed. He looked up at the big rat. *"Are you sure it's okay?"*

"Of course it's okay. It's your duty."

The small one bobbed his head and gulped. He sprang at the prisoner. It took many bites to the captive's neck. Shrieks sliced the air. Finally, the struggling ceased.

"Now," said the big rat, *"show us where it happened."*

"Yes, yes!" The pale head bobbed up and down. *"Follow me!"*

The little rat scurried ahead through the tunnels. The squad followed, dragging the limp body behind them.

CHAPTER NINE

"Death solves all difficulties."

Attributed to Stalin

Ananda sat on her bed, a sketchbook on her lap. The new art book lay open next to her; she was trying to draw her feet using a technique in the book called "continuous line." Far from teaching her how to "see how things really are," her feet looked like misshapen blobs of dough. She ripped off the page, balled it up, and threw it against the far wall.

She was too distracted to draw. Tears snaked down her cheeks until her face puckered together like a draw-string purse, and she burst into tears.

Why she was crying, she couldn't even understand herself. Was it because she'd been targeted by Litko? Yes, but that was only part of it. The whole newspaper article thing played on her mind too.

Gulping in air, she wiped her eyes with her fists.

Maybe Litko was only part of the problem, but he was the part she could fight.

The Great & the Small

Ananda began to sketch. It was a strip cartoon of Chris Litko and his goons. She cartooned close-ups of their dim-eyed, slack-jawed faces, zooming in and out at different angles as they tried to puzzle out how to spell *Neanderthal*. She gave Chris an extra-large, bushy unibrow. His plump, drooping lower lip looked very Chris.

In the last panel, she drew them dancing around a fire like the apes out of *2001: A Space Odyssey*, hooting their victory.

Ananda laughed. It was good. But that tight knot in her stomach was still there.

The newspaper article felt like a presence standing in the room with her. A malevolent presence, reminding her of how powerless she was. Of how even when she thought she was doing right, it turned out all wrong.

Shadows of early evening crept across her floor, reaching her bed. Ananda snapped on the light.

The shadows slid back into the corner.

There was a sudden rap at her door, making her heart catch.

"Dinner," called her mom.

Ananda breathed out and gripped her head. Slowly, she climbed off her bed and shuffled into the dining room.

Her dad was already seated. He looked up at her and pushed

his glasses up his nose. They hadn't spoken of the Disaster at the Market. Ignoring it meant it hadn't happened.

Ananda kept her eyes on her plate and picked at her food. Her insides still felt like a clenched fist.

"Is something wrong?" asked her mom.

Ananda raised her eyes and stared at her dad. "Ask him."

Tom shrugged. "Your mom already knows."

The casual shrug set Ananda off. She snapped, "So she knows you think I'm responsible for the coming apocalypse? Did you tell her you were *embarrassed* by me?"

Tom frowned. "Ananda, I never said—"

"You didn't have to. It came through loud and clear. You'll be pleased to know that my History teacher showed us the *same* article today. So you're right! We're all going to die, and according to you, it's my fault!"

Ananda's mouth quivered. She covered it with a shaking hand.

Her dad snorted and said, "I don't think that. You are overreacting, Ananda. I don't agree with what you did, but…" He leaned forward and clasped her hand.

"No!" She yanked it back. Her parents stared at her, round-eyed, mouths open.

"No," she said again. "Don't touch me."

Ananda screeched her chair back from the table, ran to her room, and slammed the door. She threw herself onto her bed as sobs rolled through her like waves smashing against rocks.

There was a knock at the door. "Ananda?" It was her dad.

"Leave me alone!"

"Ananda! Please, let's talk about this."

"Go away!" Burying her face in her pillow, she sobbed like a lost

child. Eventually, she heard him sigh, heard the creak of his shoes as he walked away.

Ananda cried herself dry.

Finally, she rolled onto her back. Her hair was plastered to her cheeks with dried snot. Things would be better tomorrow, isn't that what everybody said?

Everybody was wrong.

Tomorrow, she'd have to go back to that damned school.

CHAPTER TEN

"No one from this city shall be allowed to travel to infected areas, and those from infected areas shall not be allowed in."

Ordinance to restrict the spread of the plague, Italy, 1348

It was moonrise, and Fin was restless. The nest seemed to shrink smaller and smaller every moment he was in it. He wanted to go outside, to smell the air, get out of the burrow, but Papa had forbidden him to leave until he was completely healed.

Fin flexed his paw. His foot couldn't open at all now—his toes had fused together as they'd healed. But though his paw was even uglier than before, it felt pretty good. Testing his weight on it, there was no pain. That decided it: Fin was going to visit Scratch. Papa was at Council and wasn't there to stop him.

Fin limped along the old route, brushing his flank along the wall of the alley. Countless generations of Tunnel Rats had leaned against that wall to help them navigate down to the market, wearing the wall smooth.

A two-leg shuffled by. Fin flattened against the wall to make himself invisible as it passed.

The Great & the Small

It sang softly to itself, weaving back and forth as if the pavement were rolling. These kinds of two-legs were harmless—as long as one steered clear of their feet. It tottered around the corner and out of sight.

Fin scuttled across the street to the main market area, passing the statue. The creature's wings glinted in the moonlight. He could see the faint outline of the fish stall from where he stood, but it was closed, thank the Old Ones. That ugly two-leg wouldn't hurt him now.

A loud crash broke the silence. Fin froze. His fur prickled along his spine. Something was moving at the stall. The shapes were blurred, far away, but he heard whispers, a laugh, and a *thunk*.

Fin dived down the set of stairs that led to the lower alley. He pressed himself motionless against the wall, his ears swivelling to catch sound. But the market was silent.

He stayed hidden until his racing heart slowed.

The stairway up to the main market towered over him. His foot ached from running. Although the path he knew was at the top of the stairs, climbing them would be long and painful—and besides, he didn't want to go anywhere near that noise. Fin decided to find a new path to Scratch.

He sniffed along the lower alley's wall. He came to a rusted wire door that hung from one hinge. Behind it was a series of tunnels that crisscrossed under the market. Hot, moist air soaked his whiskers. Sewage. This was definitely the right way to the Lowers.

Fin squeezed through the opening. Inching down the crumbling brick wall, he dropped to a concrete slab below. A pipe snaked off from the slab, slanting lower and deeper into the belly of the hill. He caught the scent-markings of other rats in the air, hovering beneath the sewer smell.

He followed the markings like they were signposts and navigated the pitch-dark pipe by leaning against its curved wall as he walked. By fanning out his whiskers, he could "see" above and below himself. The scent markings became denser.

Fin emerged in a tunnel. Burrow openings dotted along it like hungry mouths. After sniffing around, Fin found Scratch's scent trail and followed it to a small burrow. "Scratch?" he called down. "Scratch! You there?"

A brown nose poked out of the hole. Zumi. They stared at each other, nose to nose.

Fin said gruffly, "Is Scratch here?"

"Isn't he with you?" she said. "That's odd. I thought that's what he said. But since you're here, I…" Zumi picked up her tail and began to groom it, eyes lowered. "I'm sorry about your mother." She examined something on her paw. "And I'm sorry that I was a little overprotective. Scratch is my only family. And he's so…so *gullible*." She let her tail drop and fell silent.

Fin cleared his throat. "Well, tell Scratch that—*OOF!*"

Scratch had barrelled down the tunnel, sending Fin sprawling in the dirt. Fin picked himself up. Scratch danced around him, chattering.

"Fin!" said Scratch. "*Ha!* Funny seeing you after what *I* did tonight!"

"Scratch," said Zumi. "I've been so worried about you! You told me you were visiting Fin, and then he shows up here without you! Oh, stop dancing and get inside!"

"Yes, *Sir!*" said Scratch. "Yes, *Sir!*" He gave Zumi a salute then slipped down the hole.

Zumi stared after him, shaking her head. "Come on," she said to Fin. She disappeared down the burrow, and Fin followed.

Inside, Scratch was grooming his belly. He looked up as they came in and laughed. "Zumi cracks me up! She's always so worried." Crinkling his forehead, Scratch stared hard at Fin. "Hi, I'm Zumi. I worry about everything. Is my tail clean? Oh no! There's a speck of dirt! *Ha, ha!*"

Fin snickered. Scratch did a good imitation.

Zumi glared at her brother. "What have you been up to?"

Scratch smirked, his red eyes sparkling crescent moons. "Not telling, not telling! *Ha, ha!*"

"Not telling *what?*" asked Zumi.

His smirk deepened. "Just some Tunnel business."

Fin snorted. "Tunnel business? Since when do you have *Tunnel business?*"

Scratch's face stiffened. He pulled himself up, scowling. "I've got plenty!"

"What are you talking about?" laughed Fin. "What business could you—?"

Scratch bared his teeth and jumped at him. Fin stumbled back.

"Not everyone gets to play all day, *Mister Fin!*" Scratch snarled.

"Not everyone gets to play games with ugly two-legs, maybe get squished, maybe not!"

"What?" said Fin. "You're still mad about that fish thing? I'm the one who got a paw crushed, not you!"

"It's not that, not that at all!" cried Scratch. "*No Tunnel Rat Shall Go into Cruel and Ugly Two-Leg Territory Except During...During...*Oh! I can't remember, but it's the law, Fin! *The law!* But then *you*...you just get a pat on the head! Not fair!" Scratch ground his teeth. "But now *I* am needed. Yes, poor ugly Scratch. Scratch from the Lowers. Scratch with fleas." He swung his back to Fin and sat crouched, trembling with emotion.

Fin looked at Zumi, who shrugged, her eyes wide. Keeping his voice calm, he said, "Why are you so upset? And *who* needs you? Come on, you can tell me."

Scratch shook his head. "Not telling, not telling, not telling!" He began to weep.

Zumi stepped up to her brother and nuzzled his ear. "Sh, sh, don't cry. It's okay, Brother. Don't worry. Look, I saved the best bit of cheese for you. Why don't you eat it? We'll leave you to sleep."

Scratch didn't turn around. "Yes, leave! Go!"

Zumi motioned for Fin. Fin cast a long look back at his friend and then followed Zumi out into the long tunnel.

"What's the matter with him?" he asked.

Zumi glanced up and down the passage marked with burrow holes. "I don't know. But there are too many eyes in these walls."

Fin agreed. "Do you know somewhere we could go?"

Zumi thought for a moment, and nodded. "Follow me."

The Great & the Small

CHAPTER ELEVEN

"It is important to avoid the gaze of those who are sick with plague. The plague victim must cover his own eyes with a cloth so that the illness is not transmitted."

A 1349 medical treatise on how plague is transmitted

They ran through the labyrinth of tunnels. At every cross-tunnel, Zumi stopped and sniffed, ears swivelling for danger. Fin said nothing. The image of Scratch weeping was playing over and over in his mind.

Zumi emerged onto an alley Fin recognized. The Council met farther down, under the foundations of a two-leg building—that's where Papa would be right now. Dug into concrete, the Council Chamber was cold, the walls damp. Fin had visited once with his uncle. He had pretended to admire it, but what he'd really wanted to see was the beautiful walled garden that faced it across the alley. His uncle had refused to let him go, saying, "The Forbidden Garden is only for Tunnel gatherings." There hadn't been a gathering of the entire colony since Fin was born.

A two-leg snored in a doorway, under a flickering street lamp. Other than that the alley was deserted. Zumi flitted from shadow to shadow.

"Where are you going?" Fin whispered. "We aren't allowed in the Forbidden Garden, you know. And the only other thing down here is Council."

As an answer, Zumi darted across the alley, swooped under the iron fence of the Forbidden Garden, and disappeared into the bushes.

"Hey!" whispered Fin. Glancing up and down the alley, he stood outside the iron bars. "Zumi! Come back here!" A smell wafted from within the garden that made Fin's nose quiver. The scent of leaves, of fresh earth. It made him dizzy. Suddenly he wanted into that garden more than he'd wanted anything in his whole life.

He glanced at the Council Chamber opening. No one. No one in the alley either. He placed a paw tentatively on the soil. His heart pounded. With a final look to the dark alley, he left the paved road behind and slipped under the iron bars.

Leaves brushed against his fur. Over his head, a ceiling of interlacing branches. New smells leaped to his nose. Clear air! Sweet grass! Flowers! He emerged into the clearing, gasping aloud. The moon hung in the sky like a round glowing cheese. Stars dotted the black sky. Everything—the leaves, the blades of grass, the rocks—was outlined in silver.

Zumi motioned to him from under a stone bench. A large fountain burbled next to it, which looked like an upside-down umbrella in the moonlight. Fin was too overwhelmed to move.

Never in his life had he smelled so much green! So much life! The grass felt like velvet under his paws. Joy bubbled up from him, just like the fountain. He cried out ultrasonically, *"This is beautiful! This is so beautiful!"*

The sound reverberated off the bench, the fountain, the iron-barred fence like a clanging gong.

"Are you *trying* to get us caught?" Zumi hissed.

The Great & the Small

"Sorry," he said, panting. "I didn't mean—"

It was too late. From the alley there came shouts, the sound of digging. Council's Arrest, Removal, and Management squad. The ARM was coming for them.

The grating voice of Bothwell, Councillor of the ARM, rang out like squealing metal. "Follow me, you lot! Someone's in here! We'll find out who and make short work of 'em! Bite first, ask questions later is what I say!"

Fin could hear their *tramp, tramp, tramp…*

Closer.

He hunkered low. This was all his fault. Zumi was right not to trust him. Shivers ran up and down his body. The tramping stopped a few tail-lengths away. Snuffling sounds moved toward him. Bothwell's steel-grey fur flashed through the leaves. Fin froze with fear.

"Over here, crew!" called Councillor Bothwell. "I caught me a whiff, and there's more than one!"

The bushes rustled behind Fin. "This way!" whispered Zumi.

That broke the spell. Fin dived after her. Zumi zigzagged through the garden, mixing up their scent-trail, and raced to the base of the fountain where she crouched low.

"Over here!" cried the Councillor. "They're doing a runner! Get 'em!"

The fountain was a giant stone bowl. Coiling her legs beneath her, Zumi sprang onto the bowl's rim. She leaned over the edge and whispered down to Fin, "Come on! Hurry!"

Fin clawed his way up the side with his three paws, and sat panting beside Zumi. Water burbled out of a pipe in the fountain's centre. Inky black water rippled in the basin below.

64

Bothwell bellowed, "Snouts to the ground, you lot! Don't lose their trail!" The ARM was closing in.

Zumi whispered, "We need to throw them off our scent. We need to swim across."

"But I don't know how."

"Neither do I."

They looked at each other, their eyes huge.

"Come on, Fin." Zumi dived into the black water.

Fin hesitated, then jumped in. The icy cold water stole his breath, and he plunged like a stone. But something deep inside him took over. His legs began to pump.

He broke the surface. Beside him the tip of Zumi's pale nose and ears peeked above the black ink. Sounds were muffled as he swam. He could only hear the whooshing in-and-out of his own breath, the swoosh of his paws through water. Finally, they reached the far wall and scrambled up.

They both scanned the air. A scent trail caught Fin's nose—a garbage can twenty tail-lengths away. He motioned to Zumi. Was it too far? They looked at each other.

The ARM burst through the underbrush, barrelling toward the fountain in a ball of teeth and tails. They swarmed around the base of the fountain, snuffling for a trail.

Zumi coiled her back legs and launched herself toward the garbage can. Sailing through the air, she landed silently. Her black eyes peered over the rim. Fin's turn. His paw throbbed with each beat of his heart. Cold dread gripped him. They stared at each other from across the distance.

Bothwell's voice grated. "The tricky devils went up the fountain! After 'em!" The ARM swarmed up the side.

Fin kept his eyes fixed on Zumi and jumped.

The Great & the Small

He landed short. His forepaws clung to the rim while his one good back paw scrabbled against the dented metal surface. It found a foothold. He pulled himself over the top and burrowed into the garbage next to Zumi. They waited, listening, hearts pounding.

The ARM flowed over the side of the fountain and back down to the ground. There was the sound of sniffing. The Councillor growled, "Where did those devils get to?"

"Maybe it was just a dog, or a squirrel," said one flunky, panting. "Maybe there weren't no rats in the garden at all."

"Right," said Bothwell, "and I'm an alley cat!" He nipped the flunky's ear, who yelped in pain. Bothwell barked, "Keep looking!" But after a while even the Councillor gave up. He assembled his crew at the base of the garbage can.

"Slippery devils! Vanished into thin air. But there's no need to trouble the Chairman about it, eh? We'll keep this between ourselves?"

"Right, Boss," murmured his patrol. "Mum's the word."

"You're a good lot! Now, off we go." The ARM tramped back out of the garden the way it had come and left the two trespassers to their hiding place.

CHAPTER TWELVE

"No person is so naïve and blind that he should concern himself with the care of others more than his own self."

Chalin de Vinario, physician, Italy, during the plague

F in climbed slowly out of the garbage and dropped on the ground. Zumi dropped down beside him. After a moment's silence, Fin said, "Sorry. I guess I forgot where I was."

Zumi shook her head. "At least I know you're not a Council spy. No spy would've been so dumb."

Fin snorted, but he said nothing.

The moonlight made the garden shimmer. Even Zumi seemed different in the moonlight.

She lifted her nose, breathing deeply. "This is my favourite place. Scratch has never seen it. He says it's against the rules." She lowered her head. "I'm worried about him, Fin. Scratch is…is *weak*. He needs protection. With all of the Collections going on in the Lowers, I'm afraid he'll get hurt."

"Collections?" said Fin. He pulled back. "You really believe in those?"

She looked up at him, tears glinting in her eyes. "Rats *are* collected.

Collections happen all the time. You just never see it because you live in the Uppers."

Fin shook his head. "No. The rules are the same for Upper and Lower, Zumi. Papa treats everyone the same. You can go to him— I'll go with you! We can tell him what you're afraid of and he will—"

Her mouth dropped open. "I'm *not* going to see the Chairman!"

"Papa. Call him Papa. He's not just the Chairman, he cares for each Tunnel Rat like a father cares for his pups. He will help you, Zumi. And when we go see him, we'll ask him about Scratch, okay? Don't worry so much. Nothing's going to happen."

"No. No!" Zumi shook him off, blinking.

Fin stepped toward her. "No, you were right to come to me. Council is right across the alley. We're going over right now. I want to help you."

She stumbled back. "No! I'm not going. I don't need your help."

Fin's ears burned. "Stop being so stubborn! You make everything complicated. Just like Scratch said!"

They stared, their dark eyes locked on each other.

"I need to go," she said. She slipped through the bushes and was gone.

Fin stared after her, grinding his teeth. Unbelievable! There were no Collections, and the idea of the Lower Tunnel rats being *targets* for the Council, for his *uncle*, would have made him laugh if it wasn't so pathetic. If that's what Lower rats thought of Council, it was time for Fin to step up and help change things.

He was the Chairman's nephew. It was time he started acting like it.

The moon carved the shapes of overturned stalls, tables, boxes, into unmoving witnesses. Gnaw marks scarred the legs and edges of the fishmonger's table. Feces and urine laced the floors, the counters, every surface the two-leg might touch.

That same moon reflected the matted outline of a dead rat: underfed, scruffy, unmissed. Bite marks marred its neck. Its stiffening limbs were splayed flat upon the fishmonger's table.

A warning to the two-legs.

CHAPTER THIRTEEN

"The peasant must do a bit of starving."

Vladimir Lenin

Most students ate in the cafeteria, so Ananda headed out to the inner courtyard, a garden that was maintained by the horticulture students.

She did a quick scan. No Neanderthal activity. She settled herself on a bench next to the pond.

She'd come early to school to tape photocopies of her cartoon strip in the hallways before anyone was there to catch her.

In History class, she'd sat near the door and had slipped out as soon as the bell rang without talking to anyone, but as Ananda walked through the halls to the courtyard, she saw a crowd gathered around one of the strips. She heard Litko's name mentioned. Heard snickering. She felt a stab of anxiety.

Posting the cartoons had seemed like a good idea in the morning. An act of rebellion—proof to herself she wouldn't put up with being intimidated. And she hadn't signed it. But Chris, with the canniness of a wounded hyena and the bruised ego of a Neanderthal, might figure out it was her.

Bird feeders were placed around the garden. Swarms of chickadees and sparrows flitted from feeder to feeder, their wings making that strange, wonderful thrumming in the quiet. A squadron of lemon-yellow goldfinches plucked seeds from clusters of cone flowers, their wings fluttering to keep them balanced on the swaying stalks. Watching them made Ananda's stomach unclench a little.

Other benches filled up, but no one paid her any attention. Ananda stared at the birds, wishing she could fly from flower to flower, gathering seeds. Thinking of nothing.

In History, Mrs. Zimmer had given them an assignment: pick one pivotal event in history and give a ten-minute oral report, due in a week. The research part was no problem, but the thought of standing in front of her History class with Litko smirking at her for ten minutes made her want to puke.

Ananda pulled out her book, the one she'd borrowed from her dad. It was all about Soviet Russia, about government-issued killing sprees called "The Great Terror," and Stalin the Psycho-in-Chief at the head of it all. Her dad had been right. The book *was* interesting.

Maybe she'd do her project on the Terror. She wished she could talk to her dad about it, about the ideas and the mindset of a person who could do that kind of thing. She missed those talks with him. She missed *him*.

The edges of her mouth quivered and she swallowed hard.

A shadow covered her. She looked up. Chris Litko and his Merry Band of Cavemen. By the look on Chris's face, she knew the jig was up.

Ananda put her book aside and stood up. Her head only came to Chris's chest, but she put her hands on her hips. "What?" she said.

Chris stepped closer.

"I know it was you, Rat-Girl." The circle of goons tightened.

The Great & the Small

Ananda's heart pumped, but she smiled broadly. "What was me, Chris? If I didn't know better, I'd think you were just making excuses to talk to me."

She grabbed her bag and pushed through them. "Now if you'll excuse me, I've got work to do."

It almost worked.

She was nearly at the school door, when Chris called, "Rat-Girl. You forgot this." He held up her book. Stalin's eyes winked at her from the cover.

Ananda's smile dropped from her face. She walked back to Chris and grabbed for it. "Give it over."

Chris grinned. He swooped the book out of her reach.

Blood rushed to Ananda's face. She gritted her teeth and snarled, "Give it back, you bloody hyena!"

Chris's unibrow arched at the insult. "Ooh. Such names." He held it over her head.

Ananda reached again. "Give it back! It's my dad's book!"

Chris and his pals cackled. He said in falsetto, "It's my *dad's* book!" They threw the book back and forth between them, pages fluttering. A few of the students sitting at the benches got out their cell phones and began recording.

"Give it back, I said!" Ananda's voice came out high-pitched and quavering. And then to her horror, she burst into tears.

The pack loved it. They mocked her in whiny falsetto. "G-g-give it b-b-back!"

Her mouth froze into a grimace as she sobbed. No one helped her. She was just the lunch-time freak show.

Above the noise, a voice shouted, "What is going on here?"

Mrs. Zimmer appeared at the doorway as Ananda's book cartwheeled past Chris and fell with a *phloop!* into the pond.

It drifted down. Stalin's eyes stared up at Ananda like two drilled holes, before sinking into the murk. Ananda's mouth dropped open. "That was my d-dad's book."

"That was my d-d-dad's b-b-book," said Chris.

"Idiot!" she shrieked, and pushed him so hard he stumbled backwards to the edge of the pond.

Chris's arms wind-milled for balance. He teetered, and then pitched in, butt-first. A plume of water showered down on everyone like a freshwater geyser, causing the birds who'd been feeding nearby to rise in a flurry of feathers and seeds.

The students on the far benches cheered and fist-pumped, cell phones held high. Mrs. Zimmer was drenched, her shirt and pants dripping.

Ananda backed away, her hand over her mouth.

Chris was hoisted out and thrown onto the ground like a fish hauled onto the dock.

Mrs. Zimmer looked at Ananda, then back at Chris. Snarling through dripping hair, she said, "Blake! Litko! Come with me!"

CHAPTER FOURTEEN

"For God has said, 'I will obliterate Man, whom I created, from this earth.'"

Gabriele de' Mussis, 1348

The Council Chamber was cavernous. The entrance was a tiny crack at the base of a two-leg building, almost invisible. Easier to keep it safe from two-leg eyes.

Fin squeezed through the opening and hurried along the dirt passage until it opened into the grand hall of the Council Chamber. Its walls were notched, grooved with the tooth marks of those who had carved it from the concrete long ago. Fin burst into the room and pushed through the startled Council members until he came into the centre.

Papa was standing on a carved platform at the head of the Chamber. "Now, good Tunnel Rats, I will share with you a momentous thing. I have smelled something in the air. It is something great. A gift from the Old Ones that would—"

He caught sight of Fin and stared down at him. "To what do we owe this honour, Nephew?"

"I wish to join Council!" Fin's voice reverberated through the halls.

Papa's eyes glittered, but he said nothing.

"What do I need to do? I will do anything."

"You wish to join? My nephew wishes to join me?"

Fin smiled up at his uncle. Papa had asked him to join many times, but Fin had always refused. He'd never wanted the responsibility. Never wanted to endure meetings that droned on and on.

Addressing the Council, Papa opened his arms wide. "Good Tunnel Rats! We have before us my sister's son, who has asked to join our ranks! What say you? What say you, good Tunnel Rats?"

The Chamber erupted with cheers. Papa nodded. "And my Councillors? What say you?"

Fin stiffened. He had met the Councillors before. They were so important, so lofty, that Fin had felt even more scrawny and deformed in their presence. Bothwell was there too, fresh from the chase. Would he recognize him? Fin kept his eyes on Papa. The Councillors gathered around him.

Councillor Tiv, Councillor of Information, was beautiful. Plump with lustrous black fur, she pressed close to Fin, but her dark eyes stayed on his uncle's face. "Your nephew is most welcome, Papa." The Councillor of Compliance, a withered old rat named Julian, squinted at Fin under his furrowed brow. He nodded and said, "Yes, yes, Papa! I say yes! Of course!"

Bothwell stepped out from the others. Fin forced himself not to run. A pink scar puckered one of Bothwell's eyelids closed. He looked Fin up and down with his good eye. Bothwell's quivering nostrils snuffled him.

"Is there a problem?" Papa glared at the Councillor.

Bothwell stopped mid snort. He drew back. "Nah! No problem, Boss. Your nephew is a fine sort, the *best* sort. That's what I say!"

Before Fin could even breathe out, the rat beside Bothwell stepped forward. This was Sergo, Councillor of Investigation. He had the longest teeth Fin had ever seen. He didn't look at Fin but bowed his head toward Papa. "Sergo also says yes to Papa and his nephew!"

Papa smiled. "Ah. My loyal Sergo." He raised his arms to the gathered rats, saying, "Council has decided. Council has—"

"Wait!" called a voice. All eyes turned to the sound. Fin strained to see who it was.

"Not all the Councillors have voted." A hunched figure stepped from the shadows and into the dim light of the Council Chamber.

It was a crumbling, ancient rat. His body looked like skin-covered bones. He lurched forward, weaving through the crowd, waving his nose back and forth like the white cane of blind two-legs, until he stood before Fin. He gazed at Fin with cloudy, marble eyes.

He called to Papa, "Did you forget about me, Koba? *I* have not given my approval, and I have a question for this young pup."

Fin frowned. *Koba?* he thought. *Who is Koba?*

Papa said nothing. His eyes bulged, and his mouth formed a tight line.

"I am Balthazar," said the old rat to Fin. "I was once Chairman, just like your uncle." Fin gasped and Balthazar laughed. "You are thinking, 'Impossible!' But it is true, is it not, Beloved Chairman?"

"It is true." Papa's voice was flat.

"May I ask your nephew a question?"

"You know I must allow it. It is Tunnel Law."

The old rat chuckled. "Yes. I know." His milky eyes bore into Fin. "Why do you wish to join Council, young Fin?"

Fin had been expecting a trap, but the question was simple. Yet he stammered. "I…I want to join Council…I want to…because…"

"Yes?" said Balthazar, leaning closer. He blinked his marble eyes.

"Because…because of something I heard," said Fin. "Someone told me about *Collections*. Someone told me that Council only cares about the Upper Tunnels and not the Lowers."

A hissing started in the Chamber. His uncle leaned forward, his eyes bulging.

"WHAT?"

Fin said quickly, "I know that's not true…and…I'm here to prove that. I know that Council cares for everyone."

Balthazar chuckled again. He called up to Papa. "Your nephew is here to save you, Beloved Chairman. He's here to save us all." Balthazar bowed to Fin.

Fin said, "No! Don't do that! I'm not here to——"

But the old one had disappeared back into the shadows. Fin swirled to plead with his uncle. "Papa, you know I——"

"Who said it?" said Papa. "Who is this Wrecker? Who? Tell me!"

Zumi's face rose before Fin. She had saved him. "I…I can't tell," he said.

His uncle stared at him. A hush fell upon the Chamber. Fin's breath stuck in his chest, his eyes pleading for Papa to understand.

"Can't tell, or *won't* tell?" Papa glowered at him but shook his head. "I understand. You are young, and you don't know how cruel this world is. So, now you will learn——you will learn why it is we fight. And when you do, and *only* when you do, you will join Council."

Papa nodded to Bothwell. "You know what to do."

The Great & the Small

The Counselor of the ARM barked, "Right, my crew! Line 'er up and let's go!"

Fin was jostled into one of the rows of squad members. As the squad moved out, he caught sight of Balthazar. The old rat's white eyes gazed at him.

The fishmonger was alarmed by the vandalism to his stall, in particular the small dead rat that had been positioned and left to stiffen on his table. It had taken a good deal of scrubbing with a strong bleach solution before he could use that table again.

He'd gone over the possibilities a million times in his mind, but he couldn't figure out how the hooligans had gotten in. After all, a steel grid curtain was lowered after the market closed to keep such things from happening.

"Rotten kids!" he muttered. Still, he looked over his shoulder more after that, uncertain and wary.

CHAPTER FIFTEEN

"Listen to what has happened and tears will flow from your eyes."

Gabriele de' Mussis, 1348

They plunged down the tunnel like one body with many feet, Bothwell's band of enforcers. Fin was at the very back, following the shadowy tails and legs that slithered in front of him in the dark tunnel.

"Come on, you lot!" bellowed Bothwell over his shoulder as he bounded down the drainpipe. According to the Councillor, they were investigating a two-leg Killing Chamber. To Fin, the accounts of Killing Chambers seemed as far-fetched as Collections.

Fin gritted his teeth against the throb in his foot and pushed himself forward, straining to keep pace with the hulking louts that loped in front of him. Even the smaller females dwarfed him in size. Up. Down. Squeezing through dripping holes and plowing into murky troughs filled with lumpy sludge. Running. Running. Sludge in his eyes, up his nose, through his fur. Running blind, just following the shadow tails and legs always in front of him.

The small tunnels began to change into drier, square metal ducts

that were impossible to get any traction on. Fin's claws scrabbled against the smooth surface. Once he slipped and overshot a corner, smashing into the duct wall with a reverberating gong.

"Quiet!" Bothwell barked. For the next while, except for the pinging of their claws on the metal, they ran in complete silence. Suddenly Bothwell stopped. The rest of the squad came to an immediate halt except Fin. He sailed headlong into the rump of a thick-necked brute called Squid.

"Oi!" The giant sneered down at him. "Wotch it!"

Bothwell was immediately upon them, snarling. "Shaddap, you great dumb oaf! Show some respect for the Chairman's nephew!"

Squid looked crushed. "Sorry," he mumbled to Fin. "I forgot."

The patrol had stopped in front of a fan that blocked the tunnel. Slats hung over it, but they were broken and hung askew. A hum vibrated through the metal under Fin's paws. The ARM Councillor sat on his haunches, whiskers working. Sweeping the air back and forth with his nose, he stiffened, took a few more sniffs, and then nodded.

"Right," he said. "We're here." He pulled back his lips into what was supposed to be a smile and leered at them. "Anyone feeling brave today?"

No one spoke.

Bothwell tilted his head toward Squid. "How about you—you that's all ready for a fight. You brave enough to go in and have a look?" The hulking rat stared at the floor. Bothwell guffawed. "I'm just havin' you on, Squid, you old dope! I'm thinking our Beloved Chairman wants Mister Fin here to go."

Fin's heart thumped. "He...he does?"

"That's right, Mister Fin, I believe he does." Bothwell smirked, his one eye winking at him.

"Oh, that's fine," said Fin. "Fine. Good. So, here I go." The rest of the patrol watched him.

Nosing up to a slat, he squeezed through. He flattened himself just as a whirring fan blade skimmed his ears.

Bothwell's voice floated over the humming. "Oh, and mind the fan!"

"Thanks for the warning," muttered Fin. He eased himself through the slats on the other side. As he pulled through his tail, the fan blade nicked it.

Fin was in a dark passage—another square metal tunnel. Light streamed around a corner ahead. He crept with his belly close to the ground. Rounding the corner, he stopped. Another duct fan. His tail was bleeding from the last one.

Light strobed from behind it. Fin slid under the fan—this time he knew to expect it—flattened himself against the opening, and looked down. He was at the top of a large room.

Rows and rows of cages crisscrossed the floor. Cages filled with rats.

What were they doing here?

Between the rows, a two-leg peered into the cages. It walked down the aisle and disappeared.

Fin wriggled through the slats and leaped down to the table below. Blood from his cut tail left a splotch on the surface. Before Fin could think of what to do, he heard clomping. The two-leg was coming.

Fin dived behind a pile of thin, leaf-like things as the two-leg reached the table. A trail of blood led to his hiding place. The two-leg reached down, its claw-like paw groping toward him. Had it spotted him?

Time slurred into slow motion.

The huge claw came at him— pale, blind, groping. It brushed ever so slightly against him. He trembled.

The Great & the Small

But the hooks passed by. They fumbled around a straight yellow stick that lay beside Fin. The two-leg grabbed the stick and leaned over the table, the stick clutched in its great paw, scratching marks onto one of the thin leaves. It hadn't seen him.

Fin backed away. He leaped to the floor, leaving another bloody mark, and bolted to a nearby row of cages. They rested on a metal stand with legs that had small holes all the way up. Placing his feet into the holes, Fin began to climb.

He peered into the first cage. A young white rat lay curled on his side; he looked identical to Scratch. Fin looked around at the stark, barren cage. Yellow, gravel-like material covered the floor. Water dripped from a plastic bottle hanging from the side—and obviously had for some time—dampening the gravel beneath into a damp sludge. A flaking block with a foul odour appeared to be the rat's only form of food. There was no soft nesting, no bits of delicious sausage, scrambled egg, or buttery biscuit in this barren cage. Pity welled in him.

"Hey!" Fin whispered. "Hey!"

The little one twitched. "Yeah? Who's there?"

"I'm Fin—sent by the Tunnel Council. We heard there was a Killing Chamber, but I didn't believe…" Fin's voice trailed off. For a moment all he could hear was the laboured breathing of the caged pup. "Why's that two-leg keeping you locked up?"

"Who knows?" said the rat pup. "Who can understand a two-leg? All I know is I'm trying to sleep."

"Wait!" whispered Fin urgently. "Just tell me how to open the cage, and I'll get you out of here!" Gripping the bars between his teeth, Fin gnawed furiously. But the bars remained unbroken, unmoved. Fin tried again, even more vigorously. "Come on," he growled, "open!"

"No use," sighed the pup. "We've all tried. But thanks…friend." Curling himself tightly into a ball, he wrapped his tail around his body and closed his eyes. Within moments he was asleep.

Fin wasn't giving up. Clambering over the young male's cage, Fin reached the one next to him. In it was a white rat, just like the first. Same with the next cage, and the next. The entire section of cages contained white rats. He'd thought Scratch was the only one.

Metal shelves stretched in both directions for as far as Fin could see, all covered with cages. The two-leg remained hunched over its table, making those funny scratches on the flat leaf.

It was a tall, gangly two-leg. It wore a white coat over its clothing and had a frowsy tangle of mouse-brown hair on its crown. Round pieces of glass hung before its eyes in a frame of metal that slipped down its pointy pinched nose, which the two-leg then pushed up with a long finger. Hideous, even for a two-leg. But it was too intent upon its own scratchings. It did not notice Fin.

Cautiously, Fin nosed headfirst down a shelf leg and onto the hard floor. The floor smelled of something nasty and unnatural. It burned his nostrils and made the bottoms of his paws itch.

From the floor everything looked overwhelming. Where to look? Where to go? The Killing Chamber was huge. Crawling under the shelves, he reached the far wall. The cages, crammed from one end of the wall to the other, looked identical to the ones he'd just come from. He shinnied up the leg of one of the shelves and peered into a cage. On its floor lay a mass of white fur covered with strange fleshy lumps. He thought it might be a rat, but it looked like something from Fin's nightmares.

The fur twitched. A delicate face with red eyes looked out at him. A female.

"Who are you?" she asked.

The Great & the Small

"I...I'm Fin. Council sent me."

"Council?"

"The Tunnel Council. I'm a member, or I want to be anyway."

"Why do you want to be a member?" she asked.

"Because I...I... Look, I'm not here to talk about myself."

"Why *are* you here?" Her pink eyes watched him, waiting.

He looked away. "I want to help."

"You can't help us," she said. "No one can."

A feeling rose within Fin, a feeling he didn't recognize. His heart felt squeezed. He couldn't breathe—the smells, the sounds—he had to get out. Climbing down, he ran to one side of the room and looked down the aisle. No table, no fan. "Where's the fan?" he called.

"Dunno," came a reply from one of the cages.

"What's a *fan*?" said another.

Racing under the shelves he reached the other side—it had to be over here. But rows of cages lined the wall. He sat up on his haunches and sniffed the air, waving his nose back and forth to catch the scent. The nasty stink of the floor was all he could smell.

Clink.

What was that?

Clink. Clink.

His ears rotated toward the sound. Honing in on it, he crawled toward it, under the long row of shelves, until finally he came to the row of cages with the young rats. Beyond them was the table with the fan overhead. But at the table sat the two-leg.

It was leaning over something. Fin slipped closer and hid behind a shelf leg. The two-leg was hunched over a metal pan, shining blades flashing in its claws. What was it doing? How was Fin ever going to reach the fan without being spotted?

At that moment the two-leg dropped something on the floor near where Fin was hiding. It reached down to retrieve it.

They locked eyes.

The two-leg bellowed. Its chair clattered backwards against the floor. It took off its shoe and came at Fin, circling him. Memories of the stomping boot came crushing down, but suddenly that feeling, that strange new one, electrified Fin.

He lunged at the two-leg. Digging into its leg with his claws, Fin bit into its flesh until he tasted blood. The two-leg shrieked and slapped at him. Fin lost his hold. He tumbled off. Landing on his back, Fin pedalled the air frantically, twisting his body back onto his paws. Blood smeared the floor from the reopened gash on his tail.

The two-leg gripped the shoe in its claws. It bared its teeth. As it pounced, Fin coiled his legs under himself and jumped. With his claws outspread, he flew at the two-leg's hairless face, at its blue fish eyes, and raked his nails across its flesh. The two-leg stumbled backwards and crashed into some cages.

The two-leg lay on the floor, a low groan issuing from its mouth. Fin took his chance to escape. He climbed up the wall toward the fan, digging in his claws. He climbed to the same level as the metal

pan the two-leg had crouched over. Curiosity overcame him. He crawled to the edge and looked in.

A rat was lying on its back, tied to the pan by its paws. A purple gash ran down the length of its body.

It was dead.

Below, a cage clattered to the floor as the two-leg sat up. Fin climbed to the fan and slipped through. Finally—the duct to outside.

The new, strange feeling burned inside him, making him gasp for air. As if running underwater, he saw his paws moving in slow motion. No air!

The feeling claimed him, overwhelmed him. He approached the group. Plowed through them, oblivious. Their shouts pinged off the tunnels. He did not look back.

This feeling. This new way.

It was hate.

CHAPTER SIXTEEN

"Sometimes history books must be changed and corrected."

Josef Stalin

Ananda looked out her bedroom window, chewing her lip. She'd heard the distinctive rattle of her dad's car and knew he was home. He emerged from his silver SUV, his briefcase packed with a million papers. His eyebrows were so clenched together that from where she stood they looked like a single dark, stormy thundercloud.

Whatever had upset him wouldn't be improved by Ananda's news.

Her mother said nothing about what had happened at school as the family sat down to dinner. They ate silently for a few minutes. Ananda's mouth was so dry it was hard to swallow.

Then Perrin set down her knife and fork and said, "So how was *your* day, Tom?" Her eyes slid to Ananda's.

Her dad's answer surprised them both. It gave Ananda an unexpected reprieve.

"It was awful." He took off his glasses and pinched the bridge of his nose. "A wild rat *attacked* me. It somehow found a way into the lab."

Perrin's mouth dropped open. "That's disgusting!"

"It was identical to that one we saw at the market. Identical. It jumped at my face. It *attacked* me." Tom closed his eyes and took deep breaths in and out. His jaw muscles clenched on and off like he was chewing gum. "It ruined experiments I've been working on for months."

Ananda stared at him. She and her dad hadn't really spoken since the market. Now he was talking about the rat *and* his work.

"I had to go to the clinic and start rabies shots," said Tom. He pulled up his sleeve and frowned at the bandage on his arm.

Perrin snorted in disgust. "What is it going to take for these universities to do something? At the last one it was cockroaches. Here it's wild rats? What are these people waiting for? For something to carry you off? They keep crying about funding, but this is ridiculous!"

Tom didn't seem to hear.

"It stared at me," he said. "It actually *stared* at me."

Ananda felt the hairs on the back of her neck stand on end. She and her mother glanced at each other, their eyes round.

"It stared at me," he went on. "Like...like it was..." but he didn't finish his sentence. He wiped his glasses on his shirttail then put them back on, pushing them up his nose. He gave his head a shake and looked at Perrin and Ananda, blinking. For a moment no one spoke.

Perrin raised her eyebrows.

"Ananda's news won't make you feel any better." She turned to Ananda. "Tell your father why you're suspended from school for a week."

As Ananda lay in bed that night, shadows from the trees outside her window pitched across her ceiling. Wind rattled the window-pane, clattering to come in; a storm was coming. The first fat drops of rain splattered against the house.

Scenes from the day played in her mind like a closed loop, over, and over, and over. The press of the circle of guys around her. The feeling of being threatened. Chris's face leering down. And an out-of-body shot of her own face, frozen in a cry. The book fading below the surface. And the eyes of the man on the cover, like two black holes.

The look of disappointment on her father's face when he heard what she'd done.

She lay awake a long time before slipping into a restless sleep plagued by dreams of eyes as dark as bruises.

The Great & the Small

CHAPTER
SEVENTEEN

"Their greediness, their scorn and malice were asking to be punished."

John of Reading, chronicling period of 1346–67

Fin reached the Council Chamber moments before Bothwell came bounding in, the rest of the squad behind him. Councillor Bothwell cast a dangerous look in Fin's direction, but Fin didn't care.

"I must speak!" Fin said.

He stood panting before the other Councillors: Tiv, Julian, Sergo, Balthazar, and of course, Papa.

"That was fast," said Tiv, dryly.

Julian squinted at Fin. "Didn't we just send him out?"

"I must—"

"Silence!" Papa commanded. "Councillor Bothwell. Your report."

Bothwell stepped in front of Fin. "We're back...quick as...if we'd...sprouted wings..." he panted. "Thanks to young Fin, who set a...remarkable pace..."

Fin said, "Papa! Please! I need to speak!"

Bothwell whirled around, his cheeks puffed out. "Oi! I *am* your superior, my lad!"

Fin pushed by him. "Oh shut up! Papa! Rats are dying! They're dying while we sit around scratching our fleas and talking about... about *nothing*!" He burst into tears. "They can't escape. They've tried and they can't. A two-leg has them trapped, and—"

"Silence!" said Papa again.

Fin looked up, startled. His uncle gazed down at him from the carved platform.

"Lesson Number One: There will always be those who die. For the Common Good, we who lead must rise above emotion."

"But we can save them, Papa!" cried Fin. "*I* can save them. I'll lead a squad in!"

"No. They are lost. We cannot save them from the ugly two-legs."

"But, Papa!"

"Silence! Lesson Number Two: Justice will be done. The two-legs will *pay* for this crime." The word "pay" reverberated through the chamber.

"I don't understand," said Fin. "How can we make them pay?" He looked from face to face. The Councillors watched him. The ancient rat Balthazar sat motionless, his face like carved marble.

"*That* is the question, Nephew," said Papa. "How do we make them pay?" He said this slowly, emphasizing each word.

The Chamber was silent. Papa stared at Fin, waiting. His eyes were wide, his mouth open slightly.

"I…I want the two-legs to pay for this!" said Fin. "Papa, you know I would do anything to make them pay! But-but there's no way!"

Papa smashed his fist into his paw. "Ah, but there is!" he shouted, making the rats next to him jump. "We will make their lives misery. We shall overrun them, plague them. And…that is not all." Climbing down from the platform, he began to pace in the middle of the Chamber.

The Council members circled around him.

"I have smelled something in the air," said Papa. "An ancient foe of the two-legs. It is far away right now, but it is coming. *I can smell it!*" Papa swung around. A few younger Council members stumbled back.

"I have squads searching the docks for this Weapon, this *Gift* to us from the Old Ones." Papa stood before Fin. "Nephew, it will give you your revenge. This Weapon has power to kill them all. You asked me what *Plague Rats* were, and now I—"

"ENOUGH!" cried Balthazar. He lurched to his feet. Fin stumbled backwards. Other Council members gaped at the old rat.

"Balthazar!" Papa glowered at him. "Sit down and go back to sleep before you make an even bigger fool of yourself."

"I know this weapon, or *Gift*, as you call it, Koba. Leave it alone!"

"Leave War to those who are not afraid to fight!" Papa replied.

"You forget that you are *Chairman*, not *King*," said Balthazar. "There is a Council! And leave this pup out of it." He motioned toward Fin.

Fin pushed his way between them. "I'm not a *pup*! And leave my uncle alone, you...you bully! Papa is good! He cares about the Tunnels, and he knows what's best. He's the 'Father of the Tunnels,' not you!"

The old rat swung his nose toward Fin's voice, his sightless eyes wide. Nostrils quivering, Balthazar snuffled Fin up and down, then smiled. Backing away, he bowed his head and said, "Sincerest apologies, young master."

Limping to a corner, the former Chairman dropped like a handful of sticks. Almost immediately a buzzing sound issued from him.

Balthazar was snoring.

Bothwell murmured, "Is that him making that racket?"

"Maybe it is a giant bee going *buzz-buzz* in Chamber!" said Sergo. The Chamber tittered with nervous laughter.

Papa laughed with them, but then his face became grave. "Balthazar does not mean to be harsh. It has always been that way between us, since the beginning. But I forgive him. For the good of the Tunnels, I forgive him."

He gazed at them. "Perhaps some of you believe Balthazar. You believe the ancient Weapon shouldn't be found. Even after horrors such as the Killing Chamber! But I say you are wrong."

He paced before them, looking at each one, his eyes filling with tears. "I won't turn away the Old Ones' Gift! I won't! I *accept* my destiny, no matter how difficult. I have seen too much death by the two-legs. I have seen whole colonies writhing in pain because of two-leg cruelty! I have seen my own mother's neck snapped in a cruel trap! My own father, crushed by a wheel of one of their infernal machines! And now? Now we face the torture of the Killing Chambers! No more. No more, I say!" Papa searched the faces of his Councillors. "Who is with me?"

They glanced at each other before looking back at him. "Yes, of course, Papa. Yes."

Papa's voice rang out. "We don't yet have the Gift from the Old Ones, because we haven't *earned* it! We must first prove that we are worthy by waging war upon our enemies using our bare teeth! Our claws! Our cunning! For my nephew and his paw that was crushed by the cruel boot! For the lost rats of the Killing Chamber who will die apart from their colonies! For my mother and father who died in humiliation and pain! Let us wage this war for the Common Good! All in favour?"

"Aye! Aye! AYE!" The cry rose up in the chamber.

"Let us fight the ugly two-legs!" roared Papa.

"We must organize!" cried Julian.

"We will have justice!" shouted Tiv.

"They will feel MY justice!" said Sergo, snapping his jaws in the air.

"Bothwell! More ARM squads!" cried Papa. "We need more!"

Bothwell loped out of the Chamber. One by one, each Councillor left to make war preparations, until Fin was alone with his uncle and the buzzing pile of twigs.

Papa smiled down at Balthazar's form, his eyes wistful and sad. "He used to be Chairman, and now look at him. Life is cruel to the weak, my boy."

"Yes," said Fin. "But what Weapon are we waiting for?"

"Now, now, all in good time. You trust your old uncle, don't you?"

"You know I do."

They crawled through the tunnel and into the alley, where night had fallen thick, leaving Balthazar behind. The air was warm, heavy with the smell of seaweed and fish.

"Nephew," said Papa. He squinted at the stars and breathed deeply. "Remember this night. This night when the glorious War began."

CHAPTER EIGHTEEN

"There will be bloodshed, but the land will be cleansed."

Brother John Clynn, a Franciscan friar, Ireland, 1349

After Fin's report to Council, everything changed. Rats bustled through the tunnels with a sense of urgency. More ARM squads were formed, each patrol with orders direct from Council.

Fin had his own squad. In recognition of his "heroic work" in the Killing Chamber, Council had given him Disruption of Two-Leg Feeding Stations. Every night, Fin's squad targeted a restaurant, staging fights in the middle of a crowded room, sprinting across tables loaded with food, causing two-legs to flee. It was satisfying work.

But the best part of all was that Scratch served with him. Fin had asked him to join, on the condition that he keep it quiet from Zumi. She wouldn't understand and might even get mad at Fin if she knew, even though he was helping Scratch. He hadn't seen her since that night in the Forbidden Garden.

Scratch was his old self again, head-bobbing and all. The thought of disrupting two-leg feeding stations made him giddy with joy.

"Finally those ugly two-legs will get their necks bitten, like they've done to us! Not that they have really *bitten* us. Of course they can't, they're too big and clumsy, and we are too fast and nimble! But they've poisoned us, squished us… We rats will pay them back! Pay back those ugly two-legs! Count me in! Yes, indeed!"

Fin had laughed. At least *Scratch* was back to normal.

Fin wasn't. He hadn't slept well since the Killing Chamber. During ARM forays he could usually forget. But once he was back in his burrow, memories came without mercy, images of caged rats flashing in his mind.

And then it happened during a raid.

That moonrise Fin and Scratch had been tussling in the middle of a fancy two-leg eatery. One moment Fin rolled head over tail with Scratch, snarling and clawing before the ugly two-legs, and in the next, the sad-eyed female from the Killing Chamber stood before him.

Fin stumbled—everything whirred into slow motion.

Scratch's mouth moved, but Fin didn't hear any sound. Chairs tipped over slowly. There was a rumble along on the floor, slow, like rolling thunder. The lookout shrieked ultrasonic warnings, *"The two-legs are coming! The two-legs are coming!"* but the warnings vibrated in Fin's ears like fluttering wings.

Just in time, Scratch bit Fin's ear, hard. Just in time, Fin saw the two-leg bearing down on him. Just in time, Fin leaped away as a broom crashed down right where he'd been. After that, others staged the fights.

The tall nest-towers in the area that housed many two-legs also came under attack. Each moonrise, rat squads slipped through windows, through cracks in the wall, through loose roofing tiles, to bite the sleeping two-legs. No two-leg, no matter how young, was off-limits. As the Beloved Chairman pointed out, baby two-legs grow up to be big two-legs.

The Great & the Small

MARKET NEWS

In spite of recent attempts to curb the local vermin population, vendors continue to complain about the markedly increased infestation. Management advises that although every effort is being made, it is not responsible for loss of revenue due to product spoilage or customer complaints.

THE FRESH GOURMET

State health officials have closed down yet another restaurant in the beleaguered market area, due to an escalating problem with pests. Wild rats have been terrorizing local restaurant goers and have been seen running across dinner plates, gamboling around chairs, even biting holes in pant legs while diners eat.

Multiple lawsuits have been filed against a local restaurant, amid claims that a dead rat was found in its signature soup, Market Gumbo. One distressed patron claims to have eaten part of the tail.

HARBOUR HERALD

An explosion in the rat population has harbour residents scuttling for cover. "The city should do something," said one distraught mother whose child had recently been treated for rat bites. The toddler had been sleeping in her crib in one of the city's many apartment

buildings, when she suddenly cried out. The
mother was horrified to find bite marks on
the child's cheek. She told reporters, "It was a
rat! I saw its disgusting tail before it slipped
through the window!"

The epicentre of the problem appears to be
the nearby market. "We've always had issues
here with pests, but never like this," said a
long-time vendor who refused to give his
name. Speaking candidly, he said, "I come in
the mornings, and there's rat droppings everywhere. Every morning! It's everywhere, like
they were organized or something." The man
shook his head, adding, "Sounds crazy, I know."
His comments join hundreds of others who say
this is no ordinary problem and demand the
city take decisive action.

CHAPTER NINETEEN

"Those who were dying were so blessed with God's grace as to often be joyful as they faced death, no matter how suddenly they died."

Jean de Venette, Carmelite friar, France, 1356

The shadows of night lifted, and dim morning light crept across the ceiling of the burrow. Beside him, Fin's uncle slept. Papa had been at a Council meeting all night. When he'd come in, Fin pretended to be asleep. His uncle had shuffled around, eaten a bit of the night's forage, then burrowed in and fell asleep.

Fin had returned home exhausted after his own duties, but as usual he couldn't sleep. Faces swirled before him—the caged rats, the female, the young male who couldn't wake up, the one who was stretched wide. *They* were why he was fighting the two-legs. *They* were why Fin prayed to the Old Ones to send the Gift. Anything that stopped the evil Killing Chambers was right. That old rat Balthazar was wrong. Dead wrong. And it was up to Fin to set him straight.

Fin sneaked out of his nest and slipped from the burrow. He knew approximately where the former Chairman nested. He kept to the shadows, climbing through pipes wherever he could to avoid being spotted by two-legs, until finally he reached the burrow.

Fin hesitated before the dark hole, chewing his lip. Should he just barge in? It felt ridiculous to call in politely when he was here to sort Balthazar out. Before he could decide what to do, a familiar voice croaked to him.

"Young Master Fin, what are you waiting for? Come in, come in!"

Annoyed, Fin stepped inside. Balthazar was settled on a pile of rags in the middle of a small but comfortable burrow. A mound of forage lay gathered before him. He nosed a piece of biscuit toward Fin. "Sit! Eat! You must be hungry."

Fin stood rooted by the burrow opening. "How did you know I was coming? Are you spying on me?"

The ancient rat rolled his milky eyes. "Do I look like a spy? Please sit."

Fin stayed standing. "Why do you hate my uncle?"

"Why does your Uncle Koba hate me? Sit."

"Answer my question. And why do you call him Koba? No one else does."

Balthazar turned to him, his blind eyes wide. He smiled. "Because that is his name. Long ago, when I was Chairman, little Koba played at my feet. I was quite fond of him, and he would come often, asking questions, always full of ideas. But then one day, Koba stopped coming." Balthazar looked away. He scratched behind his ear with a back paw. "The next time I saw your uncle was the day he challenged me to be Chairman. He won. Koba was gone, and Papa was born. That is all." Balthazar shrugged.

"I don't believe you. You make my uncle sound like a cheat. *You're* the cheat. You tried to stop Council from going to war. I saw what the two-legs have done, *are* doing."

"If you say so, then it must be true."

Fin exploded. "Stop trying to confuse me, you old goat! You're a troublemaker. That's all you are. You're too afraid to fight, so you make everyone else doubt! You're…you're a coward!"

The Great & the Small

The old rat only smiled.

"And stop smiling! You stupid old…I hope the Gift comes! I pray for it! If it will stop the Killing Chambers I'll take the Gift myself and kill every ugly two-leg there is!"

Balthazar gazed at Fin, still smiling, but his lips began to quiver. Tears flowed down his cheeks. "I'm so sorry…for you," he murmured.

"Sorry for me? Be sorry for yourself! We're going to win the war, and you'll see you were a coward!"

The old rat stared at Fin with his blind eyes, tears wetting his fur. "So sorry…"

"Shut up! Just shut up!" Fin backed out of the burrow, stumbling into the walls. He could still hear the old rat as he fled.

The sun burned hot as Fin travelled through as much shade and shadow as he could find. He groped his way back into the burrow, stumbled into his pile of nesting. *I am sorry…so sorry for you…* Fin dug his head into his nesting. His chest felt tighter than ever, the faces swirling around him like restless ghosts.

Beside him, Papa lay curled in a ball, his breathing deep and even.

CHAPTER TWENTY

"Has his family been arrested yet?
If not, tell me who is responsible for not arresting them!"

Stalin, after hearing of a Soviet soldier's defection to Poland

Day One: The Gulag.

Ananda stared out her bedroom window. She should have welcomed the break from school, but the humiliation was too sharp. Her only consolation was that Chris Litko was suspended too, *and* he was going to have to replace her dad's book.

She tiptoed into the living room.

Her mother poked her head out of her office room and snapped, "Start your chores. The list is on the table."

Did all mothers have hypersensitive hearing?

Ananda grunted, "Yeah, yeah." She picked up the list and read out loud, "Weed garden, clean bathrooms, vacuum house...Mom! This is way too much!"

"We discussed this. If you don't like it, next time don't get suspended."

Ananda snarled and stamped out of the house, slamming the door.

She opened the garden shed and rummaged for gardening gloves and a trowel. For the next hour she weeded. After grabbing some breakfast, she cleaned the bathroom. And then she vacuumed the house.

Every so often her mother came and checked her progress.

It was a Gulag prison camp straight out of the Soviet era. In her mind, she retorted, "Yes, Comrade Stalin, no, Comrade Stalin," to her mother's nagging. She didn't say it out loud.

In the evening, there was nothing to do. All her electronics had been taken away: no TV, no cell phone, no calls from friends—not that she had any friends. George had been incommunicado since the pond incident. Even social goddesses had limits, Ananda supposed.

She got out her sketch pad and the art book she'd bought back before the Times of Trouble started. She opened the book and did the second exercise. The first one she'd tried to draw had looked awful. This one was no better. The example in the book looked graceful and easy. Ananda's looked like a chicken had died on the paper while scribbling with a pencil between its tail feathers.

Everything felt too difficult. She smacked the book closed in frustration. She sat, her chest rising and falling. Her stomach felt like a knot of concrete. She curled up on her bed and slept.

Day Two: Drudgery and Boredom.

That evening she sketched out a cartoon of the Pond Incident: Chris Litko falling into the pond, his unibrow raised in alarm. She made his friends look like escapees from an Early Man exhibit.

Day Three: Escape.

Ananda was desperate to escape. She had to get out of the house or she'd go crazy. She stood at her mother's open office door. "Mom, I need to go to the library."

Her mother didn't look up from her computer. "No. Do your chores."

Ananda played her ace card. "But it's for school."

"School?" Perrin stopped typing and looked at her.

"Yes, I have a big History assignment. It's due the week after I get back from my…you know."

The walk to the library was heavenly.

The walk back was torture.

Ananda had five heavy books that got heavier with every step.

She was nearing home when she heard George call to her. Ananda turned around and smiled. George separated from the group of girls she was walking with and jogged over to her.

"Hey! How are you doing?"

"My life as a convict is going great so far," she joked. "No chain gangs yet, though, or murder acquittals, so my biography will have to wait." Ananda laughed.

George looked at her, mystified.

Ananda blushed. "I mean, I'm fine. Thanks for asking."

George shook her head so that her blonde hair swirled around her. "You're so weird, Ananda," she laughed, and began chattering about the news at school. Ananda nodded at the right times, but George's off-hand comment had stung. *Weird?*

By the time they reached her house and had said goodbye, Ananda was exhausted.

She dumped the books on her desk.

Ananda knew she didn't fit in at school; it didn't take Einstein to figure that out, but *weird?* Mind you, George had said it with a smile. Maybe weird was good.

When was weird ever good?

"Stop it," she said out loud. George was nice. Period. Of course she hadn't meant anything by it! Pushing it from her mind, she sat down at the desk.

The Great & the Small

She had brought home books on the plague that had happened during the 1300s. She'd dumped the idea of reporting on Stalin after the pond incident with Chris. It'd be hard enough to do her report without that grinning fool smirking at her lost book on top of it.

Besides, enough time had passed that Ananda felt silly about her overreaction to the current outbreak of plague. Of course it wasn't her fault. It had spread from India to a bunch of countries and was in the news a lot. She'd tie it in to the outbreak of the Middle Ages.

Ananda looked at the first book: *From the Brink of Chaos*. A skeleton grinned on the cover, a golden crown on his head. His abdomen had rotted away, leaving a moldering cavern where his guts had been. It was disgusting, even by modern standards.

She would need fortification if she was going to study a book with a cover that ugly.

Ananda ambled out to the kitchen and made herself a peanut butter and jam sandwich. She brought it back to her desk. Taking a bite, she opened the book:

Here begins a chronicle of the pestilence which occurred in 1348, as written by Gabriele de' Mussis of Piacenza... In 1346, from the East, a deadly pestilence struck down countless numbers. Death was instant. Soon, countries were stripped of their people. Villages, towns, and magnificent cities were left abandoned, all within either dead or having fled for their lives...

Listen to me, listen to the story of what I have seen... things so horrible it will make tears flow from your eyes. For God has said He will destroy man, take him off the face of the Earth, turn him back into dust from which he was created. So sayeth the Lord, 'I bid you weep...'

Ananda put her sandwich down. This was an eyewitness account?

As one person became ill and died, so often did the pestilence poison his entire family, too. Those pre-paring the body of their loved one, died themselves, leaving all to be buried together....

Death struck suddenly, and without mercy. It emp-tied cities and towns. It seeped through the windows and under doors....

The afternoon shadows lengthened, but Ananda kept reading.

At dinner, she was quiet. The stories of those who'd lived so long ago swirled in her head. The man who'd seen the bodies of his loved ones dug up and dragged away by dogs. The heaps of the dead thrown into pits for mass burial. The monk who'd thought it was the end of the world but had left parchment in case anyone was left alive to write about it once he was dead.

The Great & the Small

Her parents tried to pull her into a conversation but soon gave up, and they ate in silence.

As soon as dinner was done, she went back into her room and read.

Down the hill of the harbour city, within walking distance of the market, a freighter slipped into port. It was loaded to the gunwales with cargo: textiles, spices, and foodstuffs, even automobiles.

But there was another cargo it carried.

A colony of rats had inhabited the ship's hold for generations, for as long as the aging freighter had taken to the seas. Now, every member of the colony lay dead—struck down by an ancient foe.

All but one, that is.

The lone surviving rat dragged herself to the mooring rope and inched her way down to the dock below, seeking refuge. It did not take long for the ARM to discover her.

The Gift had been found.

CHAPTER
TWENTY-ONE

"Because Man is made of flesh and bone, let him become ashes and dust."

Gabriele de' Mussis, 1348

Papa burst into the nest. His eyes glinted with a strange light. "Come! You must come, Nephew!"

"But Papa, I'm—"

"Now!"

Fin obeyed. His dinner—delicious sausage pilfered from the corner deli—was left uneaten. He struggled to keep up with his uncle, who plunged down the alley. The moon was high and the alley empty of two-legs. They darted through the shuttered-up market and down the stairs to the lower alley.

Papa loped toward the Council Chamber, toward the Forbidden Garden.

"Papa...wait! I can't...keep up..."

"Hurry!"

Fin saw movement at the perimeter of the Forbidden Garden.

The Great & the Small

As he approached, he saw it was a roiling mass of rats. The entire Tunnel Colony flowed under the iron fence, a grey river of whiskers, tails, and ears.

ARM patrols stood by, watching them enter.

"Nephew! Come!" Fin was jerked out of his thoughts. Papa was on the other side of the fence, his eyes wide. "Come!" He seemed larger than ever, and his black fur gleamed in the moonlight.

"Yes, Papa! I'm coming!" said Fin. The air tingled. What was going on? Everyone seemed to feel it. Every face displayed the same wonder and excitement that he felt.

Papa leaped onto the stone bench that jutted out from the small hill. Fin stood behind him, along with some of the ARM and members of Council. Tiv, Julian, Sergo, Bothwell...and Balthazar. The ancient one sat off to the side behind Fin, hunched, his limbs as thin and frail as leafless twigs.

Balthazar did not look at the crowd, or even at the Council, but as Fin got into place behind Papa, he could feel the old rat's white marble eyes on him. Finally Balthazar turned his face forward, staring sightlessly into the throng.

Standing before the entire colony, Fin saw rats of every age—from suckling pups to toothless elders. As Papa drew himself tall and held open his arms, the crowd jostled in tighter. Mothers shushed their pups, a few receiving sharp nips on the ear.

"Good Tunnel Rats!" cried Papa to the throng below him. Hundreds of rats in the Forbidden Garden fell silent. The Chairman's gaze moved across the multitude. "You are here to witness the beginning of a new age!"

There was a scuffling beside Fin. Scratch slid in next to him, whispering, "I'm here, Captain Fin, I'm here! Here at your side, doing my duty!"

Fin nodded but said nothing. Zumi was in the crowd. Their eyes locked for a moment before her glance flickered between Fin and her brother in growing horror. Now Zumi knew Scratch was in the ARM. And she knew who was responsible. Fin looked away, but her eyes stabbed into him.

Scratch elbowed him and nodded about something Papa was saying. Scratch gazed at the Beloved Chairman, his eyes half-closed, swaying his nose back and forth to catch every morsel of sound, every whiff of action with his trembling whiskers.

Papa cried, "You may well ask why, after generations, the Forbidden Garden is open. Because we are *celebrating*!" Papa pulled himself to his full height, and his velvety black fur rippled in the starlight. He threw back his head and laughed. It was loud and startling. The gathered rats looked hesitantly at each other but then broke out into laughter too.

"Yes, good Tunnel Rats!" said the Chairman. "Yes! The world has changed! And do you know who changed it?" He stared at the audience with wide eyes. "Do you know? *He* did. My nephew." Papa pointed to Fin. Every eye in the Forbidden Garden turned to stare.

Fin's mouth dropped open. Papa's gaze was on him too. Fin forced a smile. He nodded, his ears so hot they felt on fire.

Papa called to the crowd, "Do you know how he changed it?"

A few rats yelled back, "How?"

"Tell 'em, Boss!" called Bothwell.

"This good Tunnel Rat," Papa shouted, "this *Hero* of the Common Good, my nephew, had the courage to say 'Enough!' Had the courage to say, 'Kill them all! Kill the ugly two-legs!'"

A number of rats cheered and shouted Fin's name. He kept smiling, but his teeth were gritted. Had he said that? He'd been so upset after the Killing Chamber, he hardly knew. The campaign,

Disruption and Harassment of Two-Legs, had been in force for nights and nights, but it hadn't just been Fin's idea, had it? And no one had died.

He glanced over the crowd, stumbled over Zumi's dark gaze. Fin pulled his eyes away. His back leg began to throb. Shifting his paws, he pressed his curled paw tight against his belly.

Papa hushed the crowd, then nodded to Julian. Councillor Julian stepped forward, clearing his throat. Leering at the gathering, he smiled, showing his long, yellow teeth. "Every rat is equal! Every nest for all!"

The gathering answered, "Every rat is equal! Every nest for all!"

"Dark days lie ahead, good Tunnel Rats!" cried Julian. "Wreckers will batter against us from within! Two-legs will fight us from without!"

Councillor Tiv stepped forward and cried, "Sacrifice, good Tunnel Rats! Sacrifice! Wreckers must be rooted out, traitors brought to justice. I am a good Tunnel Rat, and I am also a mother," she stared out at the rats, "but I would turn in my own pup if it betrayed the Common Good!"

The cheering crowd went silent.

Papa smiled, gazing out over the assemblage. Tiv looked at him then raised her paw and shouted, "Sacrifice! Sacrifice for the Common Good!"

Sergo strode up beside her and, shaking his clenched paw in the air, bellowed, "The Common Good! Sacrifice!"

"The Common Good!" cried Bothwell, stamping his feet. "The Common Good! The Common Good!" Like an orchestra conductor, he waved at ARM patrol members, who took up the chant. ARM members wove through the crowds. "The Common Good! The Common Good! The Common Good!"

The excitement was infectious. Rats shrieked and stamped their feet. Fin shouted and stamped his feet too. Behind him Scratch's piercing squeal could be heard over all. Papa walked back and forth on the bench, listening, smiling. Then, he turned to the gathering, arms open, and waited.

The crowd settled into a mumbled hush. Still, the Chairman stood, silent, his arms outstretched.

In the distance, a seagull squawked, its voice growing faint. A salty gust from the harbour tousled the trees rimming the garden. Water gurgled from the fountain where Fin and Zumi had swum not too long ago. Every rat in the Forbidden Garden leaned forward, their eyes riveted on their Beloved Chairman.

He spoke. "Good Tunnel Rats. The history of our beloved Tunnels would make a stone weep. We all know this history. It is whispered to pups as they play, sung in their lullabies as they sleep; it is fed to them in their mother's milk so that in the very marrow of our bones we may never forget what the two-legs have done to us. They have *trapped* us, *poisoned* us, *tortured* us, *reviled* us." With each word, Papa's arms jerked wider, as if he himself were experiencing all of those things in front of them. At the end he pulled his fists into himself and hunched over them, his breath ragged.

The Great & the Small

Sobs broke out in the gathering. A few pups began to wail. Someone shouted, "Those ugly, *ugly* two-legs!"

Papa slowly pulled himself upright. "Yes, friend, they are indeed ugly."

He began to pace again. "But there is an older story—much older—that is our history too; a time when rats ruled the earth and the two-legs were cut down like sheaves of wheat in a field. The Old Ones called it 'the Great Dying.'"

Fin gasped. Exclamations of alarm whisked through the throng. *No one* talked about that. The time when almost every living thing had been wiped off the earth from a sickness *carried by rats*. As far back as Fin could remember, a crushing sense of shame had overshadowed the history of his kind. Yes, the two-legs were cruel, and yes, rats were reviled and persecuted by every living creature…but all that was *because* of the Great Dying. The shadow of it hung over every rat like a suffocating shroud. The Great Dying was what had driven rats into the shadows, the dripping dark of tunnels, the rancid underbelly of civilization where they'd been forced to dwell.

Fin glanced quickly at the Councillors, expecting to see the same shock on their faces as on those of the crowd before him. But none showed surprise. They had *known* Papa was going to talk about this? The only Council member who was not watching Papa and nodding with agreement was Balthazar. He was asleep, his grizzled chin resting on his chest.

"Why should we not claim this history too?" asked Papa, his voice rising. "Why?" He walked slowly across the front of the park bench, gazing at each rat who sat below him. "Are we ashamed? Are we ashamed that we once walked side by side with Death? That we were its partners in bringing down the two-legs?" He walked back the other way. "Are we? Are *you*? What about you?" he asked, staring at one young rat at the front.

"No…no…I'm not ashamed, I guess…" the rat murmured, glancing at his neighbours. No one met Papa's eyes.

"Are you?" shouted the Chairman. "I don't hear you!"

"Papa, over here!" squealed Scratch, stepping forward. "I'm not ashamed at all! Not one bit! Not one little bit!"

"Scratch!" shouted Zumi, but her cry was muffled by the swarm around her.

Fin pulled Scratch back. "Come on, Scratch. Knock it off."

Scratch wrenched himself away and thrust a small fist in the air. His white fur glowed in the moonlight. "I'm not ashamed! I'm glad, Beloved Chairman! Yes, I'm *glad* the Old Ones almost got them all! All those ugly, *ugly* two-legs!"

"Ah," chuckled Papa, "the loyal friend." Scratch beamed, bobbing his head.

Council members nodded with approval, smiling at Scratch as one might smile at a beloved pup.

"Who else?" shouted Papa. "Who else is a good Tunnel Rat like this loyal friend?"

"I am! I am, Chairman!" Shouts began to thrum in the Forbidden Garden. "I am not ashamed! I am not ashamed!"

More and more rats joined in. They streamed toward the bench and swarmed on the grass below Papa. The Chairman's grin grew wide. As the mash of rats churned below him, clawing over one another to get nearer to their leader, tails became tangled.

The squealing knot of rats rolled and surged as one, careening through the crowd. For a moment it was chaos. Pups screamed, and mothers shrieked. Like flood waters, panic rose in the crowd. Rats began nipping at each other and shouting.

But as quickly as the situation had arisen, Papa calmed it down. He nodded to Bothwell, who, in his turn, nodded to the squad Captains. ARM patrols dived into the scrum, untangling tails, heaving rats back, biting to clear the throng.

Order was restored. Papa laughed. "Yes! Yes! Very good! Who else?"

Fin shook his head. How did his uncle do that? He made it look so easy, calming the chaos. How could one who commanded such devotion and adoration be related to a scrawny little rat like Fin?

He would make Papa proud if it took the last breath in his body.

He thrust his nose up. He was the nephew of the Chairman, a Hero. His uncle had said so. "I am not ashamed, Papa," he called. "I am *not* ashamed!"

The throb in his foot didn't matter. Whatever problem Zumi had with him didn't matter. This was his family. These were his brothers and sisters. And the two-legs? They had Killing Chambers and traps. They poisoned and tormented his brothers and sisters.

Stepping forward next to Papa, Fin shouted, "Kill them all! Kill the two-leg monsters!" The multitude roared with him, moving and rippling in unison like some giant beast.

"Ha, ha! Yes, Fin," chuckled Papa. "Yes, my boy."

Seeing his uncle laugh was wonderful. Fin laughed too; his heart felt like it could fly. Papa nuzzled him and nipped his ear, causing the hordes to cheer, "Papa and Fin! Papa and Fin! Papa and Fin!"

Fin stepped back next to Scratch, his ears burning with pleasure.

Scratch shouted with the crowds, "Papa and Fin! Papa and Fin!" Then he added shrilly, "And Fin is my best friend!" Rats who heard him laughed.

Papa raised his paws for silence. The cheering died. "Good Tunnel Rats! We have with us our former Chairman, Balthazar." Fin knew his uncle well enough to catch the hint of disdain in his voice.

"As Councillor of Preservation, it is his duty to tell you about the Old Ones and their sacrifice. He will tell you about the Great Dying. And teach us why we Tunnel Rats must be *proud*!"

Papa paused. "Proud enough to give the ultimate sacrifice again. For some of you will need to become Plague Rats." A few cheers went up before the words sank in, and then there was shocked silence.

Fin shook his ears as if he hadn't heard right. Plague Rats?

Papa gazed at the crowd, his eyes wide and gleaming. "You will be glorious martyrs for the Common Good. Together, we will stand, haunch by haunch, tooth by tooth. Together!" He thundered, "TOGETHER!"

The crowd went crazy. "Pa-pa! Pa-pa! Pa-pa!"

"Every rat is equal! Every nest for all!" the Chairman cried.

The crowd answered, "Every rat is equal! Every nest for all!"

Turning away, Papa leaned over Balthazar. "Wake up! Wake up! For the sake of the Old Ones, wake up!" He bit his ear.

Balthazar jerked awake, smacking his lips. "Ah, yes, Koba, I'm ready. I was merely sleeping."

"Sleep when you're dead," hissed Papa. "Council needs you. Do *not* let us down!"

The Great & the Small

CHAPTER
TWENTY-TWO

"Death alone wakes us from our dreams. Why could not I
wake before this?"

Petrarch, May–June 1349

B althazar shuffled to the front of the park bench, his ribs heaving with each wheezing gasp he took. He sat, swaying on his
haunches, nose twitching, and scanned the air.

The Forbidden Garden was silent. Reverence for the former
Chairman shone on the faces of older Tunnel Rats. The pups, however, had never heard of him. They stared at the ancient rat swaying
before them with fascinated horror.

Balthazar cleared his throat. "Friends, Council has instructed me
to tell you a story. A true story. It was told to my mother and to her
mother before her, and so on. Back through many, many lives. Ah…
one moment." Reaching up a long, boney leg, the former Chairman
scratched slowly at his ear. "Ahh…yes!" He sat up, smacking his
gums. He squinted into the vast garden.

"Balthazar!" hissed Papa.

The old rat waved a craggy paw in front of his face, as one would shoo an annoying gnat. "Yes, yes, young Koba! Patience!"

He looked out at the gathering, his white orbs seeming to see it all. "Long ago, when the Old Ones crept along the earth, the world was different. The Old Ones walked without fear. They were part of Nature's Web and were assured of their place.

"Then, from over the mountains and across the sea there came a terrible scourge, a scourge that would deal death, not only to the Old Ones, but to *all*." Balthazar raised his milk-white eyes to the heavens, his voice suddenly booming. "It was the power of Life and DEATH!"

Fin gulped and looked around.

"Death," Balthazar went on softly, "death that *we* carried, became Earth's doom. Rats who carried the scourge and died from it were called Plague Rats. Council wants you to honour those rats as martyrs."

Tiv whispered something to the Chairman. He nodded and stepped forward to whisper in Balthazar's ear. "The Streets of Plenty! Tell them about the Streets of Plenty!"

"Yes, yes! Patience!" Balthazar sighed and shook his head. "Streets that had rung with the clatter of crushing hooves and cruel boots were now still. Spoiling food lay strewn on market stalls. The streets over-flowed with hams, sausages, cheeses, and barely moulding bread!"

He paused, leaning forward, gazing across the gathering. "There were hardly any two-legs to eat the food. There were hardly any two-legs to drive off the rats. The rats who survived, lived well. Not so for the two-legs." He paused, then said, "It is told that the two-legs even wept."

The crowd gasped, but Fin snorted in disgust. Even day-old pups knew that two-legs were incapable of feelings! He glanced at Papa, but his uncle hadn't heard the old rat. Tiv was whispering something to him.

Balthazar went on. "The two-legs cast themselves out into the ocean of blood. Parents abandoned their young, husbands their wives, brother abandoned brother. The surviving Old Ones had their pick of two-leg nests. In some they even found little ones, crying and alone. But we do not care about the baby two-legs, do we? For little two-legs grow up to be big two-legs."

Shouts of "Yeah!" and "That's right!" came from Council and ARM members, even much of the crowd. But some rats were subdued. A few of the mothers pulled their pups closer. Fin had endured run-ins with little two-legs. They were loud, unpredictable, and they chased him on their stumpy legs. But Balthazar's question niggled at him.

Fin's uncle leaned forward and whispered something in Balthazar's ear.

"Yes, Koba, yes. Give me time."

Balthazar cleared his throat again. "Huge pits were dug. Pits dug to hold the two-leg dead, but it was not enough. Dogs dragged the corpses from graves to gnaw on their bones."

Papa shouted, "And did they not deserve it, good Tunnel Rats?"

Cries of "Yes!" filled the air.

The old rat paused. With his head lowered, his breathing laboured, he was silent. Council members glanced at each other. A rat sneezed in the crowd, muttering, "Sorry." A pup began to whine. A few more joined in. Still the former Chairman of the Tunnels was silent.

"Balthazar!" hissed Papa.

The old rat's sides began to heave. A small cry escaped him. When he spoke, his voice sounded thick. "Do not weep for the two-legs. Do not think of their horror. After all, two-leg hearts are cut from stone. They do not feel as we feel. Or so says Council."

Fin's head jerked to attention. What had he said? Had Council told him to say that? Fin looked at Papa. Papa's eyes bulged, his mouth opening and closing like a fish at the market. The other Councillors stared, speechless, at the former Chairman.

Balthazar was going against Council.

Balthazar was a Wrecker.

The Great & the Small

The ancient rat raised his face, tears streaming from his eyes. "So much suffering…for the Plague Rats, for the two-legs!" he wailed. "So much…! And Council wants to bring that doom again? I say NO!"

A sound rose up from the gathering, like a thousand hissing snakes. Shouts erupted from Council. Tiv shrieked words that Fin could not hear over the chaos. Julian's jaw dropped open. Papa nodded to Bothwell and Sergo, flicking his head toward Balthazar. They crouched, legs coiled, and sprang. But the old rat was surprisingly nimble and stepped aside. Bothwell and Sergo overshot their mark and tumbled off the edge with a roar of frustration and scratching fury.

Balthazar cried, "Do not allow Council to wreak this doom! Do not let them unleash this scourge!"

ARM squads from the back pushed through the crowd and streamed toward the bench. Pups in the crowd wailed. Mothers screamed, clutching their babies close. Fin wanted to scream as well. His eyes found Zumi's. Hers were round with terror.

Over the chaos Balthazar's voice rang like a bell. "Do not their hearts beat like ours?" he shouted. Papa charged at him, but again Balthazar eluded capture. ARM squads leaped up the bench.

Scratch bounded across the bench to join the squads. "Scratch!" called Fin, but his voice was lost. The ARM surged toward Balthazar. Bothwell and Sergo clawed their way up the bench legs.

"Truth! Seek *truth*!" called Balthazar.

Fin's fur stood on end. He stood frozen as the ARM surrounded the old rat. As Sergo lunged forward, his teeth bared, Bothwell leaped on Balthazar's neck.

"… Council… Poison… Words are poison!" the old rat was struggling to be heard. "Do not believe their lie—!" Balthazar's voice stopped as rats swarmed over him.

Over the crowd Fin heard Zumi wail, "No! Balthazar!"

He watched her swim through the mob and climb the bench leg where he stood. ARM squads swarmed below and surged over Zumi, covering her.

"Get off her!" he shouted. But she was buried. Without thinking, Fin launched himself off the bench. He threw rats off with his teeth, his bad leg trailing behind. He reached a large rat who was holding Zumi to the ground.

He bit into the rat's haunch and pulled him off her, just as he was knocked backwards by fleeing rats. "Zu—!" A paw stepped in Fin's open mouth. A claw scratched near his eye. He couldn't catch his breath. "Stop! Get off of me…! Help!"

"Fin!" It was Zumi. Her voice was faint over the noise. "Fin!"

Over the chaos Papa thundered, "Fin! Where is Fin? Find him!"

Can't breathe…!

"There! Get him!" Squad members hoisted him out of danger, back onto the bench, where he lay panting for air. By the time he was able to stand, Zumi was gone.

The rat that had escaped from the freighter was dead, killed by the Gift. But before she died, she infected the patrol that had found her. Now, the dying patrol members sat in isolation, waiting for their final orders.

They would not have long to wait.

The Great & the Small

PART TWO

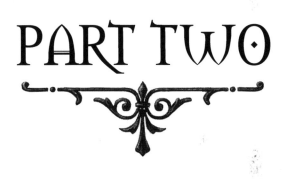

CHAPTER TWENTY-THREE

"Some believed that the way to keep free of the plague was to drink heavily, making merry all day and night."

Giovanni Boccaccio, author and poet, Florence, Italy (1313–75)

*C*urled into her side, he is wakeful, his belly full, and he is warm. Yet he is restless.

He tucks his muzzle under her, squeezes his eyes shut.

"No, Pip," says Nia. "You must see."

Burrowing in deeper, he pretends not to hear.

"Open your eyes."

Still he doesn't move.

"Open them!" Her voice is insistent. He opens his eyes a sliver and when he does, he sees a shadow lunge and she is gone from his side—but he can still hear her.

She is shrieking.

Over and over she calls a name. Whose name? But before he can put the sounds together, make sense of them, she is silent.

The thick shadow blankets him. Fin squeals, struggles, and bites.

Teeth sink into his paw, biting clean through, and he is dragged from his nest.

The Great & the Small

The freighters hovered like floating mountains in the hot, shimmering heat. In the nights since the gathering in the Forbidden Garden, summer had come. Fin had been looking forward to the heat. He had never experienced summer before. But before Papa and Fin reached the railing overlooking the harbour, the thrill of the new experience was gone. Baking hot pavement roasted his feet, and his back paw became swollen and heavy.

Once they reached the walkway that cut below the market, his uncle leaped easily onto the railing. Fin jumped too but fell short. Smacking against the railing, he clung by his paws and tried heaving himself up. But the railing felt sizzling under his feet. He slid, *plop!* back onto the walkway. His uncle gave no sign that he had noticed.

Fin found a shady spot farther down the walkway. He rolled onto his back, lifting his feet so they could sweat and cool his body. Papa stood on the railing, watching the wharf below.

"What are we doing here in the daytime anyway?" asked Fin irritably.

"Surveillance, dear Nephew. You do remember that word, don't you?"

Fin grunted. He was too hot to be teased.

Time passed. The Chairman's coat shone in the afternoon light, jet black against the blue sky. He scanned the air with his nose.

Fin's mind wandered back to the Forbidden Garden. So many questions. Had Zumi escaped? Was Balthazar okay? Where was he now? Why had there even *been* a meeting? To announce that they were at war with the two-legs? They were *already* at war with the two-legs! And Plague Rats...? It made Fin's head spin. Plague Rats were from the Great Dying, not now.

Suddenly Papa bellowed, "Ha!"

"Agh!" said Fin. "You scared me!"

"Ha!" Papa bellowed again. "They made it in! Except the one— but the rest got in!"

"What? Who? Who's in? What are you talking about?"

His uncle didn't answer. Swivelling on the railing, Papa sprang toward the market, soaring through the air like a strange black bird, and landed at the mouth of a broken air duct. Slipping through the slats on the duct, he disappeared.

Fin stared after him, his mouth hanging. "Hey! Hey, wait a minute!"

But at that moment his uncle thrust his head back out between the slats, a wide grin on his face. With his velvet ears pinned under a slat and his nose poking through, the Beloved Chairman looked ridiculous!

Fin laughed. "What are you—?"

"Coming, slowpoke?" Papa leaped back out onto the pavement. To Fin's delight, his uncle began to dance a jig. A couple of pigeons pecking at the ground raised their heads to gape at him.

Fin laughed until his stomach hurt. Clutching his belly, he gasped, "Goofball! My uncle is a goofball!"

"Ha! Ha! Don't you know it, Nephew! Don't you know it!" Papa swooped back into the duct and out of sight. Still laughing, Fin scrambled after him.

Throughout the night, as they foraged the corners and crevices of the closed market, Papa remained jovial. He wouldn't reveal what he'd seen, but Fin was just glad to see him happy.

The Great & the Small

The death squad had honed in on their target—a small hole in the side of the building near the docks. Wriggling through, the Plague Rats had gone in, one after another, except for the last one. Sicker than the rest, the rat named Meena had been exposed to the pestilence earlier than the others as punishment for suspected Wrecking. Near death, she staggered blindly in front of the hole, blood frothing from her nose.

"Stop stalling, you ugly Wrecker!" hissed an ARM member. He and another member were watching from a distance. "Get in the hole, and do your flipping duty!" Reluctant to get any closer for fear of the pestilence, the two squad members hid behind a shrub and peered at the rat.

Meena collapsed on her back, her hind legs kicking the air, her whole body convulsing.

"Get in the hole before you die, you blinking moron!" the ARM member barked. "You're no good outside of it!"

"She can't hear you, stupid," said the other.

"You're stupid. There, go give her a bite. A sharp one, right on the tail to move her into that hole or we're both in for it!"

"Me? Why should I do it? You do it!"

But neither of them needed to bother. Meena was already dead.

CHAPTER TWENTY-FOUR

"People make friends with sin and wrongdoing,
while the children die for the sins of their parents."

Anonymous fourteenth-century poem on the pestilence

Just before sunrise, Fin and his uncle returned to their nest. Papa fell asleep right away, but Fin lay awake. The questions had left him alone while he and Papa were out, but now the questions were back. The bedding felt scratchy and hot. Fin squirmed to get comfortable. When he finally slipped into sleep, the dream came.

Heat shimmers. Freighters float over the water. The Chairman stands against a hazy sky, on the railing overlooking the wharf. There is no shade for Fin. His thoughts run like a mouse on a wheel...must find shade...

The Chairman turns. But it is not Papa anymore. It is Balthazar. He looks at Fin, his eyes marble-white. "Come, young master," he croaks. "Do not be

afraid." Grabbing Fin by his scruff, he leaps into the sky.

"No!" shouts Fin. "We'll fall!"

But the old rat sprouts wings, grey and sturdy like the wings of a pigeon, and climbs high into the sky, his now-glossy fur fluttering in the wind. He holds Fin tight.

Fin struggles, his legs thrashing, until he notices his back leg—the curl in his paw is gone! Stretching it, he wriggles his toes. There is no pain.

Unafraid now, Fin gazes around. They are flying over the harbour. Seagulls wheel far below. He takes a gulp of air, and it is fresh and cold in his chest. Joy flashes through him like sunlight dancing on water.

At that moment, blood drops down on him from above. Fin looks up to see blood foaming from Balthazar's mouth.

Their eyes meet. The old rat's eyes are shining black, no longer white. His thick fur begins to peel back, away from his body, like sheets of wax melting in the sun. Balthazar smiles as, layer after layer, he fades away until there is only sky.

Fin is alone. "Balthazar!"

Screaming, he falls. A black dot lies far below. As Fin plummets, the ground grows larger, rushing at him.

It is Papa.

Fin woke up gasping for air, feeling himself falling. Oh, thank the Old Ones, it was only a dream! He climbed out of the nest, still panting.

Papa was awake, hunched in the corner. He was finishing off a pastry from last night's plunder. He licked his paws and rubbed them over his whiskers until they gleamed. "Finally awake, eh? Pleasant dreams?"

"No," said Fin. "Horrible."

His uncle stopped his grooming. "Eh? Tell me."

But the images that had been so real evaporated like fog in the morning light. "I...I don't remember," said Fin.

Papa chuckled. He licked his paws again and began to groom his fur. "Pah! Another white strand of fur? Soon I'll be like that old carcass Balthazar."

"Balthazar!" cried Fin. "That's right! It was Balthazar! He had wings, Papa! Just like the creature in the market! He looked just like it! He was flying, and he held my scruff between his teeth, and we...I flew in the sky, just like a bird! And then...there was blood, and then he disappeared and...I fell. I fell into *you*."

His uncle stood frozen, paw in midair.

A feeling of dread buzzed in the pit of Fin's stomach. "Where is he, Papa? Where's Balthazar?"

Papa growled, "Why do you care?"

"Did he die, Papa?" Fin stepped toward him, searching his eyes. Papa turned away.

"The ugly Wrecker asked to leave the Tunnels," Papa said. "Council is merciful and allowed it."

The buzzing increased in Fin's belly. "When he told the story of the Great Dying, he *cried*, Papa. Not just for the Old Ones, but...but for the *two-legs*."

"Do not mention that Wrecker again, Nephew!"

"But Papa, he *cried* for the *two-legs*."

The Great & the Small

Papa swung around and glowered at Fin. "Silence! Do not speak of it! Wreckers are liars, and anyone who talks about them is a liar too! Are you telling me that my own nephew is a *Wrecker?*"

Fin looked down so that his uncle couldn't see the doubt in his eyes. "I was just wondering…"

"Just wondering?" said Papa. "Questioning, more like it. Questioning me!"

Fin nibbled a biscuit, his eyes fixed on it.

"Council asked Balthazar to do his duty," continued Papa. "To tell the story of the Great Dying, *for the Common Good*! And that old carcass, that *Wrecker*, betrayed us! Betrayed us all! There are *more* Wreckers, m'boy. They shall be rooted out! Rooted out and exterminated like common vermin!"

The biscuit tasted like dust in Fin's mouth. What little he'd had sat like a lump in his belly. "Let's just forget it," he said. "Let's go down to the market—"

"Forget it?" Papa sputtered, licking his lips. "You ask questions like a Wrecker and we are to forget it? Who gives you such thoughts, eh? Maybe that ugly albino? White fur, bulging red eyes… Is he a Wrecker?"

"No," said Fin. "No! Scratch is—"

"Well, then maybe his mousy sister, eh? What's her name? *Zumi*, isn't it?"

Fin's ears burned and tears pricked his eyes. "No! I mean, yes, that's her name but—"

"Oh, ho! It is *her*, isn't it? When you came to Council and you wouldn't tell us who your Wrecker friend was!" The corners of Papa's mouth were damp with saliva. He took a step toward Fin. Jabbed a claw at him. "Could've had you there, m'boy!"

"Stop it!" choked Fin. Tears streamed down his face. "Stop it, Papa!"

His uncle stepped back like Fin had bitten him. He stood panting, licking his lips over and over again, his eyes wide and confused.

At that moment a voice called from the burrow's opening. "Chairman? Is the Beloved Chairman there?"

Blinking rapidly, Papa said, "Yes? What is it? I am here."

"Private message from Council, sir."

"Yes, yes! Coming!" Papa swept his paws over his ears in a quick groom and, smoothing his fur, went out into the passage, leaving Fin alone in the nest.

The mutter of voices bounced off the tunnel walls, surging and receding. A deep weariness came over Fin, like the fog that rolled in every night from the harbour. Staggering to his mound of rags and feathers, he burrowed his way in between the layers and slept.

"Get up, Nephew, get up!" Papa crowed joyously. "Get up! Get up!"

With his fur still damp with tears, Fin sat up.

"It has started, my boy. Finally, it's started."

"What?" said Fin.

"Chtt! Chtt! Listen!" Eyes squeezed closed, Papa held up a paw to silence Fin. Music was playing—tinkling, whimsical music that wafted up from the two-leg eatery on the hill below their nest.

Papa began to sway. Eyes still shut, he swayed back and forth to the music. He popped one eye open to peer at Fin.

"Come! Come! Why so glum, Nephew? It's finally started!"

His uncle's glee shot through the nest like a shaft of sparkling night air, but Fin was having none of it. He turned his back. "No. Whatever's started, I don't care."

Papa surprised him by leaping to his side. He nuzzled him, snuffling Fin's ear. In a sorrow-filled voice, he murmured, "Forgive my temper, dear Nephew. Forget it…please. I cannot bear for you to be angry with me."

The Great & the Small

Fin looked away.

Papa sighed. "Ah me. I can be an inconsiderate oaf. A big, horrible, offensive, brutish *oaf.*"

"You're right," said Fin. He still didn't turn around.

"Nephew, I tell you what. You come to the Council meeting, and all shall be made clear. Please?"

"No!" Tears streamed fresh from Fin's eyes. "You threatened my friends! You threatened me! I didn't like what you said, Papa. I didn't like it at all!"

But again his uncle surprised him. Instead of being angry at Fin's challenge, he chuckled. "Yes, there is that fighting spirit. But come, Nephew, forget all. Yes? Can we not celebrate together?" He laughed, swaying back and forth to the music, and motioned for Fin to join him.

Fin stood frozen.

His uncle stopped dancing, and his shoulders drooped. "I tell you, dear Nephew, you must ignore the ravings of a tired old rat. Forgive your poor uncle." The smile wiped from his face, he looked forlorn and weary. A few white hairs marked his cheeks. His eyes, glimmering with tears, did not leave Fin's.

The anger that had felt so powerful to Fin just moments ago now seemed petty. It was a sign of greatness to admit one's mistakes, wasn't it? And who else had the love of the Beloved Chairman? Love and forgiveness radiated from Fin's heart for his hot-tempered old uncle, his uncle who'd raised him from a pup.

With a smile tugging at him, Fin said, "As usual, you're right. You *are* an oaf!"

They both laughed.

Fin took his place beside his uncle. The tinkling music swooped up and slid down. Around and around the burrow Fin and Papa danced, swirling, leaping, and gasping with laughter.

CHAPTER TWENTY-FIVE

"In the year of our lord, 1348, the great mortality struck our
excellent city."

Giovanni Boccaccio (1313–75)

Fin limped through the Lowers, his squad behind him. Council
had given him the assignment of collecting Wreckers and
bringing them in for investigation. It was a huge responsibility, and he didn't want to mess it up. But his foot bothered him, he
hadn't slept well in ages, and he had no clue what he was doing.
Trying to hide his discomfort, he called down into a nest opening.

Filth and raw sewage lay strewn about. "Hey! Is there a Hobbs
here?" There was shuffling and then silence. "I know you're in
there!" called Fin. "Come out and make it easier on everybody."

A squad member named Mink said, "Can I go in after him, Boss?
Can I?" Mink's eyes shone like those of a rat pup asking for a treat.
The hulking brute's whiskers twitched in eager anticipation.

Fin repressed a shudder. "No. Let me do this my way." He shouted
down into the nest. "Hobbs! Come out before you get hurt. Don't
force me to send the squad in after you!"

The Great & the Small

"No...no!" squeaked a voice. "I'm coming!" A small shape emerged from the nest opening. An elderly rat gazed up at Fin, worry wrinkling his patchy fur. His eyes bulged with dread.

"Nothing to worry about, if you cooperate," said Fin with what he hoped was an encouraging smile. The terror in the rat's eyes didn't waver.

Fin's smile dropped. "There are reports of extensive Wrecker activity in the Lowers, Mister Hobbs, reports that pinpoint this area. Council believes you are involved."

"I... I dunno..." Hobbs muttered. "Can't remember! I swear, I can't remember!"

"Mister Hobbs, that's not what I heard," said Fin.

"I...I..." The grey-muzzled old rat chewed his lip. "I...can't remember!" Tremors shook his body, making the ends of his whiskers dance.

Fin scowled, trying to hide the uncertainty that gripped him. Hobbs hadn't confessed. Now what?

There was an uncomfortable silence. Everyone's eyes were on him, waiting for him to take action.

The old rat's eyes darted back and forth between Fin and the other squad members. He looked bewildered. One of the squad yawned and scratched her ear. Another sighed.

"Well," began Hobbs, "if that's all, young feller, I'll just be gettin' along—"

"Of course that's not all!" snapped Fin. His mind raced. What would Papa do?

Screwing his face into a sneer, Fin leaned in close. "You leave me no choice! My…my first priority is to ensure the safety of these tunnels. So…as sorry as I am for you, either tell me what you know, or… *you know.*" Fin wasn't sure what "you know" would be. He hoped Hobbs wouldn't want to find out.

It worked. To Fin's surprise, Hobbs burst into tears. "I dunno! I dunno!" Hobbs sobbed. His teeth chattered so much that drool trickled down the side of his mouth.

Mink sidled alongside the suspect and thrust out his haunch in a fighting move. The frail rat slammed against the tunnel wall.

Hobbs squealed, "Agh! Don't…don't hurt me!"

Mink grinned and looked over at Fin, awaiting orders.

Fin could hardly breathe. He struggled to keep his face impassive. He couldn't take the old rat's screams anymore. "Let him *go!*" he gasped.

"Huh?" said Mink with a snort. "I don't think so!"

"By order of Council, you big stupid oaf, let him go!" shouted Fin. "Let him go!" Rushing at Mink, he bit him hard on his neck.

"Yagh! Yes sir!" said Mink. "Sorry, sir!"

"Go! All of you!" Fin shrieked. The ARM squad fled, casting backward glances at Fin like they thought he was off his cheese.

Once Fin and Hobbs were alone in the tunnel, the old rat babbled, "Oh thank you, thank you, young feller! I knew you weren't no thug like the rest of 'em…"

"Shut up!" Fin's head pounded so hard it felt like it was going to shoot off his neck. He wanted to leave. Let the poor old rat go. But Papa was counting on him. The Killing Chamber rats were counting on him.

Fin choked out, "You're…you're just an ugly Wrecker! NO! Don't deny it! Stir up any more trouble, and I'll come back and finish what Mink started! Understand?"

The Great & the Small

The old rat stared at Fin, his eyes like glass marbles.

Tears pricked behind Fin's eyes. *"Do—you—understand—me?"* he shrieked.

"Y-yes…yes…" Hobbs's chin quivered uncontrollably. Tears clouded the old rat's eyes. "I…I understand you."

"Good! Now *go!*" Fin's voice was shrill as it ricocheted off the walls. Hobbs scrambled down into his burrow.

As soon as he was alone, Fin burst into tears.

After he'd recovered himself a little, he dried his face and went to give his report to Council. Sticking out his chest, he gazed around at the Councillors with his eyes steady and managed to convince them that he'd planned the whole thing from the start. "And now the dirty old Wrecker will spread the word about the no-tolerance policy for Wrecking!"

Council believed him. He even fooled Papa. Not easy to do when you're lying through your teeth.

After that first horrible experience, Fin went to Tiv, Councillor of Information, to get the background on suspected Wreckers *before* he collected them. That way, when the excuses started (and there were always excuses) he'd know the real story. He'd stay strong.

Scratch went with him on Collections now and was granted new quarters by Council. He had a nest in the Uppers, close to Fin's. Scratch talked non-stop about his new life. "I could get used to this, I won't lie! I could get used to this!"

It was nice to have his buddy by his side, but sometimes Fin worried about him. Scratch was so gullible, so easily led. Zumi had tried to tell Fin that a long time ago.

Zumi had refused to move with her brother and had stayed behind in the Lowers. She'd avoided them both since the Forbidden Garden.

Fin's feelings for Zumi were a giant tangle. Zumi had saved his life. He'd saved hers. She was exasperating, but also honest. And whatever else she was, Zumi was brave. When Papa had accused Zumi of Wrecking, Fin knew why it had upset him so much—because he knew it was true.

As nights went by, Fin carried out Collections with greater and greater effectiveness. Questions didn't trouble him while he was awake. There was too much to do, too much responsibility on his shoulders. But every sunrise, when he curled beside his uncle, dreams crowded his sleep.

Nia nuzzles his ear. Sighing, he tries to wriggle in closer, but suddenly she is gone. There is nothing there, and he is alone.

Whimpering, Fin noses around for her in the dark. She was there a moment ago, but her scent is cold. Where did she go?

From the shadows in the grey tunnel beyond, creatures emerge, ghostly and shimmering. Plague Rats. Their fur hangs in shredded strips. White bone glimmers.

Fin looks away. Where is Mother?

The Plague Rats slowly approach, bones creaking. One reaches for him, and he shrinks back until he recognizes her. "Pip," says Nia. Her eyes glimmering, tears fall down her face and wet his fur.

CHAPTER
TWENTY-SIX

"I closed my ears to the sound of children crying and women weeping…
I believed I was doing what was necessary. What was right."

Lev Kopelev, a young Soviet activist

It was Saturday afternoon. On Monday, Ananda would go back to school after her suspension. Every time she thought about it, she broke out in a cold sweat. She tried to push it out of her mind.

She hadn't told anyone about what Litko and his goons had done to her, how they had humiliated her. And how every single person in that courtyard had watched them do it but had done nothing.

Nothing. Would she have helped if it were someone else being bullied? She liked to think she would. After all, wasn't helping that rat escape in the market the same as helping someone who was being bullied? It seemed the rat incident had been the start of a series of events that were unravelling beyond control. But even if she was the instigator, the one who'd started it all off, Ananda wouldn't change what she had done. She couldn't have just stood by and watched.

Tears stung her eyes. She would never, ever just stand by.

Ananda sat on her bed, drawing, the sound of charcoal on paper rasping in her ear. Using a hand mirror, she was drawing a self-portrait. She had mapped out the "gesture" of her face. She was just starting to add shadow contour when her mom rapped on her door.

"Ananda, don't forget you've got to clean the basement today."

Sigh. "Yes, *Mother*."

The floorboards creaked as her mother walked away.

The murmur of the television in the other room floated below the sound of the charcoal. Her mother's voice broke through every so often, talking to someone on the phone—probably Ananda's dad, who was at the lab.

Smudging the charcoal with her thumb, Ananda deepened the shadows around the bridge of her nose. She held up the mirror and studied herself. The drawing did look like her—kind of. Something was off, but she couldn't tell what.

She was hesitating, her hand hovering over the paper, when she caught a few words that drifted in from the TV.

"Bubonic Plague…the city's waterfront…public not to panic…"

Setting her sketchpad aside, she climbed off the bed and cracked open the door.

Her mom sat braced on the edge of the couch, her back to Ananda, watching the news. Perrin was pointing the remote at the TV with one hand and holding the phone with the other. Beyond her mother, Ananda saw the TV screen filled with shots of the wharf. "Tom, did you hear that? Yes, just downtown, near the docks or something… wait, wait, hold on!"

The image on the TV switched to a female reporter standing in front of a downtown hospital. In the background, people bustled

The Great & the Small

around wearing surgical masks and protective gear. The reporter spoke to the camera.

> *"There are three confirmed deaths at this point from what appears to be an outbreak of plague. Health officials say it's too soon to say if it's the same strain that has been ripping through South Asia and parts of Europe. Although details will not be released until next of kin are notified, we know that two of the dead were members of the Golden Age Seniors' travel group, visiting from the UK. I was just told that a worker from a local tourist shop may be the third victim…"*

The plague? *The* plague? It was here?

> *"Public health officials are investigating the case. As you can see behind me, containment procedures to stop the spread of contagion have been put into effect.*
> *"Officials are acting quickly, determined to avoid another SARS or Ebola crisis. If you recall, in the case of the 2003 SARS and 2014 Ebola outbreaks, hospitals around the world scrambled to keep up."*

Her mom said into the phone, "Are you listening to this?"

> *"Although officials won't say why the individuals died so suddenly, some experts are raising the specter of 'super bugs'—pathogens resistant to drugs, pathogens that have the ability to mutate over time. That, along with the over-prescribing of antibiotics, has created what some experts are calling 'a public health time bomb.' One moment…"*

The reporter held the earpiece closer to her ear. She nodded before continuing.

"We are receiving breaking news that five more people, again that is five other people, which my sources tell me includes a local high school student, have been admitted to hospital with very suspicious symptoms. It is not clear if they are infected, but health officials are—and I quote—'acting with an abundance of caution.'"

"Oh my God, Tom! Don't tell me not to panic! This is exactly what you were afraid of!"

The hair on Ananda's arms and neck stood on end. Her eyes stayed locked on the reporter who dug into the deadly history of the plague with obvious relish.

"Nicknamed the 'Black Death,' the plague struck medieval Europe, killing an estimated one-third to one-half of the population. The highly contagious pestilence is believed to have originated in the East and was transported by trading vessels to Europe. Public officials have reportedly been considering whether this current pestilence was also transported to North America through international cargo ships in a true case of history repeating itself…"

"Three people already, and maybe five more!" said Perrin. "And one of them's a teenager!"

"In a breakdown of medieval society," the reporter continued, "plague victims were often sealed alive into their homes by panicked neighbours, and red crosses were painted on their doors. Once sealed in, very few survived…"

"No, no, Ananda can't hear me! She's in her room…"

Ananda quickly, quietly, shut her door. She sat on her bed, her hands shaking. The sketchbook lay beside her, the face on its page staring up at her.

CHAPTER
TWEПTY-8EVEП

"I hear you, evildoer, whispering in my ear."

Gabriele de' Mussis, 1348

The ARM squad circled the burrow hole. Fin shouted into it, "Come out! We know you're in there."

No answer.

There had been a recent attack on an ARM squad. One squad member had been killed in the ambush. Resistance against the Plague War was gathering force. Council's orders to Fin were clear: quash it. Find the Wreckers and bring them in. The alleged ring-leader lived in this burrow. "Get him out," said Fin to Mink.

The big rat dived into the nest, followed by a shrill cry from within. Mink emerged, gripping the scruff of a sable-grey rat between his long teeth. The grey rat's four paws pedalled the air wildly. Unable to speak, he gave off ultrasonic squeaks.

"Drop him," said Fin. Mink opened his jaws, and the grey rat plopped on the ground where he sat huddled.

Fin walked around him. An oozing gash on the rat's rump, a cut ear crusted over with a fresh scab—this rat had been in a fight. He was their Wrecker.

"Get up," said Fin. The rat made no move. Fin jerked his head to his squad. "Get him up."

The grey rat was brought to all fours. Blood already rimmed his nostril. "I'm...I'm innocent..." he stammered.

"You all are," said Fin dryly. Turning to Scratch, who was standing beside him, he asked, "Would you like to handle this one?"

Scratch puffed out his chest. Bobbing his head, he said, "You betcha, Boss, you betcha! Let me at this ugly Wrecker!" Hopping forward, he reared up before the prisoner. "You," he sputtered, "are nothing but an ugly, ugly Wrecker! Don't deny it!"

"I...I..."

"Tell me your name, Wrecker," said Scratch. He leaned in close, his red, beady eyes narrowed. "Tell me your name, or so help me, I'll—"

"Oliver." The rat's eyes were huge. "My name's Oliver, but I swear—"

"*Oliver*? Well, save your excuses, Oliver! We've got the goods on you. The goods! You've been reported!"

"For what? I haven't—"

"Quiet!" said Scratch. "You've been *reported*!"

Oliver looked back and forth between the squad members. "But I'm telling you—"

"Shut up!" shrieked Scratch. "If you're so innocent, then why are you scared? A Wrecker should be afraid, they should be very afraid, but if you're innocent, you shouldn't be, so what do you say to that?"

Oliver blinked at him. "I don't understand your question..."

"You've been reported, stupid!" said Scratch. He stamped his foot in frustration. "Don't you get it? Fin, he's too stupid to get it!"

"This is taking too long," grumbled Mink.

Fin sighed. Moving Scratch over, he said, "Oliver, if you don't talk, not only you but your family will be collected, and anyone who knows you. Your mate just had a litter of pups, didn't she? One by one your pups will be dragged out—"

"No! Please, no!" Oliver started to sob, sagging forward. "Oh...! By the Old Ones, please no! They haven't done anything!"

In the nest behind Oliver, little faces watched. They were curious, no doubt, to see their big strong father crying like a pup.

Fin hated this part of the job. If the stakes weren't so high there would be no way he'd do it. But there was a war on. Lives were at stake. He had to stay strong. "Bring out the pups," he said through gritted teeth.

"No! No!" shrieked Oliver. "I'll talk! I'll talk!" The grey rat burst into a flurry of tears.

Fin breathed out, silently thanking the Old Ones it would go no further. "Take the prisoner to Councillor Sergo for investigation," he said. Turning in the small space of the tunnel, he bumped right into Zumi.

Nose to nose, they stared at each other, her eyes round with horror. She'd heard everything. Suddenly Zumi pushed him with her strong hind legs, making him stumble back. She turned and darted down the tunnel. Fin watched as she disappeared.

"What's wrong with my bossy sister now?" asked Scratch, coming up beside him.

Fin said nothing but stared after Zumi long after the squad had left with the prisoner.

The Great & the Small

CHAPTER TWENTY-EIGHT

"This plague caused such terror that brother abandoned brother... The worst though, were parents who refused to care for their own sick children."

Giovanni Boccaccio (1313–75)

The moon was high overhead, casting the alley in deep shadow. Fin was going to a Council meeting about the Plague War. The cobblestones, which burned Fin's paws in the heat of day, were cool, but that didn't abate the burning he felt inside. He felt sick, confused.

As he limped down the alley toward the Council Chamber, he passed the metal fence that enclosed the Forbidden Garden. Memories of that place flashed through his mind: Bothwell and the ARM, close on his tail; Zumi popping through the brush behind him, saying, "Follow me..."

Why did Zumi have to come up behind him when he was collecting that Wrecker? Now she would think he was a monster. She wouldn't understand he was only doing his duty.

Collecting pups was his duty?

The ugly question clamoured at him, joining all the other questions. Fin pushed it away. The Common Good was bigger than any of them—bigger than what Fin liked or didn't like.

Reaching the tunnel that led to the Council Chamber, he squeezed through and emerged on the other side into the cool darkness. He scanned the air. There was the tang of wet stone and concrete. As he padded along the narrow, uneven tunnel, his whiskers fanned out to feel his way and guide him.

He became aware of other smells. Mingling with the smell of damp earth and stone, Fin detected the usual scent markings of individual Council members, each member's comings and goings crisscrossing the tunnel in bright strands of odour, like a catalog of events. But weaving through them were other scent trails, other ones he knew. Wreckers. Wreckers *he* had Collected. Wreckers *he* had sent here.

The Wreckers left a sour, bitter smell as they passed. The odour reminded Fin of something—something terrible. It made his stomach knot, and for a moment he leaned against the wall, gulping air. "Snap out of it!" he muttered to himself. But then it hit him.

The tunnel smelled like the Killing Chamber.

Fin stumbled and fell. The passage buckled around him. He squeezed his eyes shut, but he couldn't keep the faces of his captives from rising before him like sheets of fog off the sea.

The old rat named Hobbs, crying, drool running down his chin. Oliver weeping for his pups, their faces innocent and confused. And there were others, too. Lots of others, their faces, all terrified…

And they all blamed Fin.

He couldn't do this anymore. He was no hero…and yet he had promised the Killing Chamber rats. Despair swelled up inside of him. Tears stung his eyes. Whichever way he turned he hurt someone.

The Great & the Small

He pulled himself off the ground and staggered to the opening. In the Council Chamber the Council members were hunched in a circle.

Papa looked up. "You're late!" he snapped.

Fin nodded wearily.

"Your report?" asked Papa. His black eyes burrowed into Fin's.

"Oh, our Fin's a busy one," cut in Bothwell, jovially. "Collects them Wreckers, Boss, and how! Finds 'em in the bloody woodwork, 'e does!" He winked at Fin with his puckered eye.

"That's good, that's very good," said Papa. "Now——"

"Don't matter 'ow much they carry on! Weeping and chattering, it don't matter! Our boy is all business!" chirped Bothwell.

"Wonderful," said Papa. "Now Fin, can I please hear your——"

"I quit," said Fin.

The Chamber froze.

Bothwell was the first to stir. He looked around, blinking. "What did 'e say? I could swear 'e said——"

"He said *shut up*, idiot!" muttered Sergo.

"No, I'm sure 'e didn't say that."

Tiv began to laugh her high tinkling laugh.

"Quiet!" said Papa. He scowled at Fin. "This isn't the time to joke around, boy. We are at war!"

"A war *you* started," murmured Julian.

"I'm…I'm not joking, Papa," said Fin. "I'm sorry, but I can't do it anymore. I can't bring in Wreckers. I hate it. I hate collecting them, hate using what they love most to make them talk."

"Then you hate war," said Tiv. "Because that's what war is. It's dirty, and sometimes you have to get your paws mussed."

"War!" said Sergo. "It is a dirty, dirty business!" He didn't seem too upset by it. He smirked as he said it.

"Quiet!" said Papa. The smiles dropped from the Councillors' faces. They looked at him.

He studied Fin. "Nephew, you are young. Things bother you now, but in time you will see the wisdom in all of this. Even in the cries of your enemies, dear boy."

Fin said nothing. He shook his head. Tears tugged at his eyes, but he gulped them down. He would not cry in front of Council.

"None of us doubt that you are a good Tunnel Rat," said Papa, glancing sharply around the room. The other Council members murmured agreement. "So what is behind all this?"

"Well," said Fin. "I don't want to collect Wreckers. I…I just want to stop the Killing Chamber."

"Then that's what you shall do," said Papa. "Finish your duties this day, and tomorrow you will captain your own squad of Plague Rats. You may lead them into the jaws of Doom, if you wish, as long as you shut down that Killing Chamber."

"Really?"

Papa smiled. "Really."

Bothwell piped up, "But mind you, keep your distance, Mister Fin! Don't catch no fleas from that lot!"

Everyone laughed. And in that dark, damp room it was as if the stars had risen in the sky. Finally, Fin would help the Killing Chamber rats with the blessing of Council. With the blessing of his beloved uncle.

Fin said, "Oh thank you! Thank you! I won't let you down!"

"No, my boy," said Papa. "I know you won't." Turning to the others, he said, "And now, honoured members of Council, we have matters that require attention. Councillor Sergo, what is your report on…" Fin's issue sorted, Council moved on to the next item on the agenda.

The Great & the Small

Fin didn't stay to listen. Wandering back out through the passage-way, the smells assaulted his nose again, but it was all right. One last afternoon of collecting. He could do that.

CHAPTER
TWENTY-NINE

"You who were once so rich, are now just food for worms."

Gabriele de' Mussis, 1348

Fin listened as his first lieutenant relayed his last collection orders from Council. There were three suspected Wreckers to deal with, the first two being the usual sort. They'd been overheard saying that the Plague War was wrong. Fin wished they could see the Killing Chamber for themselves! Handling those two would be easy. The next one stunned him.

"It's his sister, Boss," whispered the lieutenant. She jerked her nose toward Scratch, who sat cleaning his whiskers.

"Zumi?" said Fin.

"Yep, that's her. Council wants her. Says she's a bad apple. Hey, wasn't she the one who kicked you earlier?"

Fin ignored the question. Keeping his voice even, he said, "We're going after the two Wreckers, full force, all of us on it. No splitting into groups. Got it?"

The Great & the Small

The lieutenant's brow wrinkled. "But wouldn't we get more done if we split up? I can handle a little pip like Scratch's sis—"

"Are you going to follow orders, or shall I report you?" said Fin.

Flustered, the lieutenant said, "No, no, sir. I'm on it, sir." As she bustled off to prepare the squad, Fin ambled over to Scratch who was digging at an itch behind his ear.

"Scratch," whispered Fin. The other squad members were in a huddle, listening to the lieutenant. They were too far away to hear Fin. "Go and warn Zumi. Tell her to leave the Tunnels."

"Now why would—?"

"Council wants to bring her in," hissed Fin.

Scratch squinted at Fin. "Why? What's she done now?"

The lieutenant glanced over. Fin smiled and nodded at her. He forced himself to speak slowly. He whispered, "Scratch, they'll interrogate her. Do you know what that means?"

"Yes, yes. It means we find her, and we get her. We bring her in to Councillor Sergo for investigation." Scratch blinked at Fin. "I'm not dumb, you know."

"We *can't* take her in. You know what might happen."

"But it's an order," said Scratch. Confusion clouded his face. "An order from Council. From the Beloved Chairman, who also happens to be *your* uncle! Besides, what's it matter to you? You don't even like her!"

Fin's ears burned. "She's your *sister.*"

"So? If she's innocent they'll let her go, right?" Scratch kept blinking at him like it was all so simple. Fin had told himself the same thing over and over again with the Wreckers he'd pulled in. If they were innocent, they had nothing to worry about. *If.*

Fin glanced nervously over to the squad. He couldn't stall them much longer. His lieutenant had already looked over a few times. Fin whispered tersely, "I'm in command here, I'm Captain, and I *order* you."

Scratch's mouth dropped open. "Does your uncle know what you're up to? Switching orders? That's not good, Fin! That's not good at all!"

Fin pulled himself up to his full height. He held Scratch's gaze even though his heart felt like it would hammer out of his chest. "The Beloved Chairman who—as you keep reminding me—is *my* uncle, doesn't want me to bug him for every little thing that comes up. But if you won't follow orders, I'll ask someone else."

"Oh no you don't!" snapped Scratch. "I'll tell her, *Captain* Fin! Bending laws back and forth, just like in the market when your paw was crushed to jelly! It's up to Scratch to obey. It's up to Scratch to follow orders!"

"Come on, Scratch," wheedled Fin. "Don't be mad!"

At that moment, the lieutenant called over. "Captain?"

With a final pleading look to Scratch, Fin turned and puffed out his chest. "Who's ready to hunt some Wreckers?" he called. He swaggered over to the group.

The squad members cheered. "I am, Boss!" "You know it!" "Let's go!" As they set out, Fin risked a glance back.

Scratch was gone.

That moonrise, Fin was assigned his new mission. While the Plague Rat squad was being prepped, Fin would go to the Killing Chamber to get information on the cruel two-leg who kept them

prisoner. He would then return to the Tunnels and lead the Plague Rats to their target.

When he left for the Killing Chamber, Fin still hadn't seen Scratch. He did his best to ignore the questions that batted around his head like buzzing flies.

CHAPTER THIRTY

"You cannot make a revolution with silk gloves."

Josef Stalin

Heat shimmered off the pavement as Dr. Tom Blake drove into the parking lot. Sweat soaked his shirt in spite of the car's air conditioning, which had only managed to blow a slightly cool, musty vapour.

He parked the car, got out, and locked the door. As he walked across the lot a small grey and white rodent streaked across his shoe, causing him to stumble.

"What the…?"

He stared after it as it galloped across the grass with an uneven gait and slipped under a shrub at the research department's entrance. There was something familiar about it—the colouring, the size, even the limp. Maybe there was an infestation of lame grey and white rats in the city.

Tom cut across the lawn. Dry grass crunched under his shoes. At the front doors, he knelt and peered under the bush. There was a flash of white and grey. It was a rat, all right. A rat that looked just like the one that had bitten him. And like the one at Middle-Gate Market.

The Great & the Small

This was getting weird.

Don't make too much of it, he told himself. *There's a reasonable explanation. I have no idea what it is, but there's got to be one.*

In his office, Dr. Blake called the custodian. "Yes, it was a rat, and I think it broke in before. Yes, I know rats usually try to break *out* of here...yes, I *know* you're busy...then put out *more* poison!" He slammed down the phone.

As Tom worked that day, the incident in the parking lot weighed on him. His progress felt slow. He turned on the radio in time to hear the DJ announce that there would be soaring hot temperatures today. "Thanks, Einstein, I hadn't noticed," he muttered. A few scattered rain showers were expected for tomorrow night. Something to look forward to. Sweat trickled down Tom's forehead, dripping onto the table where he worked.

"The city's death toll has now reached twenty-three," the news announcer said. *"Health officials blame the continuing hot weather for the rising count. A concerned citizens group has launched a multi-million-dollar lawsuit against the city, stating that local government neglected to take action quickly enough..."*

The room felt stuffy—closed in. Tom switched off the radio and worked in silence.

The news *was* alarming, but was there real reason to worry? The hospital had emergency containment procedures in place. Families of victims were in quarantine. Theoretically, the plague wouldn't spread much beyond what it already had.

Theoretically.

The reality was that no one could predict exactly what would happen. The deadliness of the plague had surprised everyone. It had not responded to antibiotics. And the heat wave was making a bad situation worse.

Tom remembered reading about the Black Death in his university days, but he hadn't read much. His interest had been in stopping the modern plague of cancer. Ananda had been reading up on the Black Death for a school project. Maybe he'd borrow one of her books.

The moon was up when Dr. Blake finished for the day. A breeze blew in from the harbour. It was warm and balmy, with that ever-present tar smell from the waterfront.

He balanced a box of papers on his hip and dug in his pocket for his car keys. Wrong pocket. He shifted the box to his other hip, fumbling a bit. Then, with a *whump*, it slipped to the ground. The lid fell off, and Tom's research papers took to the air, gusting across the parking lot like a flock of origami birds.

Cursing, Tom sprinted after them. He cornered the last of the escaped papers and stuffed it in the file box with the others. He roughly set the whole thing on the back seat of his car, and with a final curse or two, he got into his car, started the engine, and drove out of the parking lot.

Tom Blake drove home through silent streets, humming tunelessly along with a jazz song playing on the radio.

He had no idea that he wasn't alone.

This time, he hadn't seen the flash of white and grey, hadn't seen the rat as it slipped into the box he had placed in the back of the car.

Relieved to finally be home, Tom turned into his driveway and brought the shadow of the plague right to his front door.

CHAPTER THIRTY-ONE

*"It was unusual that in a house where one person died,
others did not follow."*

Brother John Clynn, 1349

Finding the two-leg's nest had been surprisingly easy. Fin had staked out the Killing Chamber all day, had watched the ugly two-leg walk across the pavement to its machine. And when it had dropped the box it was carrying, Fin slipped in. The poor dumb thing had taken Fin *right to its nest.*

After the two-leg had turned off its machine and got out, it reached into the back seat for its box. That's when Fin had had a little fun. Galloping up the two-leg's arm, he leaped onto its mousy head then vaulted through the air. Landing on the grass, Fin dived under a shrub.

From his hiding place Fin chuckled, watching as the two-leg screeched, flapped its arms, and slapped itself on the head. The two-leg's round pieces of glass flew from its nose and settled near Fin's paws. Patting the ground, it had crawled on its knees, sounds of anger hissing from its mouth. Finally, the thing got up and hid inside its tall nest.

Alone outside, Fin sniffed every corner, every windowsill, every crack of the wooden nest until he found a way in: a slight gap in a small window frame, which was only a tail-length up from the ground. On the night of the attack, Fin need only gnaw an opening the Plague Rats could fit through.

Running back home to the Tunnels, Fin mapped the way in his mind, memorizing every smell, every dip in the pavement, every pattern of light and sound. He repeated to himself over and over, *I will keep my promise. I will keep my promise. I will keep my promise.*

"That's the target we're hitting tonight, Lieutenant Scrubbs," said Fin. He glared at his second-in-command. "That's an order."

She glared back. "It's too far away! I've deployed death squads before and—"

"I know, and this is my first time. But *I'm* in charge."

Scrubbs pointed at the Plague Rat squad. "Captain Fin, look at them. They've peaked! They're almost gone!" The ragged group huddled together several tail-lengths away. Clearly they did not have long to live.

Fin gazed at the rats. They looked miserable. Chewing his lip, Fin fought back the pity that swelled up inside him, that pricked at his eyes. *No! There is no time for this! They are martyrs for the Common Good. There is no greater honour.*

"Then we'd better hurry up," said Fin, gritting his teeth.

A light rain began to fall as the Plague Rats stumbled after Fin. Progress was slow. "Hurry up!" Fin yelled over his shoulder. His foot was aching—he'd done too much running already. He forced himself forward. Drizzle beaded on everyone's fur and whiskers like a fine gauze. The only sound was of gasping breath and the scratch of claws on pavement. The Plague Rats were slowing, but so was he. Fin's paw felt like it was on fire.

Lieutenant Scrubbs puffed along beside him. "Captain Fin, the squad needs a rest." She looked pointedly at his paw. "It seems you do too."

"No...need," panted Fin. "We're...here." On the other side of the street sat the two-leg's tall nest. A light shone from one of its windows.

"Stay here," said Fin. "I'll call when you're to bring them."

"Captain, I should be the one—" began Scrubbs, but Fin had already started across the road.

Fin felt the lieutenant's sharp eyes on him and tried not to limp. On the other side, he climbed up the lawn. The grass was cool and wet and eased his paw's throbbing a bit. Sitting up on his haunches, Fin sniffed the air until he caught the scent trail he was looking for.

Since his eagle-eyed lieutenant couldn't see him now, Fin limped heavily to the low window. He sniffed at it: the ledge was just a tail-length up from the ground. He could jump it, no problem. But when he leaped up his leg was so stiff that it knocked clumsily against the ledge and forced him backwards into the grass. He jumped again. This time he dug in his claws and managed to hoist himself up.

The whisker-thin gap ran the length of the window. Choosing a spot in the frame that was rat high, Fin bit into the wood then spat, flakes of bitter paint sticking to his tongue. Wrinkling his nose, Fin gnawed at the hole. When he thought it was big enough, he tried fitting his head through. Too tight. He kept chewing.

After spitting out mouthfuls of paint and chewed wood, Fin tried squeezing his head in again. This time it fit, which meant the rest of him would too.

Sniffing his handiwork, Fin nodded, his part of the mission done. He opened his mouth to call ultrasonically for Scrubbs to bring the Plague Rats but clamped his mouth closed again. It had been *Fin's* idea to come here. *Fin's* mission to save the Killing Chamber rats. But he wasn't allowed to go in? Only the Plague Rats? It wasn't fair. Orders or no orders, chewing a hole in a window frame was nothing.

Fin had to see where the cruel two-leg would die. It would only take a moment, then he'd call the squad. No one would ever find out.

Fitting his head in the hole, Fin eased through one paw, and then the other. The inside ledge was just below. He dug his claws into the wood to brace himself, and, flattening his ribcage, squeezed his chest through.

He pulled through his good back paw. His curled paw was still on the outside, hanging like a market ham. As he pulled it through, it caught on the frame.

His claws popped out of the wood and his front paws pedalled air. Yanking his leg free, Fin tumbled and fell sprawling onto the ledge below.

He lay frozen, not daring to move, not daring to breathe. Slowly, Fin lifted his head and sniffed his surroundings. He was high up. Below him was plunging darkness. Thank the Old Ones he hadn't fallen down there.

He carefully picked himself up. Grey shapes poked out of the gloom. Scent trails of cooked food could be detected in the air, coming from somewhere above him. It mixed with the sharp smell of concrete that surrounded him here in the nest's lower part.

This was it? This was where the monster lived? He'd expected something else. Something that spoke about the evil of the Killing Chamber. Maybe rows of cages. The moment he'd imagined over and over in his head, the triumphant moment of stopping the two-leg, of getting justice for the tortured Killing Chamber rats, felt bitter in his mouth, like the flecks of paint.

He shouldn't have come in.

The gnawed hole was a few tail-lengths up. Fin clawed up the concrete wall and, reaching the window frame, fit his head into the hole. But as he tried to lever in his shoulders, his swollen back paw threw off his balance. His hind paw gave way, and he slithered back down.

Frowning up at the hole, he dug in his claws and pulled himself up one paw at a time. But as he fit his head to the hole and pushed forward, his hind paw gave way once again. Again he slid down.

He peered up. His heart pounded a drumbeat in his ears. Again he hoisted himself into the hole. Again his paw slipped and he fell back down.

Panic buzzed in his ears like a swarm of angry bees. Coiling his haunches, he leaped. He stabbed the wall with his outstretched claws and clung to it. The tips of his whiskers quivered against cold concrete. The hole was overhead—a reach of the paw, that was all. He stretched his paw toward it slowly…

His foot slid out and he fell straight back, passing the ledge. He plummeted into the dark, his paws flailing. He squealed, "Help me, Papa! Help me!"

He hit bottom. Metal jaws snapped around his paw.
Red washed over his eyes. Everything went silent.

CHAPTER THIRTY-TWO

"In our modern times we are drowning in sin."

Archbishop of Canterbury, July 15, 1375

Papa lay on his side, his body halfway off his pile of nesting and sprawled on the dirt floor of the burrow. There was a scuffling at the entrance. A guard peeked timidly around the corner.

"Beloved Chairman? Here is your forage. I brought sausages and—"

Papa reared up and bit the rat's shoulder. "Get out! Get out!"

"Agh! Yes, Chairman! I'm sorry, Chairman!"

"And take your filthy sausages with you!" shouted Papa, scooping his nose under the food and flinging it after the retreating rat. He slumped down onto the dirt again.

Tears shimmered in his eyes. It was never supposed to be like this. Not after Nia. He had already lost so much. And now Fin…

Even as a tiny pup, there had been something about Fin. The pup's father had been a dirty Wrecker, but Papa had always loved

Fin. Fin could be trusted. In the Council where enemies hid behind smiles, his beloved nephew was the only one he could believe.

They had gotten the news while in the Council Chamber. Fin's second-in-command Scrubbs had told them that Fin was lost. She'd said other things—the death squad dying without being deployed—but Papa brushed that aside. The Plague Rats were going to die anyway, and there were always more. But his beloved nephew had been very much alive. And now he was gone.

The Council meeting had been contentious. Julian had "issues" with using Plague Rats, wanted the deployments stopped. Had actually called for an *end* to the war. Oh, not the puny little war that they had fought *before* the Gift; according to Councillor Julian, the Tunnels could contin-ue its campaign of Disruption and Harassment. But not the *real* war.

The burrow was so empty. Papa shivered, even though it was so hot outside that even the dirt under his claws felt scorched. He felt hollow. All of his plans…

Papa had made Fin into a War Hero. The crowds had loved him. Loved them both. "Papa and Fin! Papa and Fin!" the Tunnel Rats had roared in the Forbidden Garden until Papa's ears had thrummed. Together, they would have been unstoppable.

Papa groaned as he pulled himself up. "What am I to do?" he asked. The walls of the burrow stared back at him. He looked down

The Great & the Small

and noticed that his coat was covered with grime. He leaned back on his haunches and, spreading his fur with his paws, groomed his belly, nibbling out bits of dirt.

"Eh? What's this?" White fur salted his belly. Where had it come from, all of a sudden? "Pah!" he spat, slapping down the ruffled fur until the offending white shafts were covered.

Papa carefully licked his paws and drew them over his ears and down his whiskers, one by one. And then he saw it: one long white whisker sprouting amongst the black. He breathed deep to steady himself, rocking back on his haunches.

Papa was getting old. Old rats did not stay Chairman for long.

This was the time when Fin should have been by his side, when he was needed most. And now that buzzard Julian was circling. Must have seen Papa's greying muzzle. But Julian was too old to be Chairman, even older than Papa!

Tiv wasn't. And hadn't he seen Tiv nodding her head when Julian had spoken about the Plague Rats? Were the two of them in this together?

Papa's eyes glinted as he realized the truth. Tiv and Julian were plotting against him.

Papa had underestimated them, had believed their hollow oaths of loyalty, while they schemed under his very nose! He knew it now. Papa realized that deep down inside he'd *always* known it.

Wreckers. Wreckers *everywhere.*

Who to trust? If only Fin were here.

But there was one. Sergo could be trusted. Papa's "loyal dog" would do anything Papa asked of him. Yes, he would send for Sergo. There was no time to lose.

CHAPTER
THIRTY-THREE

"Be assured, comrades, that I will give all to the cause...
even my life's blood, drop by drop, if need be."

Josef Stalin

Ananda gripped her books to her chest as she walked across the school parking lot toward the front doors. She hadn't slept well. Correction: she hadn't slept *at all*. Litko's face loomed before her every time she closed her eyes. What was it with that guy? Why did she let people like that get under her skin? She trudged, head down, and gulped in air to try to stop her heart from racing.

Closer to the school, the buzz of high-pitched voices, of crying, made her jerk her head up. Students milled around out front like an anthill that had just been stirred up. Some were sobbing, others had tears running down their cheeks. She slowed down, stopped.

A girl with long blonde hair pushed by her. Ananda stumbled, and her notebook fell to the ground. The girl looked back. "Oh, sorry— Ananda!" It was George.

"Oh, Ananda! It's so awful! How he died! Oh my God, you must feel awful! He was out of school because of you!"

Around them, the pitch of crying and general hysteria had raised. More students gathered into the press. Ananda couldn't breathe.

"What?" gasped Ananda. "What's going on?"

George looked at her, round-eyed. "You haven't heard?"

Students turned around to stare at her. A few pointed. "She was the one who pushed him…" "I saw her do it, I was there…"

"Shut up!" Ananda snapped at them. "George! Tell me!"

"It's Chris. He's dead. He caught the plague! I mean, *the plague*? Who dies of plague anymore? It's crazy—" George kept talking, but Ananda didn't hear her.

Chris Litko was dead.

Ananda's first thought was, *I'm saved.*

Her second thought was that she was a disgusting human being for thinking such a thing. But as the chaos continued, with students flinging themselves into each other's arms weeping, she couldn't help but feel relief.

Chris Litko, a.k.a. "Hyena Boy," unibrowed tormenter and modern-day Neanderthal, had died of Bubonic Plague. He was the "local high school student" in the news.

By the time school started and the crying mass of students was shepherded inside the school doors, grief counsellors had been brought in. By midday the halls were empty. Parents had come early to pick up their kids, cars parked bumper to bumper, spilling out onto the road in front of the school. Buses were called in early.

Ananda's mom pulled up with her car, and Ananda climbed in. Her mother grabbed Ananda to her, awkwardly pinning her to her chest while she squeezed her. "I am so glad you're okay…I'm so glad…"

Instead of pulling away, Ananda hugged back. Her throat suddenly felt like it was being squeezed by a vise.

"Mom!" she choked.

"It's going to be okay, honey," said Perrin. "It's going to be okay."

Ananda pulled back, wiped her nose, and burst into tears.

Perrin looked at her, eyes streaming, and nodded as she put the car
in drive. "It's going to be okay," she said again, as if she could make
it true by sheer will.

That afternoon, Perrin had to go out to an appointment. She had
stared into Ananda's eyes and asked her about a million times if it
was okay for her to go, and insisted that if Ananda said the word she
would change her appointment in a heartbeat. But Ananda needed
some time alone to think.

She curled up on her bed and pulled the covers over herself, even
though it wasn't cold out. It seemed surreal. Like a joke. These kinds
of things happened to other people, in other places. Not here. Not
to her.

"It didn't happen to you, stupid!" she hissed to herself. "It happened to Chris."

She turned over and buried her head in her pillow, hating herself
anew. She lay like that until she fell asleep.

A clanking sound jarred her awake. She jerked her head up and
looked around her room, blinking groggily. "Mom?"

No answer.

The Great & the Small

She climbed out of bed, opened her bedroom door a crack, and peeked into the next room.

Nothing.

The noise started again. A scraping noise coming from the basement. Visions of Ebenezer Scrooge being visited by the ghost of Jacob Marley in Dickens's *A Christmas Carol* ran through her mind. In her case, it would be Chris Litko wearing the huge chain, covered with plague sores and pointing his rotting finger at her. Her mouth went dry.

She reached for the basement door with a shaking hand. She opened it a crack. *CLANK! Scraaaape.* She slammed it shut.

Pinning the door closed with her body, she grabbed her phone and dialed her mom's cell number.

She hung up. She had promised Perrin that she could handle being home alone.

Dad was at work, and his lab was too far away. Besides, what were they going to do? If whoever was in the basement came up after her, she'd be made into sausages before her folks had even gotten into their cars.

The scraping started again.

What about the police? She picked up the phone again, but her finger hovered over it. Whoever or *whatever* was down there was awfully noisy. Too noisy to be a murderer.

She put down her phone and eased the door open. Patting along the wall, she found the light switch and flipped it on. She stepped slowly down the stairs and peered into the room. The light bulb cast harsh shadows across the concrete floor. "Hello?"

Something moved. Ananda stifled a scream. A small lump quivered under the window, in a mess of metal, wood, and fur. Her dad's trap had caught something.

She moved closer. The creature's eyes were half-closed. Soot-grey fur capped its head and ran down its back. White fluff trembled between wire and wood jaws. And then she saw its tail: naked and pale, stretched out like a bristly snake.

A rat.

Ananda jumped back. The thing twitched and its eyelids fluttered, but it sank back onto the floor, ribs heaving.

She crept closer. Her shadow flickered across the creature.

Its eyes popped open.

It squealed, thrashing against the trap. Fresh blood seeped onto the concrete, adding to the dried pool already there. Ananda stepped back and the rat went still.

Wearily it closed its eyes. Its head slumped down.

What was she supposed to do now? Was it somebody's pet? It looked like the rat from the market, but that was impossible.

Ananda leaned forward to see how badly it was hurt. The rat went crazy again. It squealed shrilly, biting at its trapped leg to free itself.

"Okay! Okay!" she said, and moved back. This was *not* someone's pet. It was wild, no matter how it looked. And that meant it might have fleas. Fleas infected with plague bacilli.

Backing up the basement stairs, Ananda turned and raced out the back door and to the shed. She hauled open the rickety door and scanned the shelves. There were thick gardening gloves. She put them on. A dusty cinder block sat on the shed floor. She picked it up, staggered back a step under its weight, and waddled into the house and back down the stairs.

Standing over the rat, she gripped the cinder block with both hands. She'd try to make it painless.

The Great & the Small

CHAPTER THIRTY-FOUR

"There will be fierce battles
and much killing, biting hunger and death."

Brother John Clynn, 1349

Fin couldn't move. His hind leg felt bitten in two. Some evil thing had its teeth into him. Why didn't it just kill him? What was it waiting for?

The floor was cold. A chill crept through his fur, into his bones. The red curtain of pain shifted. He thought, drifting, *It's not so bad...*

The peaceful dark was shattered. Buzzing light split the gloom. Red pain bit into him again. He pressed his eyes closed, trembling.

A shadow moved over him. Fin opened his eyes a crack and saw two boggle eyes staring down at him. He thrashed against the cold teeth. Bit at his leg to free it. "Help! Help! Papa!" he screamed.

The bulbous eyes floated away. Panting, Fin stopped, listening. He couldn't see it, but the thing was nearby. He could hear it breathing. Lifting his nose, he feebly scanned the air and froze. There it was, an odour rank and pungent: two-leg stench.

The eyes hovered close again, its foul smell filling Fin's nostrils. He shrieked, "Let me go! Let me go!" yanking at his pinned foot. Once again the ugly two-leg moved back. Was it toying with him? Like a cat toying with a mouse?

Barely able to make out its blurry shape, Fin threw ultrasonic screams at it, calling it every insult he could think of, but his cries fell like stones, unheard. The thing was too brutish to understand him.

He was grateful Papa couldn't witness his shame. He was no Hero of the Tunnels now.

When the two-leg stood over him one last time, Fin did not feel a thing. He had already fainted.

Warm water cocoons him. He is suspended in warmth, but something grips Fin around his body, presses along his leg, probes the edges of jagged bone. Pulls it straight. Pain shoots him back into the darkness.

"Remember, Pip. You must remember," says Nia. *She holds him into her side and curls her tail around him. "You must see. When will you open your eyes and see?" She licks his foot, licks the blood from his leg, licks where bone meets broken bone, pulls him close.*

The two-leg comes into focus. Nestled in a soft towel, Fin peers at it with sleepy eyes. There are bars between him and the two-leg. He is in a cage? Fear clutches at him. But the sounds coming from the two-leg's large pink mouth are strangely soothing. His eyelids droop. He sleeps.

"Do you remember, Pip?" asks his mother.

"Remember what?"

Something strokes him. Gently. Behind his ear. Soft sounds. A piece of cooked egg is held under his nose. His leg aches, but it is a dull pain. A good pain. It itches.

It is there again. It looks at him with its enormous eyes. But it has brought more egg.

CHAPTER
THIRTY-FIVE

"You're not Stalin and I'm not Stalin…
Stalin is who I am in the newspapers and portraits."

Josef Stalin, speaking to his son Vasily

Looking down at the helpless creature, Ananda had known she could not kill it.

She lugged the cinderblock back out to the shed. "Now what?" she muttered. Rummaging through the shed, she looked for anything that could give her an idea.

There was a box of dog supplies from Belle, their golden retriever who'd died when Ananda was twelve; no one had been able to give away her things. Inside there was a grooming brush, a folded leash, Belle's dog collar. But tucked in the bottom of the box was an unopened bottle of flea shampoo.

Armed with the shampoo, some rubber gloves, and a can of bug spray, Ananda ventured back into the basement.

The rat hadn't moved. She could tell it was alive by the feather movement of its ribcage. Dousing herself with the bug spray,

The Great & the Small

Ananda pulled on the rubber gloves, then, crouching over the rat, she examined the trap. Never having used one before, she wasn't sure how to open it—and how to keep it open.

There was a wire bar on a spring that was embedded in the rat's leg. Another long straight wire lay beside it—the pin that held the bar in place and loaded the trap. Carefully, she pried the bar up, trying to hold it open. But the spring was too strong, and the bar snapped back onto the rat's leg causing fresh blood to flow. The creature was unconscious and didn't move.

Ananda looked around the basement until she saw an old pair of running shoes. Again she pried up the bar, but this time jammed the toe of the running shoe under it. It held.

The rat's leg, glued to the bar, was now raised off the floor. A cold sweat broke out on Ananda's body. "You can do this," she murmured to herself. Gently, she grasped the tiny leg—it was awkward in the rubber gloves—and pulled gently until the leg peeled off. Her breakfast lurched up in her throat. She swallowed several times, gulping air until her stomach settled.

Gingerly, Ananda picked up the little creature and cupped it in her hand. It looked so forlorn.

She filled the laundry sink with warm water and squirted the flea shampoo onto the rat's fur. Using her gloved fingertips, she worked it into a lather. But as Ananda rinsed the soap from its injured leg, she noticed its paw. It was curled over, a thick white scar cresting the top, almost like it had been branded. "I bet you've got a story to tell, little guy. If only you could talk."

She set it on a towel laid out on the washing machine. Pressing lightly along its leg, Ananda felt the raw edges of bone lying at sickening angles. She leaned on the sink's edge with her elbows, her head below her hands, fighting back the wave of dizziness.

"Just do it," she said. After she had straightened its bone, she threw up in the sink.

While the rat was unconscious, Ananda scrubbed out her old guinea pig cage. She pulled out the moving boxes that were still in the cupboard under the stairs then pushed the cage to the back. When she wasn't there, the boxes would be staged at the front of the cupboard, so no one would see the cage, even if they looked in.

Wrapping the animal in a small towel, Ananda placed it in the cage and then vacuumed the basement like her life depended on it. Putting the vacuum bag *inside* a garbage bag, she sprayed it again with bug spray and then ran it outside to the garbage, in case any fleas survived all that.

The trap was still bloody and needed to be cleaned. Manoeuvring the shoe out, she scrubbed at the blood and the peanut butter her dad had daubed onto the trigger. Next she placed it back under the window. With its trap sprung and all traces of bait gone, it was perfect: an enigma for her scientist father to work out.

When her parents came home, Ananda said nothing about what had happened. After dinner, Tom went to check the trap. He was frowning when he came back up, wiping his glasses. "I don't get it. There's a gnawed hole in the window frame, the trap is sprung, but there's no rat. Am I missing something? And what's that funny smell in the basement?"

Ananda shrugged and said, "Sorry, Dad," before leaving the kitchen.

Over the next few days, scraps of dinner—cheese, broccoli, egg, toast—made their way to the basement without Ananda's parents finding out about the visitor beneath the stairs.

The little rat began to look more bright-eyed. And although it

The Great & the Small

didn't go crazy when she approached like it had before, it had ripped off its gauze bandage and would sit, licking its wound, eyeing her suspiciously.

In honour of having survived her father's trap, Ananda named the rat Tom Little.

CHAPTER THIRTY-SIX

"Let your house be aired out and filled with the smell of herbs."

Bengt Knutsson, mid-fifteenth century, on prevention of plague

L ife in the cage was strangely pleasant. Fin's injured leg knit itself back together, and he'd never eaten so well in his life. The bulbous eyes of the little two-leg became familiar to him. With those eyes came a mouth that made soft sounds and hands that brought bits of cheese, apple, and raisins.

As he grew stronger, when he heard the two-leg coming he would poke his head out of his nest to see what it had brought him. Sometimes funny snorting sounds would come from its lips and it would bare its teeth. The first time it happened, Fin dived under the towels. But when it happened again and again, he realized the funny sounds, and even the bared teeth, meant the two-leg was happy. What surprised him was that it made him happy too.

When he felt really silly, he would dart around the cage. Stopping abruptly, he'd bob his head up and down, then zoom to the other side. He'd do that over and over, until the two-leg snorted with

The Great & the Small

laughter. Sometimes he would even laugh, which surprised him even more. Those were good days. But every so often, the little two-leg tried to pick him up, and he'd squeak at its pale claws until they retreated.

CHAPTER THIRTY-8EVEN

*"Ideas are more powerful than guns. We would not
let our enemies have guns, why should we let them have ideas?"*

Josef Stalin

The news was always on at Ananda's house. She was sick of it. They only reported *bad* news: *"Over forty-three hundred confirmed deaths worldwide, with hundreds of suspected cases being investigated daily…Global hysteria…"* Blah, blah, blah.

She wanted to tell her parents that there was good news, too. That Tommy's leg was getting better. That the little guy wasn't so afraid of her anymore and that he'd put on some weight. But she didn't. They wouldn't understand. Ananda wasn't sure *she* understood. The plague was killing people, and she was nursing a wild rat back to health? It made no sense. But, all the same, it felt right.

For hours, she sat under the stairs, on the pretext of doing laundry. While the clothes were washing and drying, she sketched him: Tommy eating; Tommy washing his ears; Tommy sleeping. She kept the sketches hidden in her book so her parents wouldn't see them.

And her parents were delighted that Ananda had finally "taken responsibility for some of the housework." A win-win.

One day Ananda dangled her fingers in Tom Little's cage. Usually he ran for cover, but this time he didn't. His eyes not leaving her hand, Tommy nibbled a cracker. He began to wash himself. Licking his paws, he pulled them down over his ears.

She moved her fingers a little closer.

He paused, watching her with alert eyes.

With the tip of her finger, she brushed against his ear. Tommy trembled for a moment but didn't run. Gently, so gently, she stroked his head.

Suddenly Tommy zipped to the other side of the cage, where he stopped and bobbed his head up and down. Zooming to the other end, Tommy stopped and bobbed his head again. Up, down, up, down, like a dance. He streaked the other way, this time running under her fingers like a car going through a car wash. What was he doing? And then Ananda realized: Tom Little was playing.

She began to laugh.

Tickling his back as Tommy zipped around, Ananda laughed harder and harder until she burst into an earsplitting coughing fit. With a single leap, Tommy jumped under his towel and hid.

Ananda cleared her throat, and waited.

It didn't take long. The little guy was so curious. He stuck his head out, peeping from under his towel. Ananda tried not to laugh—she really did!—but the towel draped across his forehead made him look like a tiny nun. ·

She erupted into another fit of laughter and coughing. Tommy pulled back his head abruptly and the towel flapped shut.

"I'm s-sorry, Tommy," she wheezed.

One afternoon, Ananda was reading, propped comfortably up in bed, snacks surrounding her like a junk-food buffet. Her mother was out, and the house was beautifully quiet, for once.

A flash of movement outside her window caught her eye. It was unusual for anyone to be out nowadays, so she craned her neck to see who it was.

It was George. Ananda tore out of bed and cranked open her window.

"George!" She waved. George looked over and walked up the driveway.

Ananda ran to the door and opened it. She suppressed a gasp. George, usually perfect, looked terrible. Her hair looked uncombed, pulled into a messy ponytail. Dark circles framed her eyes.

"Hi…how are you?" Ananda asked.

George raised one side of her mouth in a half-smile, as if raising both sides was too tiring. "Hi," she said.

"Do you want to come in?" said Ananda, holding open the door, adding, "I have junk food." She smiled. George shrugged and came inside. She followed Ananda to her room and stood, looking around in silence.

Ananda suddenly felt awkward. She grabbed a chip bag and said, "Want some?"

George frowned at the proffered bag, blinked, and shook her head. More silence.

Ananda took a chip and chewed it, its loud crunching reverberating in the tomb-like silence. She swallowed, but swallowed wrong and began furiously hacking. George raised her eyebrows as Ananda waved and choked, "I'm fine…really." Her face felt hot, and her eyes watered. Still coughing, she sat on the edge of her bed.

Again, silence loomed.

Ananda cleared her throat. "So, how are you?"

George slowly swivelled her head to stare at her. "How am I?" She laughed so unexpectedly that Ananda jumped. The sound was bitter, grating. Like screeching metal.

Ananda recoiled, but George leaned in, her eyes round.

"How am I? People are *dying*, Ananda, that's how I am. They're all *dying*." Without blinking once, George's eyes glazed over with tears. Then, like someone had pulled a string that connected her features, her whole face tightened into a knot. She hunched forward, still standing in the middle of the room, holding her face in her hands. Her shoulders shook with silent sobs.

Guilt flooded Ananda. After the initial shock over Chris Litko, the problems of the world had been firmly locked outside her door. She'd not only locked them out, she'd felt relief that she didn't have to go to school. Her whole focus had been on Tommy.

People were dying.

Tears stung her eyes, but whether from grief or from guilt she couldn't say. She stood and patted George's back. "It's okay. It's going to be okay." Her hand felt like a piece of ham, like it didn't belong to her, as she patted this stranger's back.

She kept patting for a minute, but George showed no signs of slowing down.

"Hey," said Ananda, "I'll show you something that'll cheer you up! Come with me." She gingerly took George's hand and led her to the basement door. "You can't tell anyone. Promise?"

George said nothing, tears streaming down her face. They walked down to the basement where Ananda positioned her in front of the cupboard, and opened the door.

She hauled out the boxes and pulled the cord for the light bulb that hung from the low ceiling.

Tommy raised his head from the towel he was snuggled in, blinking in the sudden light.

"Look!" Ananda said to the motionless girl. "George, look!"

George focused on her for a moment, then stooped and looked in. Her eyes went wide. A vein pulsed on her temple.

Ananda knew right then that she'd made a big mistake. She began to jabber, as the blood rushed to her head. "Ha, ha! I know, he's cute, and he's harmless, totally, and his name is Tom Little because I rescued him from my dad's trap, but he's not really wild, he's such a sweetheart, but I named him Tom Little because my dad's name is Tom and…"

George was still staring.

Ananda's mouth went dry. She laughed, but it sounded more like a cough. "Rats are really nice when you get to know them. He's really smart, and he's friendly, too—"

A low moan started from George's mouth. It sounded like an animal.

Ananda's hair stood on end.

The Great & the Small

George's eyes bugged out. The moan grew into an open-mouthed scream.

Ananda jammed the boxes back in front of the cage and slammed the door shut. "It's okay! It's okay!" she said. "Stop screaming! Stop it! George!"

George backed away, shrieking, until she was in a corner.

Ananda approached her. "George, stop it! Tommy's harmless! He's not going to hurt you!"

George thrashed at her as Ananda came near. "Murderer! You've killed us all!"

As if it had a mind of its own, Ananda's arm swung back and she slapped her friend, hard. "Shut the hell up!"

A red handprint rose on George's cheek. She stopped mid-scream, jaw hanging slack, and stared at Ananda. She raised her hand to her cheek. "You hit me."

"I'm so sorry," said Ananda. She made a move toward her.

George crouched back and spat, "Keep away from me!" She sprang past Ananda and bolted up the stairs, two at a time.

Ananda ran up the stairs after her. "I'm sorry I hit you! But don't tell anyone about Tommy! George! Please!" She heard the slam of the front door.

Ananda fell against the nearest wall, slid down, and crumpled into a sobbing heap. A few minutes passed. When she heard the door open again, she leapt to her feet.

"George?"

"Ananda?" Perrin. "Help me carry in these groceries."

"Coming, Mom!" She flew out the door and began hauling bags of groceries from the car.

"Who's George?" said her mom, as they carried in the last of the bags.

Glancing over to George's house, Ananda saw the curtains were drawn. It was quiet, as if the shrieking hysteria that had occurred only minutes before had never happened. But it had. The shrinking, sick feeling in her stomach told her this was real.

And if George told anyone about what she had seen, Tommy was dead.

"No one," said Ananda.

The Great & the Small

PART THREE

CHAPTER
THIRTY-EIGHT

"The plight of the lower and most of the middle classes was even more
pitiful to behold. Most of them remained in their houses, either through
poverty or in hopes of safety, and fell sick by thousands."

Giovanni Boccaccio (1313–75)

The strange squalling of the other two-leg passed quickly, and
Fin was left, once again, in peace. He had never felt so good.
Under his little two-leg's care, his leg was strong enough for
him to run again. When the two-leg tickled him, Fin couldn't contain the glee that made him shoot around the cage. Or the feeling of
love that welled up in his heart.

But when the two-leg wasn't there—playing with him, feeding
him snacks—he couldn't forget where he was. This was also the nest
of the big and cruel two-leg.

But the little one had saved him. The thought that it could have died
from Fin's Plague Rats? It made him sick. Now he knew Balthazar
was right: two-legs *could* feel. Or at least one of them could. The little
one had proven it.

The Great & the Small

When it was happy, it laughed. When it was sad, it cried. Just like Fin. How would Fin ever be able to lead another death squad without wondering if the targets were good two-legs or bad ones?

The question confused him.

Papa said there were *no* good two-legs. He'd said that the Old Ones meant for *all* two-legs to die. But they couldn't have meant this little one, could they? There must be some kind of mistake.

The little two-leg was a gentle creature. Fin loved its funny bared teeth that meant it was happy. Loved its bulging shiny eyes that were more familiar every day. Loved how it scratched on its flat white leaves with a small black stick, watching him. The two-leg was strange, yes. But he loved it.

It was all too much for Fin. Who was he to question the Old Ones or his uncle? He was never meant to decide such big things. And yet everything had changed.

Papa would never understand. He would see Fin's refusal to lead a death squad as betrayal. And wasn't it? Fin had told his uncle to "Kill the two-legs!" Had shouted in the Forbidden Garden that he wasn't ashamed. Had promised to stand by Papa forever. He'd even promised to save the Killing Chamber rats.

He had failed.

The night he left was horrible. More painful than getting his foot bitten in the metal teeth. More painful than the dreams that haunted his sleep.

Fin found his chance when the two-leg left the cage door unlatched. The wire latch rested on the bars but wasn't clipped shut. Climbing up, Fin nosed open the door and slid through. Even then, he wasn't sure he could go.

You can't stay, he told himself.

Why not?

You know why not. You came to kill it. You don't belong here. You don't belong anywhere, now.

The gap below the door of the fort-under-the-stairs was plenty big for a rat. Squeezing under, Fin peered around the basement room. A lifetime ago he'd lain there, bleeding, terrified. The cruel teeth were still there, metal jaws open and waiting, its spring baited with peanut butter.

Edging around it, Fin reached the wall. With his leg healed, he scaled it easily. Climbing up to the ledge, he found the hole he'd gnawed plugged with a rag. Fin tugged at the cloth with his teeth and dropped it into the darkness below.

From the open hole, cool night air blasted him, riffling his fur. Smells of the city, of his home, came rushing back to him. But the burst of joy was squelched by what lay ahead. And by what he was leaving behind.

Goodbye, he thought.

Wriggling through the hole, he was gone.

The Great & the Small

CHAPTER
THIRTY-NINE

"What can we do, we who have lost everything? We can find no peace."

Petrarch, in a letter to a friend, 1350

Over the next few nights, Fin wandered, missing the little two-leg, missing Papa. Unable to see either one. The damp side-walks only dimly registered on his paws. Whorls of fallen leaves tumbled past without Fin noticing.

When he would see a little two-leg coming toward him on the street, he'd force himself not to run to it. Hiding behind a water pipe or a dumpster or a garbage can, he would watch. Was it his? All of the two-legs now wore thick white cloths on their faces, but as the small one passed, he would see it wasn't his little one.

One moonrise, strong odours cut into his thoughts. Startled, he sniffed the air. The familiar aroma of sausages, butter pastry, and fish prickled his nose. He'd wandered to the market! Fin turned and ran in the opposite direction before he was seen by an ARM squad.

All moonrise he travelled. Just as the sun broke over the buildings, Fin found himself in an open, cobblestoned square. Giant trees with trunks many tail-lengths wide towered overhead. Benches lined the area.

There was the scent of rotting food in a nearby garbage can, mingled with a sharp, sour smell he couldn't identify. But the square was quiet; it seemed safe.

Fin edged into the clearing, his whiskers trembling on high alert, ears swivelling to catch any sound.

He scurried under a bench and hid behind its metal leg. Just then, noise exploded in his ears—rasping, furious barking. It came from over his head. What was it? Fin's fur rose at the nape of his neck. Should he run? Would the barking thing grab him if he did? He trembled behind the bench leg.

Foul odour surrounded him. A dark shape loomed over, leaning down from the bench.

Phtt! A wad of slime shot past Fin's hiding place. It made Fin jump.

The looming shadow paused, leaned closer. Huge bloodshot eyes glinted at Fin from under two hairy caterpillar eyebrows. White bristles covered a fleshy chin and sprouted from flared nostrils. A two-leg. A really, really old two-leg.

The two of them stared at each other.

Its few teeth clung to its gums like kernels of corn, and from its withered mouth came a low, rumbling sound that Fin now understood to be laughter. It worked its lips around, like it was chewing on something. It sat up and fumbled in its pocket. Then it held out a lump of cheese to Fin. From its mouth came a clucking noise as it waved the cheese back and forth.

Fin didn't move.

The old two-leg tossed it. The cheese landed in front of Fin. The smell of it made Fin's nose twitch. Sharp, tart, delicious. With one eye on the two-leg and the other eye on the cheese, Fin inched toward

The Great & the Small

his prize. Seizing it, he darted behind the bench leg and gobbled it down.

More deep rumblings from the two-leg. It tossed Fin a crumb of cookie. He gobbled that down too. The old one's odour was foul and sour, but it was sharing its food, and it seemed kind.

More treats were tossed before Fin. But as he was eating a morsel of cracker, the old two-leg dropped a rag onto the pavement.

Fin froze.

The old, watery eyes watched him. Soft sounds rumbled from the withered mouth. Leaning down, the two-leg nudged the rag toward Fin with its fat sausage claws.

Fin crept from his hiding place. Without taking his eyes from the two-leg, he grabbed the edge of the rag in his teeth, then pedalled backwards, dragging it to safety. Bunching it into a ball, he burrowed inside. He could hear the two-leg rumbling.

Fin realized this was a good two-leg, just like his little one, but the thought troubled him even more. *Two* good ones? Were there more?

Fin would not think about it now. He would think about it later. Besides, what could he do? He was just one rat.

Wriggling into his rag nest, he tucked his nose under his paw and curled his tail around himself. As the ancient two-leg welcomed the dawn with its snores, Fin drifted to sleep.

Shouting awakened Fin. From his nest, he saw white covered legs stride by. Down the square there were more two-legs, also in white. Their heads, faces, and eyes were covered by clear screens they could look through. White, noisy machines encircled the area. On top of each machine, a light pulsed and flashed, around and around.

The old two-leg sat up as white legs approached. Gloved hands reached for it, but it fought against them, swatting at them and bellowing. Fin trembled in his rag. What was happening?

More white legs. More hands on the two-leg. It was hoisted up. String that was wrapped around its feet came loose on one foot. The shoe flapped open, exposing a foot that was grey and pale, like an oyster shucked from its shell.

Slowly, the white legs hauled the old one to a white machine with back doors that were open. As Fin watched, they loaded the old one into the back. The two-leg's chin shook, as did its sausage hands. Its eyes were wet.

Fin buried his head in the rag. It was too much, to lose his new friend—the only friend he had left in the world. He couldn't bear to watch. The old two-leg had shared its cheese, its bits of cookie and crackers. *Don't look away*, Fin told himself, forcing himself to look back. *You owe it that much.*

Other two-legs in the square were also gathered up. A few struggled and swung their arms. Their bellows bounced off the building in the square, making Fin's ears ring, but the white legs did not seem to hear. The two-legs were lifted up from the benches, over to the waiting white machines, and into their gaping mouths.

In a few minutes the square was empty. The white legs jumped in the noisy machines and slammed the doors shut. With lights still pulsing, the machines rumbled away.

When the next swarm of machines buzzed up, Fin knew he was in trouble. White legs poured out of those too, but these ones had shiny blue claws and two bulbs that stuck out from their faces. Their breath sucked in and out through the bulbs. No soothing sounds, only shouts.

First, they emptied garbage cans. As they moved, the white legs beat the bushes, grabbing food wrappers and empty pop cans. He'd seen two-legs take garbage away before, but this was different. This was swift and deliberate. And they were heading toward him.

The Great & the Small

"Glad I'm not you," said a voice above him.

Fin jumped. A big grey seagull was perched on top of his bench.

It screeched over to a white leg, "Hey! Over here! There's one over here!"

"Stop it!" said Fin. The bird cackled. Lucky for Fin, the white legs didn't seem to understand the seagull, but they were scouring the bench next to him. They'd find him if he didn't move, and Fin was starting to get an idea of what all of this was about.

If they caught him, he'd be dead.

"Over here, before it gets away!" the gull screamed.

The white legs moved to Fin's bench. One of them pointed to his coiled rag. Masked eyes peered closer. Fin shrank back.

"Too late! Ha! You left it too late!" said the seagull. "Now you're in for it!"

"Why don't you shut up!" said Fin. He sprang from the rag and up the bench leg. As blue gloves came smashing down, he was already gone, launching into the air. There were muffled shouts. More white legs came stumping over, swarming after him. Zigzagging across the square, Fin raced through the forest of stomping boots.

The seagull flapped above, screeching, "Over here, idiots! No, not that way, fish-for-brains! Over here!"

Except for the white machines that surrounded the square, the street beyond was empty. Fin dashed across the street and into the alleyway on the other side. He slipped behind a pipe that stuck out from the wall. White legs stood on the other side of the road, staring down the alley. "It's here!" screamed the gull, wheeling over Fin's head. "Hey! What are you giving up for? It's right here!" But the white legs had turned away. Landing beside Fin's hiding place, the bird fixed its eye on him. "I guess I'll have to do it myself, rat."

"You...you...!" sputtered Fin. "What'd I ever do to you?"

"You're all the same! Garbage on legs!" Flapping into the air, it dived close to Fin, snapping its orange beak. *Snap! Snap!* "Nest-robbers! Flea-gatherers! Filthy, disgusting—" *Snap! Snap! Snap!*

Fin crouched low under the pipe. "Leave me alone!" he said, his voice shaking. From where he hid, he could see its webbed feet approach.

"Come out, come out, wherever you are!" the gull sang. "Come on, rat. Gully wants to play. Ratty isn't scared, is it?" The bird bent low, peering under the pipe with its head cocked to one side. Its beady black eye looked straight at Fin. Lifting its head, a second later the gull brought its beak down hard. *Snap!*

Fin leaped to one side. Grunting, the seagull pecked again. Fin dodged it easily. He realized that the bird couldn't see him and peck at him at the same time.

The gull screamed in frustration. As the beak came down a third time, Fin bounded out from under the pipe, grabbed the seagull's scaly leg, and dug in his claws.

"Yagh!" screamed the gull. It waggled its leg, but Fin held on. He was about to sink in his teeth when he saw a familiar face staring up at him from the ground. He lost his grip, slid off the leg, and tumbled onto the cobbled pavement.

The seagull pounced. Pinning Fin under its rubbery foot, it lunged at him with its beak.

Fin couldn't move. He squeezed his eyes shut, waiting to feel the beak slice through his head, but the beak snapped harmlessly above him.

"Yowch!" the gull screeched. "All right! All right! Just let go!"

Fin's eyes popped open. "Huh?"

Blood streamed down the bird's leg where a small brown rat had bitten it. The gull wept, "Let go, I'm begging you!"

The brown rat stepped back, the gull's blood dampening her fur. "Leave!" she said.

The gull took off, flapping crookedly into the air, shrieking, "I hate rats!"

Chuckling, the brown rat watched it go, then turned.

"Hello, Fin," said Zumi.

CHAPTER FORTY

"The death of one man is a tragedy. The death of millions is a statistic."

Josef Stalin

When Ananda discovered Tommy's empty cage, she cried, but she was also relieved. Now it didn't matter what George did or didn't do. Tommy was beyond her reach. Ananda knew that he'd made it outside, because the rag in the hole was out. Smart enough to have avoided her dad's horrible trap, now Tom Little was in even more danger. The world was at war with rats.

When George's mom knocked on the door with George by her side, and Ananda's parents were led down to the nook under the stairs, there were only boxes. Ananda had shrugged and said nothing when George had told them all about a rat Ananda had named "Tommy something."

George was led back out, her mother looking worried for her daughter. Ananda felt bad for lying. George had left her no choice, she told herself.

The months left in the school year passed slowly, now that Tommy was gone. Home felt like a prison.

The Great & the Small

The end of the school year came and went. Summer made the boredom of the spring look like a holiday. The hot weather made the number of plague deaths soar. September arrived with no resumption of school. The last school year would need to be repeated, and possibly this year's, too. That is, if there was any need for school once the plague had played itself out.

Every day the news had updates on the plague. Plague Watch, they called it. The rising death toll flashed in red at the bottom right of the TV screen. The worldwide death toll was now around 84,000 with over 2,000 in the city alone. It was getting worse, and people were terrified.

News channels gave dire warnings about the hazards of leaving out trash:

> *"Residents are urged to clean all garbage, litter, and garden waste from their properties in an effort to reduce habitable areas for rats. Again, authorities urge everyone to keep children and pets away from baited traps. Only yesterday, a toddler in a suburb of Toronto found a bait box and…"*

Ananda lay on her bed. She didn't feel like drawing. The house was silent, except for the buzz of the TV in the next room. Her bedroom was like an oven—the relentless sun streamed through the window.

A fly bashed itself, again and again, into the window, scudding down the side of the glass, before starting the whole thing over again.

It was sticky and so muggy Ananda felt like she was suffocating.

Outside was no better. It was the hottest fall on record. The experts kept promising that the coming cold weather would slow the plague's spread. Winter couldn't come soon enough. Her mom had done the whole "Let's talk" thing, and her dad had suggested they play board games in the evening. Yeah, that was the answer. While the world died, while Tommy was hunted down and savagely killed, they would chat and play board games.

It was too much. Everything was too much. The walls felt like they were closing in. There was no relief from sickness, from death, from worry. She'd even dreamed last night that her driveway was lined with stacks of corpses, with Tommy's small body curled on top. If she didn't get away, she'd explode into a million pieces.

She opened her door a crack. Her mom was in her office.

Ananda crept down the hall and snuck out the back door. On the porch, she hesitated.

The air was still, like the world was holding its breath. The neighbourhood was silent. Before there would have been people walking dogs, people jogging, moms with strollers. Not now. Now there was silence.

George's house was still closed up tight, curtains drawn. Ananda looked away.

George had been taken for psychological testing, was "under the care of a physician." Guilt stabbed at Ananda, but she brushed it away. George had left her no choice.

The sky was a clear pale blue. A wisp of air brushed her hair back from her face, cooling it.

Ananda stretched out her arms and filled her lungs, but as she did so, she had the strangest feeling she was being watched. She lowered her arms and gazed around. She glanced at George's window again. No, the curtains hadn't moved.

Yellow leaves ruffled across the lawn. The huge oak stood leafless and naked in their front yard. There was nothing there. No one was watching her. No pile of bodies in the driveway. And no little rat lying dead on the top.

She unlocked the shed and hauled out her bike. Just a quick ride. She'd be back before her mom knew she was gone.

A small streak of movement flashed in her peripheral vision. Tommy? Her heart began to thud. Ananda peered closely, leaning over to look under the shrub by the door. It wasn't Tommy. Its fur was dark, but she couldn't see what kind of creature it was. It was either a squirrel…or a rat. She hesitated.

Stop being paranoid. It's a squirrel.

Before she changed her mind, Ananda pulled her bike onto the driveway and hopped on.

It was heaven to feel the wind on her face. She pedalled along to the end of the street where it sloped downhill. Ananda threw out her arms like she was flying, balancing on her bike, and soared down the hill.

Scrubbs waited under the bushes, her squad nearby. It had taken a lot of sniffing and grunt work to find this target again. Blast Fin! Leaving her to clean up his mess! Only for the Beloved Chairman would Scrubbs do this.

The captain had gone into the target's nest to chew a point of entry for the squad. Simple, and yet he'd still failed to do it. He never came out, leaving Scrubbs to explain to the Councillors why their mission had failed. To the Chairman. Her whiskers trembled thinking about him.

There was no movement at all from the two-legs' tall nest. It was hard to keep focused on the mission.

Her thoughts drifted back to the Chairman.

She didn't blame the Beloved Chairman for being angry. "Go back and finish the job!" he'd ordered. Magnificent. Terrifying. Scrubbs had only seen the Chairman from far away. To be so close to him...

The back door opened.

Scrubbs leaned forward, whiskers twitching. A small two-leg came out. The thatch on its head was hideously long, sprouting only from the top (as with all ugly two-legs) and swinging down like dead grass in the wind. The rest of its body was pale and hairless.

It raised up its thin, stick-like arms, then dropped them suddenly, looking around. It drew its gaze to where Scrubbs lay hidden. She held her breath.

The moment passed. The ugly two-leg walked down the stairs and onto the grass.

The squad looked at Scrubbs. She shook her head.

It entered a small building in the yard. Scrubbs nodded, and the Plague Rats began to advance, but it swung open the door, and the rats retreated to their hiding places.

The two-leg hauled out a big-wheeled machine that it then mounted. And before Scrubbs could give the command, it rolled off, riding the machine.

Scrubbs stared after it. She had been sloppy, and now the mission was in jeopardy. Again. This time, because of her.

Failing twice was not an option.

Keeping a safe distance, Scrubbs arranged the death squad around the yard. If the two-leg came back, it might return the big-wheeled machine to the same place.

She positioned the largest rat by the building. Others were placed in a half-circle around the door, so the ugly two-leg's escape would be cut off.

The Great & the Small

Scrubbs found a good vantage point behind a garbage can. All she could do now was watch and wait. And pray to the Old Ones the two-leg would return.

The sun touched the tops of the tall nests.

Where was the two-leg? The squad was peaking, close to death.

She knew the squad members would perform, if they could survive long enough. Each dying rat knew that their families would be exterminated if they rebelled. But now disaster loomed: Scrubbs's mission might fail.

Where was the two-leg?

It came back as the sun dipped out of sight. The two-leg's cheeks were pink from riding its two-wheeled machine.

Breathing prayers of thanks to the Old Ones, Scrubbs nodded to the large rat stationed near the shed. The rat crouched, ready, but foam dribbled from his mouth. He was fading.

Scrubbs watched. *Come on…come on…!*

The two-leg wheeled its machine back to the building. It reached out its hook to open the door.

Now!

The Plague Rat leaped, burying his claws into its knobby knee and sinking his teeth in deep. The two-leg shrieked. Flinging its machine to the ground, it swatted at the Plague Rat, hooks slapping wildly at its naked legs. The other Plague Rats moved in, leaping onto the two-leg until it fell under a carpet of rats.

The nest door smacked opened. A large two-leg jumped down the stairs, screaming, waving a board in its hooks. Scrubbs was stunned. Another two-leg?

Without waiting for the Plague Rats to refocus their attack, Scrubbs hurtled toward the big two-leg, teeth bared. This one was hers.

For the Beloved Chairman.

Scrubbs leaped for its face as the big two-leg swung the wooden board.

CHAPTER FORTY-ONE

"I bid you weep, for the time of mercy is over."

Gabriele de' Mussis, 1348

Papa paced in his nest. A movement by the entrance caught his attention.

Sergo had come. "Come in, come in, dear friend!" said Papa. "Why do you stand at the door like a stranger?"

Sergo stepped into the chamber. Papa had never invited him to his nest before. The large rat's eyes darted eagerly around the room, then back to Papa.

The Chairman began pacing again.

"Perhaps you are wondering, dear friend," said Papa, "why I have asked you here. Here to my nest."

Sergo cleared his throat. "Yes, Beloved Chairman. It is a great honour for this humble Tunnel Rat."

Papa lowered his eyes. "Nonsense, dear fellow! Every rat is equal! Every nest for all!"

Sergo bowed.

"Now," said Papa, sighing deeply, "as Chairman I must do what is best for the Tunnels. Even if it means terrible sacrifice. Do you agree, Councillor?"

Sergo bobbed his head. "Of course, Beloved Chairman."

"And I know you will sacrifice; you will do what is best, as well," continued Papa, "but others are not so loyal. There are Wreckers, Sergo. Wreckers *within* Council. Within the ranks of *Councillor*."

The big rat's eyes grew wide. He glanced around the nest, nervously this time, as if the Wreckers might be lurking in the shadows. Clearing his throat again, he said, "Oh?"

"Perhaps you know of whom I speak?" asked Papa softly.

Sergo shook his head, his eyes still darting from side to side. "No, Beloved Chairman. I am sorry, I do not."

"Ah, my friend." Papa smiled wistfully. "You are simple—an honest soldier for the Common Good. A refreshing innocent in these dark times." He laughed, but his laugh was joyless, like a dry leaf skittering in the wind.

Leaning forward, Papa said, "Shall I tell you who it is?" He gazed into the other rat's eyes. "I warn you, friend, the truth is ugly. Can you bear it?"

Sergo's eyes bulged from their sockets. "Tell me! Tell Sergo!" He leaned close, ears cocked forward, whiskers quivering.

"Ah...good!" sighed Papa. "I knew I could trust you, dear, loyal Sergo. Here, sit, sit! Have a biscuit...here you are. And now, let us talk...."

CHAPTER FORTY-TWO

"Even as we speak we are drifting away…becoming shadows."

Petrarch, 1350

"Zumi," said Fin. He stood blinking at her. She had grown thinner, but her eyes hadn't changed. Still something shining inside. "How did you—I mean, where—?" They were in the middle of the alley. At that moment the seagull's shadow flitted overhead. It was coming back.

"Quick!" said Zumi. She dived down the alley. Dodging in and out of shadows, she led Fin through a tangle of alleys toward the warehouses along the wharf and disappeared into a drainpipe.

Fin followed. On the other end, he found himself in a small burrow.

It was close enough to the road that the growl of two-leg machines could be heard—what few there were—but the burrow itself was safe and dry. A pile of rags, leaves, and feathers were arranged into a tidy mound of nesting.

Fin limped further into the burrow, suddenly aware that it was just the two of them. The last time he'd seen her, Fin had been collecting rats—and their pups. His mouth felt dry.

Zumi seemed to feel awkward too; her ears were a deep pink.

Fin broke the silence. "I want you to know that I'm not…I'm not collecting Wreck—I mean, I'm not…" His voice trailed off. More silence.

Zumi grabbed her tail and began to groom, her eyes lowered. "You ordered Scratch to warn me. You saved my life. Why?"

Fin shrugged. "I don't know."

"Scratch was going to let them do it," she murmured.

"He thought Council would protect you if you were innocent," said Fin.

"And if I wasn't?" Zumi looked up and stared at him defiantly.

"I…I don't know," said Fin.

A lone two-leg machine buzzed by outside, its sound forlorn. Zumi listened, her ear cocked. "The war is getting worse. Hardly any machines go by now. The two-legs are dying. But maybe you think that's a good thing."

Memories of his little two-leg came to him. Fin didn't answer.

"You hungry?" she asked, and pushed a hunk of bread crust to him. He nodded, not trusting himself to speak. They gnawed on the crust, sitting across from each other.

Feeling better with something in his belly, Fin sat back on his haunches and watched as Zumi licked her paws and wiped her whiskers clean.

"So how did you find me?" he asked.

"It was pure luck—or maybe the Old Ones led me to you, I don't know. I was late getting back from foraging when I heard you with your new 'friend.' What did he call himself?" Zumi paused. "Gully?"

The Great & the Small

Fin chuckled. "Yep, good old Gully. Only tried to murder me!"

They both laughed and then fell silent.

He looked at her. "Thanks, Zumi."

Her ears blushed a rosy pink. "I just wanted to pay back the favour."

At moonrise they went out foraging. With the two-legs disappearing, food scraps were getting harder and harder to find. The two-legs who were left had made things tougher for rats: litter was cleared, dumpsters covered, garbage bins emptied.

Traps baited with tempting tidbits were everywhere—but the only rats who ate from those were dead rats. Still, in the rougher areas, food could be found.

Zumi led Fin behind a tall building filled with two-leg nests where the sound of shouts and loud thumping music made the ground vibrate under their paws. The garbage had a foul reek to it, not like the tasty finds from the market. Overhead a streetlight buzzed and cast everything in a garish light.

Zumi must have found something good. She was tugging at it to try to get it loose. Fin waded over to her. The tip of a steak bone poked through a plastic bag. Bracing himself, Fin gripped it too, and together they hauled it out. A few bites of gristle still clung to it.

He glanced at Zumi, who was gnawing at the bone, her usually tidy brown coat thick with mats from wading through garbage, spikes of oily fur sticking straight up on her head. She caught him looking and grinned. "Welcome to my neighbourhood, Mister Fin. It's a long way from your precious market!"

"Oh yeah?" he said. Biting the piece of gristle, he pulled it from her paws and ran.

"Hey, you thief!" Zumi raced after him and tackled him.

They somersaulted over each other, landing in a tangle of tails, paws, and ears. Zumi lunged for the gristle, but Fin dodged back and forth, keeping it out of her reach. Finally she nipped him on the ear.

He yelped and dropped the gristle.

She wolfed it down and smacked her lips. "Delicious!"

Fin bowled her over. Zumi tumbled backwards through the garbage where she lay flat on her back, panting.

She laughed. Her fur was greasy, and her tail was covered with filth, but her eyes smiled at him. Without thinking, Fin nuzzled her ear.

Zumi gasped. Then she sprang up, first darting one way, and then another, before scurrying off to different part of the garbage.

Fin was frozen with horror. He burned with embarrassment from tip to tail. *Of course* Zumi didn't like him. She was being nice to him because he'd ordered Scratch to warn her.

Wishing the Old Ones would suck him into the ground, he waded over to her.

"Sorry," he said. He tried to sound casual. "I was just playing around. I mean, we don't even really like each other, right?"

Zumi looked at him. "Right," she said. "You were just *playing*. That's what I figured. Let's just forget about it."

For the rest of moonrise they foraged in silence. When the sun began to glimmer on the horizon and the streetlights winked off, Zumi led the way back to her nest.

Inside the burrow, not sure what to do with himself, Fin stood in the entrance. It was sunrise. Time to sleep. He felt awkward being alone with Zumi, especially after what he'd done.

Dragging over some rags to the other side of the burrow, Zumi said, "You can sleep here." She climbed onto her nest and disappeared from sight.

Settling into the rags, Fin said, "You know it meant nothing, right? I'm always playing around. It's just because of Scratch that we're here together."

"Right."

There was a long silence. She must have fallen asleep.

Fin was wide awake. He hadn't just been playing. He'd felt something for her, something he'd never felt for anyone before, and if he was honest, he'd felt it for a very long time. Zumi was argumentative, bossy, and most likely a Wrecker. She was also intelligent, loyal, and incredibly brave.

And Fin loved her.

CHAPTER FORTY-THREE

"We should follow Jeremiah the prophet's writings and not do evil, but do good, and humbly beg forgiveness for our sins."

Bengt Knutsson, fifteenth-century bishop, on prevention of plague

They were foraging behind the tall two-leg building again. Frost hung in the air. Zumi was silent, picking through the garbage. All moonrise, she had only communicated to Fin with curt nods.

Swinging around to him suddenly, she said, "You've got a lot of nerve, you know that? You show up, you sleep in my burrow, eat from my forage, and then you say, 'It's just because of Scratch! We don't even like each other!' Well, thank you very much!"

"What? But I didn't mean—"

"Go back to the Tunnels and to your Beloved Chairman if you don't like it here! Don't torture yourself being with Scratch's 'ugly sister' from the Lowers."

Far off, a two-leg voice warbled a slurred melody.

Fin's ears burned. "I…I don't *want* to go back. And I think you're beautiful."

The Great & the Small

Zumi's mouth dropped open. "What?"

Fin swallowed hard. "I said, I think you're *beautiful*."

Zumi's eyes went as round as moons. Even in the pale lamplight Fin saw her small perfect ears—like dainty seashells—deepen to crimson. "You…I…but…oh!" She stepped toward him. "Fin!"

Pulling her close, he whispered, "Zumi."

The next moonrises and sunrises passed blissfully. The troubles of the Tunnels, of the Plague War, and even of missing Papa and the little two-leg, seemed far away.

The cobbled pavement around their burrow was cold to the paws now. Winter was on its way. But it didn't matter to Fin.

Zumi loved him.

Every moonrise they set out foraging, side by side, their breath puffing into the air like icy swans. Sometimes Zumi asked Fin why he had left the Tunnels, or why he wasn't in the war, or if he missed his uncle. But always he'd steer the conversation away. "Don't worry about that now," he'd say, nipping her ear and tackling her. Rolling down the alley in a big furry ball, they'd scratch and bite at each other like two pups.

Fin had never felt so happy, so in love. For the first time in his life, Fin felt confident and content. There was no talk of being a leader, no talk of what good Tunnel Rats do or don't do.

There was only him and Zumi.

CHAPTER
FORTY-FOUR

"The cemeteries overflowed, but still there were always more dead.
Trenches were dug and bodies were placed in, layer upon layer."

Giovanni Boccaccio (1313-75)

Winter arrived.

There was a chill in the air that cut through small fur coats, cut into thin bones. Food became even more scarce, forcing Fin and Zumi to forage farther out of their range.

One moonrise, they decided to forage along the wharf, by a section of warehouses they'd never been to before. Fog hung thick over the pavement and wrapped around the dark buildings. The cobblestones were slick with frost.

A light snow fell, landing on their ears and whiskers. Fin had never seen snow before and had looked forward to it. Now, all he felt was cold.

"I don't like it down here," said Zumi. "Two-legs don't live this far down, and the streets are deserted. I don't think we're going to find food." She sniffed the air warily.

The Great & the Small

Fin looked at her. Her once thick coat was a little shabby, and her cheeks were sunken. She needed food. Fin did too. He'd never known hunger before. This constant gnawing in his belly was new.

Not for the first time Fin wished he was more like his powerful uncle. Papa would have found a way to get food. He wouldn't have let his mate starve. At the thought of his uncle, Fin's heart ached.

"Fin!" Zumi was staring at him. "Are you listening?"

"Of course I am," he replied. "You said no two-legs live down here and you don't like this place."

Zumi nodded but eyed him suspiciously.

Closer to the waterfront Fin caught a whiff of fish. "See? What did I tell you?" They followed the trail to a dark warehouse where a splotch of fish guts had frozen onto the cobblestones. Two-legs must have spilled them there earlier that day. Most of the guts had been scraped up, but there was still plenty for two small rats.

After a few mouthfuls, Zumi's eyes got their old sparkle again. It made Fin feel proud. Even if he was a puny little mouse-rat, he could take care of his mate.

The two of them laughed and joked and gorged themselves on fish. After Fin's belly was as round as an egg, he chortled, "So, Miss Zumi! Who was right this time?"

"You were," sighed Zumi. "For once!"

"Ha!" said Fin. "Hey, what's wrong?"

Zumi was sniffing the air, frowning. "Can't you smell it?"

"No, what—*ugh!*" An odour had drifted overhead on a slight gust from the harbour. Heavy, cloying, the smell squeezed out the aroma of fish, leaving only itself. Fin and Zumi stared at each other, their eyes wide.

It was the smell of Death.

Whatever had died must be huge. The smell was everywhere now. Like a gossamer snake, the foul odour coiled and glided deep into the alley. Fear bristled along Fin's spine.

"What do you think it is?" asked Zumi. She huddled close to him.

"I don't know," said Fin.

They crept forward together, ears swivelling, noses twitching.

The fog grew thicker as snow began to dust over the cobbles. The scent trail led to a warehouse, its metal doors chained and bolted. A swirl of the sickly-sweet odour eddied around its opening, confirming that the doors had rolled open that day.

The stench came from inside.

Dread seeped into Fin. He could sense the clinging smell of *many* dead things—not just one. "Let's get out of here!" he said.

Zumi stared at the door. "Fin, I know what's in there. Balthazar saw it."

"Balthazar? *Balthazar?* What's he got to do with—Zumi, *no!*"

Zumi had darted under the doors. Into the warehouse.

"Come back! Zumi, come back!"

She didn't answer. The doors loomed overhead.

Fin approached the doors. His whole body shook.

He crawled under.

Inside there was darkness. Strands of putrid odour leaped at him, clawed his nose. Using his whiskers to feel his way, he took a step. The smell was so thick it smothered his senses. He felt blind. Sounds were deadened, like something was blocking them.

There was a flutter of muffled weeping. "Zumi?" called Fin. "Are you okay? What's the matter?"

From far away, he heard her sob, "He was right! He was right! Oh, Fin! They're everywhere."

Fin's eyes bulged. He swivelled, looking behind himself. *Where? What? I don't see—*

Look! Open your eyes! They're all around you! Why can't you see them?

Wide columns began to emerge from the dark. One was directly in front of Fin. He'd almost walked into it. He took a step forward and sniffed along the bottom.

It wasn't a column. It was a *stack.*

Long objects lay one on top of the other, wrapped in bags. The sweet, foul odour of death wound around each bundle like a shroud.

"Wh-what are they?" asked Fin, and then his heart began to race. He knew. He knew what they were. Horror pumped into his veins. His teeth began to chatter.

"Not *what,*" came Zumi's voice. "*Who.* They are two-legs, Fin. *Dead* two-legs."

The room swam. Stacks sagged and whirled around him as if he were tumbling through the air. "Two-legs?" he croaked. His voice sounded strange, like it belonged to someone else. *"Two-legs?"*

The face of his little one rose before him.

Bubbling stench filled his nose. His pounding heart muffled his ears.

The words of Balthazar sprang up. *Over the mountains and across the sea there came a terrible scourge…a scourge that would deal death not only to the Old Ones, but to ALL.*

He panted, "I need to get out…Zumi…need to go…now!" Anguish twisted his heart. He couldn't breathe. "Zumi…"

The two-legs cast themselves out into the ocean of blood…

Another stack emerged before him. Bodies of two-legs lay sandwiched on top of each other. No bags on these. A pair of small feet stuck out from the jumble. A little one.

Two-leg children cried out, calling for their parents…but we do not care about two-leg little ones. Do we…?

The door! Squeeze under…cool air…he is free! Running…running back, through the dark alley, over damp pavement where snow has gathered. But always, always, the face of his little one hangs before him.

Zumi calls to him from behind, pleads for him to wait.

His legs do not, *cannot*, listen.

Hurtling through the drainpipe, he dives into the nest, burrows into the rags. But still the voice of Balthazar can be heard.

It is told that the two-legs wept.

The Great & the Small

CHAPTER FORTY-FIVE

"A lie told often enough becomes the truth."

Vladimir Lenin

The season's first snow swirled outside Ananda's hospital room window. Out in the hall, her father peered through the small rectangle of glass on the door that separated him from where she lay in a coma. He hadn't been allowed to get near her. Not since that day.

Perrin had been hysterical, and Tom could only piece together what had happened. Perrin had been inside, working. Hadn't realized Ananda was outside until she heard the screaming.

She'd run outside. What she described then sounded impossible: rats swarming over Ananda's body. Grabbing a piece of wood, Perrin had beaten them off. She was in quarantine now. So far she showed no symptoms.

Not so with Ananda. After Perrin had done away with the rats, Ananda began vomiting. A specially-equipped ambulance had rushed her to a quarantine ICU at the hospital, but by then she was unconscious.

Lumps the size of eggs swelled Ananda's eyes shut, making her look like she'd been molded from clay. The lymph nodes around her neck and under her armpits were as hard as baseballs. Even unconscious she moaned and cried out.

A nurse rushed by, heading down the hall. "That's my daughter in there," Tom said to her. "Nobody's telling me anything!"

"Let go of me, sir," said the nurse. Tom looked down and realized he was gripping her arm. He let go and stepped back. The nurse was dark-skinned and young, her eyes bloodshot with exhaustion. "I'm sorry, sir. That's not my patient, but I have dozens of others that are just as sick."

"I'm sorry…" said Tom to her back. She had already hurried away.

He'd found Ananda's bag of long overdue library books on the Black Death. The people who'd written the eyewitness accounts had all turned to dust ages ago, but he felt close to them.

One man stuck out to him. The man had lived 650 years ago in Italy with his wife and five children. When the plague came, it took everything he had: his work, his city, and his entire family. He'd buried his children with his own hands and had written a chronicle of everything he'd seen. Tom could feel the man's anguish through the pages, and strangely, felt comforted. He wasn't alone. Others had gone through this.

Tom didn't even know how long he'd been here. How many days. It had been a long time, going back and forth between his daughter and his wife, catching a few naps hunched in a hospital chair, brushing his teeth in a public restroom. He hadn't been home since this happened. Hadn't been to the lab…*the lab!*

Had anyone taken care of the rats? Were his assistants still working? He fumbled with his cell phone, but the battery was dead. Should he go?

The Great & the Small

No, it was too late. In his heart he knew it had been too long.

The rats were dead.

The floor seemed to tip toward him, and he sagged against the door. He could feel tears pushing up, trying to burst through. He swallowed. They were rats, for heaven's sake! He'd *dissected* them! But that had been for something, to fight cancer. Their deaths now? Needless.

It was too much. Too much death.

He broke down and, like a dam that had finally been breached, sobbed into his hands. He slid down onto the floor, and in the antiseptic light of the hospital ward, he bellowed out tears until strings of snot dripped through his fingers and his mouth felt frozen into a cry.

He felt a hand on his back. "It's going to be okay, sir." He looked up, blinking through bleary eyes, and saw the same nurse crouched next to him. She held a wet washcloth. "We've got to be brave. They need us to be brave." She pointed with her chin at the hallway lined with doors, behind which lay countless other souls fighting for life.

He nodded and took the washcloth. Wiping his face, he choked, "Thank you."

She held her hand on his back for another moment, looking into his eyes, and then stood up and walked away. On to the next crisis.

Tom watched her, a small woman, her head high and her shoulders back, although she carried the weight of the world on them. He breathed out.

Slowly, he rose to his feet and looked through the glass in the door again.

Breathe in. Breathe out.

Wiping away tears that would not stop, Tom Blake prayed for his little girl and for all of the doors that stretched down the long hallway.

CHAPTER
FORTY-SIX

"The town is only recognizable through the buildings and homes which still stand. The people who teemed through its streets are all gone."

Jean Baptista Spinell, Naples, Italy, July 10, 1656

J ulian! Come in! Come in!" said Papa heartily. The Councillor's eyes darted nervously around the Chairman's burrow. "What?" said Papa. "You don't trust me, old friend? Ha, ha!"

Julian frowned. "I know you are angry," he said. "But you must understand, I am only acting for the good of the Tunnels."

Papa stopped him. "First, a nibble between friends, and then we talk." Bustling to his reserve of forage, Papa carried a chunk of apple fritter back in his mouth. Its smell filled the burrow. "Guests first," he said, pushing it toward Julian with his nose.

Julian raised his eyebrows. "I'm…not hungry."

Chuckling, Papa ate the fritter until the sweet aroma was all that remained. He smacked his lips. Then he began to groom himself. He pulled first one whisker through his moistened paws, and then another. And then another. Papa glanced up at Julian and flashed him a brilliant smile.

Julian watched warily.

Papa sat across from him. "Old friends should never doubt one another. I trust *you*, Julian."

At this, Julian's grizzled eyebrows rose in surprise. "You do?"

"Yes," said Papa. "We have our differences. What friends—what *brothers*—do not?"

Julian nodded. "Yes, I have considered you my brother, Koba. But I was not sure you felt the same since I called for an end to using Plague Rats."

Papa began to pace. "We go back a long way, Julian. Back to when the two-legs ruled with cruelty and without justice, when we huddled in dripping sewer pipes, when we made plans for a new way. You and I, Julian."

A smile transformed Julian's face. "I am relieved to hear you speak like that, dear, dear Koba. So glad! May I speak to you now, then, as brother to brother? The market has become a ghost-town. And so many Collections from the Lowers! The Tunnel Rats are becoming rebellious. Change is needed, dear Papa, change is needed now. That's why I said that the death squads must cease. It is not because I love you any less as my brother."

Papa sighed. "Yes, change is needed. And right away. A change is essential."

Julian nodded his head, his watery eyes round with joy. "Really? Oh, I'm so happy, so relieved."

"My first allegiance is to the Tunnels," said Papa. "I pledge to do whatever is necessary to protect them."

Julian said, "This *is* good news."

"Yes, Julian. It is."

The Great & the Small

The Councillor sat up on his haunches, a grin gathering his drooping skin into furrows. "Every rat is equal!"

"Every nest for all," answered Papa.

They touched noses in farewell. Julian moved toward the nest opening, then stopped. "You are wise, my brother," he said. "Very wise indeed." Julian hobbled out into the tunnel.

Papa gazed after him, listening. A breath of movement, scuffling, a muffled shriek. Silence.

"Ah, Julian," he sighed.

He would miss the old goat.

CHAPTER
FORTY-SEVEN

"You who had been given so much,
who had countless joys and pleasures…
now you are headed to the same tomb as those who had nothing."

Gabriele de' Mussis, 1348

Councillor Tiv yawned and stretched, arching her back. The Council Chamber was empty, with the only sound a *drip-drip-drip* from a leaking pipe in the corner.

A shift in the air riffled her fur.

"Hello, I'm waiting!" she called. No answer. She sighed, shaking her head. Licking her paws, she pulled them over her velvety ears. First one and then the other. She sank her paws into the fur on her ample belly and combed them through, pausing to nibble at a fleck of dirt.

A noise made her freeze. She sniffed the air. Then shook her head again. "At last you show up!" she said. "I have been waiting."

The figure standing in shadow at the entrance said nothing.

"What is this all about?" said Tiv. "What was so very important, so *secret*, that it couldn't wait for Council?"

"Don't you know? Haven't you guessed?"

A smile pulled up one side of her mouth. "Oh, I've got my ideas about it, I admit."

She took a step toward the dark opening, whiskers twitching. "Why are you hiding? There's no one else here. Now tell me, what did you have in mind?" She shook out her fur, smoothing it.

"Come here, lovely Tiv."

She scanned the air with her nose, sniffing the darkness.

The figure chuckled. "Don't worry! There's no one else here. Now come to me."

"You'd better not be trifling with me." She took another step. Leaning forward, she closed her eyes, a smile on her lips.

The movement from the shadows was swift.

Before Tiv could make a sound, her spine was bitten in two. Tiv's eyes flew open. Her body slumped onto the ground.

"Goodbye, my lovely Tiv," murmured the voice.

Tiv blinked once, then closed her eyes.

CHAPTER FORTY-EIGHT

"Alas! God of all mercy, when will you help me in my misery?"

Heinrich Suese, fourteenth-century German mystic

Fin didn't move when Zumi came in. He could sense her standing next him, waiting. The only sound was the faint hum of a two-leg machine outside.

"I know you're awake."

Still he said nothing.

"You left me. I was scared, Fin, and you left me."

"Leave me alone."

"No. Why did you run away?"

The face of the little two-leg sprang to Fin's mind, its brown eyes, its big nose—so different from a rat's delicate point—the snorting laughter that came from its mouth…those things that had terrified him at first but that he had grown to love. He squeezed his eyes shut against tears.

"Oh, Fin." Zumi's voice was soft. She nuzzled away a tear that had escaped down his nose.

The Great & the Small

He began to weep. "After…after I saw you in the Tunnel that day, when I…and those pups…you know."

"I remember."

"Well, I went to Council and I quit. I told them that my fight was with the two-legs, not with other Tunnel Rats. Let the Council deal with Wreckers!" He looked at Zumi, the defiance and liberation he'd felt standing up to Council strengthening him for a moment. "So Papa said I could have my own Plague Rat squad after I finished that day's work. I only had a few more Wreckers to collect. But I found out you were one of them. I sent Scratch to warn you."

There was silence. Zumi stared at him. "So, it's true? Council is using collected rats as Plague Rats?"

Fin chewed his lip. "I don't know. Some volunteer, but others…I don't know."

She nodded, but her brows were furrowed.

"I…I thought I was done with…with feeling so guilty!" said Fin. "But it's worse than ever." He climbed out of the rags and paced fretfully. "After you and I argued in the Forbidden Gardens, I joined Council to see the truth for myself. For my first assignment I was sent to investigate a Killing Chamber."

"Oh!"

"Yeah…I saw a two-leg there who…who was so *cruel*." Tears washed down his face. "I swore I'd kill the two-leg for what it had done."

"So what happened?"

"I was assigned my Plague Rats, and before the mission I went back to the Killing Chamber. I hid in a box, and the two-leg drove me to its tall nest. It was easy. Next moonrise, I led the squad right to it. I chewed a hole in a window frame so the Plague Rats could get through."

"Why?"

"They were supposed to climb into the tall nest and infect the two-legs…and then die. That was their mission." He'd pushed aside the pity he'd felt for the miserable, dying rats because it was easier. Shame suddenly choked Fin. "But that's not what happened. My orders were to leave and let the death squad do their work, but I didn't. I wanted to see where the two-leg would die. So I went in, but my leg got stuck in the hole and I fell into its nest. I fell a long way. At the bottom, huge metal jaws bit my leg and broke it.

"Oh, Fin!"

"I thought I was dead. But then something happened that I can't explain." Fin's fur stuck out in wet tufts on his cheeks. "A little…a little two-leg saved me," he finally said.

"Oh!"

"It should have killed me!" said Fin. "After all, I was there to kill it. But it didn't. It saved me and hid me, and every moonrise and sunrise it came and fed me."

"Weren't you scared?" asked Zumi.

"I was at first. But then…then…I grew to love it."

Zumi's mouth dropped open.

"I love the little two-leg," Fin said, gulping. A fresh rain of tears spilled from his eyes, down his cheeks. "The little one was good to me. I almost stayed, but I couldn't. Not with…with what I had tried to do. But I couldn't go back to Papa, either. I've been hiding out, trying to figure out what to do." He looked at her. "I'm lost, Zumi. I don't belong anywhere."

"Yes, you do. You belong with *me*!" she said, nuzzling him. "And you and I are going to fight this Plague War and stop it. You've got to go to your uncle, Fin! You're the only one who can tell him to stop the war!"

"No! No way!" Fin's head pounded.

"What do you mean, *no*? You just told me that you love a little two-leg. An innocent little two-leg who saved your life! Your uncle is back in the Tunnels trying his best to kill every last one of them. *Including the one you love.*"

"Zumi! It's not that simple." Fin pulled away and began pacing. The doubt and worry that had been festering in the back of Fin's mind now clamoured at him. "It's not like I can just stroll in and tell him to stop!"

"Why not? You're his nephew. You're the only one who *can* stop him!"

"You didn't see the Killing Chamber!" cried Fin. "You didn't see the rat with no name, covered with lumps!"

"You mean the Killing Chamber where my mother was?" said Zumi. "Why do you think Scratch is albino? Our mother escaped from a Killing Chamber, so if anyone has the right to hate the two-legs, it's me, not you!"

"Then why don't you?" said Fin.

"Because hate doesn't change anything!"

Fin ground his teeth. "Zumi, the two-legs have been killing us, torturing us since the days of the Old Ones! And now, just because I—"

"Just because you love one of them."

"That's not what I was going to say." Tears choked Fin's voice. "This has nothing to do with my feelings."

"Then what does it have to do with?"

Fin took a breath. "Zumi, we have a chance to be happy. You and I. I'm no Balthazar. I just want to be left alone to live my life. Let's find him and get *him* to stop the war."

Zumi stared at him. "Balthazar is dead. You saw him die."

Fin shook his head. "No. Papa said that Balthazar asked to leave, and Council let him. We just have to find him."

Zumi shouted, "Your uncle lied to you! He's lied to you about everything! Balthazar is dead!"

"No! Papa wouldn't lie to me," said Fin. "Just because you hate him doesn't mean *I* have to hate him too! He's my uncle!"

"He lied. He's not like you, Fin. Your uncle is evil."

"*Evil?* Now you sound like you did in the Forbidden Garden. I don't want to fight you, Zumi. I love you. We have each other. Why isn't that enough for you?"

"What about your little two-leg?" asked Zumi.

Fin froze. His mouth opened and closed as he struggled to speak.

A wave of red surged over his eyes. He screamed, "I. Said. I'm. Not. *Going!*" He charged at Zumi, running at her, his teeth bared. Zumi stumbled back and gaped at him.

Fin stopped himself. Remorse struck him like a crushing boot. "Oh...Zumi, I'm sorry! I'm sorry!" He tried to nuzzle her.

She shrank back, her breath coming in ragged gasps. "Go—go back to your uncle! Kill all the two-legs! Get every last one! And when they are all dead, and when the Lowers are dead, and the market is dead, YOU WILL STILL HAVE EACH OTHER!"

Fin crept toward her. "But Zumi, I love you..."

With a cry she pushed by him and scrabbled out of the nest, out the drainage pipe, into the bleak sunlight, away from him.

The Great & the Small

A gaping hole split open inside Fin. An emptiness that swallowed any good thing he had ever tried to do, any good feeling or intention he'd ever had.

He was a monster.

Blindly, Fin staggered through the pipe and into the glaring light. As he ran, trying to outpace the despair that lapped at him, shapes danced, dark smudges in the sun. He kept on, not knowing, not caring which way he went.

He ran until he couldn't run anymore and then collapsed to the ground. He dropped into a feverish sleep. Immediately, nightmares leaped up, clawing at him.

She is there, warm. Her body curved around his. But now Fin knows what is coming. He tries to sit up, to warn his mother. But sleep is too heavy on him, and he cannot move.

A brushing sound—he shudders. His mother shudders too. Rearing up, Nia lunges at the intruder, but the voice speaks to him, mocking him.

Fin shakes his head, no—no—no.

Nia screams, "Listen, Pip! Can't you hear?"

The voice laughs. "Fin is deaf."

"Open your eyes, Pip!"

"Fin is blind," laughs the voice.

Struggling to open his eyes, Fin finally opens them a small slit. His mother lies with her back to him, a crimson ribbon of blood flowing from her neck, staining the dirt.

She is dead. But before he can cry out, her head turns and stares at him. It is not his mother now. Eyes that are brown stare at him, pierce him. The two-leg.

Lumps the size of apples circle her neck, swell her face. She tries to speak from pale, bloodless lips, but the crimson river spews from her mouth, her nose, her eyes.

When Fin awoke, it was moonrise. Snow filtered down from the dark sky, settling on the bench over top of him and tracing an outline on the cobbled ground. The winged statue stood nearby, head bowed, so like Balthazar. Just ahead he could see the fishmonger's stall, its steel curtain lowered.

The market. He had found his way home, without knowing how he'd gotten here. But as he gazed around, he realized *why* he was here.

There was work to do.

CHAPTER FORTY-NINE

"Let us discuss the things we have seen, and show
the terrible judgment of God."

Gabriele de' Mussis, 1348

The Chairman paced back and forth in the Council Chamber. Sergo sat stiffly, his eyes not leaving Papa. Bothwell was hunched over a chicken wing that he'd filched from a dumpster. It was just the three of them.

"Ah, Julian," sighed Papa. "What to do? And now dear Tiv."

Sergo's eyes met his. Sergo opened his mouth to say something, but Bothwell interrupted.

He crunched noisily. "Well, I'm just sayin', we're runnin' low on Councillors, ain't we? I mean, first, there's old Balthazar, then Julian, and now Tiv! I'm watchin' me back," he said with a nod. "That's all I can say!" Bothwell sucked through his teeth and picked at them with a claw.

Sergo stared at him, his lip curling. "Yes," he muttered. "Never know what happens in dark tunnel."

242

Bothwell took another bite, fixing his good eye on Sergo. "Some might take that as a threat, my lad."

Papa smiled. "Now, now. Councillor Bothwell, you raise an excellent point. We can't be too careful. Wreckers are everywhere, right, loyal Sergo?" The Beloved Chairman's gaze rested on the large rat.

Bothwell snickered. "Sergo's loyal all right. As loyal as a flipping dog—and as ugly!"

"Idiot!" said Sergo. He lunged at Bothwell and bit his ear. A drop of blood appeared.

Bothwell sniffed the blood. He snarled. Throwing down his chicken wing, he faced Sergo. "You'll pay for that, you will! You'll bloody pay for that!" He dived at Sergo's haunch. Sergo was too swift, and the ARM Councillor's jaws snapped the air.

Bothwell reared up on his hind legs, his teeth bared. "By the Old Ones," he hissed. "You've been askin' for this a long time!" He lunged again, but missed. He snarled, circling Sergo.

"Ha! Ha!" taunted Sergo. "You missed me, little Mouse-Captain! Maybe I stand still for you, huh? Then maybe you catch me?"

Bothwell hissed at him. The two rats circled each other, panting, their eyes locked.

Papa said nothing, just watched.

Bothwell thrust his head forward one way, then bobbed the other. The manoeuvre threw Sergo off balance. Bothwell bit deep into Sergo's shoulder, then darted out of reach.

"Aaggh!" roared Sergo. "Buffoon! Idiot! You are joke to Council! Papa does not ask BUFFOON for special favour! Only Sergo! We do not need buffoon Captain!"

"I'm a buffoon, am I? And what 'special favour'?"

"Tell him, dear Papa! Why don't you tell him! Tell buffoon Cap—!"

The Great & the Small

But as Sergo spoke, Papa lunged forward. He threw Sergo to the ground and drove his curved incisors deep into Sergo's hip.

Sergo screamed. Blood began to spurt from the wound. Papa stood over him, blood dripping from his mouth.

Bothwell jumped back. His eyes blinked rapidly at the dark red bloom growing in Sergo's fur. Then he blinked at the blood around the Chairman's mouth.

Sergo's mouth opened and closed without a sound. He stared up at Papa. His eyes were as round as a pup's.

"Right…" said Bothwell. Edging behind Papa and Sergo, he paused before the entrance. His eyes darted between them. He turned and ran out.

Papa and Sergo were alone.

The Chairman stood over Sergo. "Wrecker," he said.

"What? But why…?" groaned the other rat. "Ohhhh…"

"There are many ways of Wrecking. Many."

"But…"

"All I ask is *loyalty*!"

Sergo began to protest. "But…but Sergo *is* loyal…"

"SILENCE! Leaking secrets! Spreading lies! Who else did you tell? Eh?" Papa thrust his face into Sergo's.

"No one," gasped Sergo. "I told…no one!" His blood puddled around him, tears flowed down his cheeks. "Papa…does not…*trust* Sergo?" choked the huge rat.

The Chairman's eyes were as cold as two stones.

Sergo exploded into sobs.

"Loyalty," said Papa.

"No…!" choked Sergo before bursting into a fresh flurry of

weeping. Struggling to get up, he collapsed. Front paws scrabbling at the dirt floor, he dragged himself toward Papa's feet.

The Chairman stepped back, his brows drawn together, his jaw hard. Walking to the entrance, he paused without looking back.

"Goodbye, Sergo." He climbed through the hole and was gone.

The large rat pulls himself through the tunnel with his forelegs; he can see the light from the market ahead.

Squeezing between the gap separating the Tunnels from the world of the two-legs, he hauls himself onto the snowy street. He is in the alley below the market, but it is deserted. Perhaps there are two-legs in the market above.

He claws himself up the icy stairs, leaving a steaming trail of blood behind him.

There must be at least one two-leg left. One who can do this last act of mercy. Suddenly there is a shout, the thud of boots.

A shadow blots out the sun. Smashes down.

And then, silence.

The Great & the Small

CHAPTER FIFTY

"When God made his creation he never imagined it would come to this."

Gabriele de' Mussis, 1348

Papa trudged along the alley. It wasn't a long walk from the Council Chamber back to the Uppers, but he was tired. The meeting to elect new councillors for the Organs of Council had been short. A list of candidates had been given to Papa, and he had decided yes or no—that wasn't the problem.

The problem was age. It was catching up to him.

He crawled into his burrow, sighing deeply. He couldn't even remember the new councillors. They all looked so young! Like that new Councillor of the ARM, which, on top of everything else, he'd had to find. Blast Bothwell!

After seeing Sergo's punishment, Bothwell had vanished. Papa had sent the ARM after him, an irony that even the dull-witted Bothwell would have appreciated—if he'd lived long enough. The coward's body had been dragged back for all to see. An example, as Sergo was an example, to show that no one was immune from justice.

Papa's heaped nest of feathers and soft rags looked inviting. He ambled over and yawned, nosing the layers of cloth. The cloth was soft, wonderfully soft. Stolen for him by new Councillor What's-his-name. Smart of the young pup to bring it. The recent rash of councillor deaths made everyone eager to please the Beloved Chairman.

Fear is good. Fear is useful.

Papa circled until he found a good spot then collapsed with a sigh, his tail curling around his body. Sleep beckoned. But just as he was nodding off, he heard a scuffling.

Someone was in the burrow.

He threw off the nesting. "Who's there?" he demanded.

There was no one.

Lowering his head, Papa's ears remained pricked and alert. But soon, his eyelids began to droop.

"*Papa,*" said a voice behind him.

He jumped straight into the air. As he did, he twisted his body around. He landed facing the other way, teeth and claws drawn.

There was no one.

"What is this trickery?" he bellowed. His eyes darted around the room.

"*Papa.*" The voice was loud in his ear.

He whirled. There was only the dirt floor. "Show yourself! Or are you a coward?" The only sound was his breathing.

Someone giggled in his other ear.

He bellowed and reeled around. Again, no one.

The Chairman licked his lips, his eyes flicking around the nest. That voice. It was familiar. A thought struck him. Was it Fin? Had Fin returned? He wasn't dead! It would be just like Fin to play a joke on his old uncle!

"Fin!" he called. "Fin! Is that you? Fin?"

Out of the corner of his eye, Papa saw the bedding twitch. His fur

prickled as the mound of nesting began to move. A scream grew in his throat.

The lump wormed its way under the rags. It was coming toward him.

He stumbled back. "Who is there?" His voice rose to a shriek. "Come out, you devil!" Lunging forward, he ripped the rags away with his teeth.

Underneath, nothing.

He staggered to keep his balance. "What is this? Who are you?"

Another giggle behind his ear.

Papa spun around but now his legs were as wobbly as a pup's. He tripped. Floundering on his back, his paws pedalled the air.

"*Ha, ha.*"

Heaving himself upright, the Chairman roared, "Show yourself!" Then, whirling around, he stood nose to nose with her. Nia.

"*Hello, brother,*" she said.

Papa shrieked. He jumped up-wards and back so violently that he crashed high against the bur-row wall. His claws scrabbled at the dirt wall as he tried to stop himself from sliding.

Nia waited at the bottom.

Her lidless eyes glittered as she grinned at him. Her fleshless jaws opened wide.

Still shrieking, Papa fell into her mouth. Felt her teeth close, sever his neck. Blood spurted onto the burrow wall. Puddled on the floor.

He sank to the ground. *Head so heavy. Can't hold it…* His head snapped free from his neck and rolled from his body. It bounced across the dirt floor…

He was still shrieking as he lurched awake.

"Oh," he gasped. "A dream! Just a silly dream." He had not dreamed of his sister since…since….

Forget it. It's over. His paws trembled as he drew them over his head and along his whiskers. Usually grooming calmed him, but he couldn't stop shaking. He snorted, began to pace.

Perhaps a snack would clear his head. Papa looked through his stash of food. Picking out a chunk of pungent cheese, he nibbled. He couldn't stop seeing his sister's face. Nia's face. Her skin hanging on her…shrivelled eyes that stared…her curving teeth…

The lump of cheese stuck in his throat. Papa spat it out, gagging, as a voice called, "Chairman?"

Papa screamed.

"*Sir?*" asked the voice.

"Leave me, Nia!" he shrieked.

A head peeked around the corner of his burrow entrance. The guard. A young pup who looked like it had just been weaned from its mama. The guard's eyes were huge. "Are…are you okay, Beloved Chairman?" he stammered.

Papa glared at the guard, his chest heaving. "Stop staring at me or I'll rip out your eyes and feed them to the gulls."

The guard's head ducked back behind the corner. "Y-yes, sir! S-someone to see you…Mister Chairman…sir!"

"Well then send him in, imbecile!" hissed Papa.

A figure filled the entrance. "No need, I'm here. Hello, Papa."

Fin. He was back.

The Great & the Small

CHAPTER FIFTY-ONE

"How he worried about you, you who travelled this wrecked world.
Then, when he heard you were well, he threw off his fears."

Petrarch, 1350

Fin stepped into his uncle's nest.

"Fin!" cried Papa, and bounded to him in one leap.

Circling, bobbing, climbing over each other, paws touching faces, whiskers trembling, Fin realized how much he'd missed his uncle.

Their words collided, tumbling over each other.

"Oh Papa! I'm so glad to see you…!"

"My boy! My boy has returned!"

"I missed you so much, Papa!"

"Knew you were alive, boy! Knew it…!"

But suddenly Papa stiffened. Sniffing Fin up and down, he said, "Where've you been, boy?"

Fin pulled away and didn't say anything, his eyes fixed to the floor.

Papa scowled. "Where have you been, boy?"

"I—I have seen so much, Papa," said Fin. "There's so much I want to say." Pulling his gaze up, he looked his uncle in the eyes. "That's why I came back."

"Back from *where*? What are you talking about, Nephew?"

"Well, I got...hurt," began Fin. "I led my squad of Plague Rats to the target, but then I hurt my paw. It got stuck in some metal teeth and was broken. Until it healed I couldn't go far. Luckily I found a park that had lots of benches and trees. I foraged there until my paw healed. Then I came back."

"That's it?" Papa's eyes hadn't left his nephew's.

Fin could see that Papa knew he was hiding something. "Yeah," he said, his ears burning. "A stupid seagull almost got me. I escaped by a whisker."

"By a *whisker*, you say? Hmm." Papa's brows furrowed. "Seagulls are cruel, yes, but stupid?"

"I just meant that the thing almost killed me. It was jabbing its beak, and—"

"That's when the seagull got your foot."

"No! No, I mean, I had already hurt my foot—"

"Oh?" Papa's eyebrows raised. "Where was this park, you say? Near the target? It would have to be if your paw was hurt so badly that you could not return."

"Look, I'm back now, okay? Don't you trust me?"

"Of course I do," said Papa, but his eyes narrowed. Fin looked away. His uncle continued. "I talked to your lieutenant when you didn't return. Scrubbs, wasn't it? I ordered her to complete the mission with a different squad of Plague Rats after you went missing. Got her head bashed in attacking the two-leg."

Blood thrummed in Fin's ears. Papa was speaking again, but Fin couldn't hear him. *Attacking the two-leg.* Was it dead? Was his little two-leg dead? Because of him?

The Great & the Small

Papa was staring at him. Fin babbled, "Sorry, my…my paw has been hurting me, and I'm just a little tired." Then, with an effort, he said, "I'm sorry Scrubbs is dead."

Papa snorted. "I'm not. It could have been you."

"Did they…*kill*…the target?" asked Fin.

"Ha, ha!" laughed Papa. "A good Tunnel Rat to the end. Sadly, there's no way to know, Nephew. Our weapon does not work *that* fast. Ha, ha!"

"No, of course not."

"Come now, make a nest in your old corner——"

"I'd like my own burrow," said Fin quickly. He added with a smile, "I'm not a day-old pup anymore, you know."

Papa looked surprised. "If that's what you want. My nephew is back from the dead. If he wants his own nest, he *gets* his own nest." Papa smiled, but he looked weary. More white streaked his once jet-black fur, and there was a hunch to his back that Fin hadn't seen before.

"Are you okay?" asked Fin.

Papa rested his cheek against Fin's and murmured, "I am now, Nephew. I am now."

CHAPTER
FIFTY-TWO

"Without knowing it, we were carrying death on our lips."

Gabriele de' Mussis, 1348

"Hello in there!" Fin called down a hole. He was in the foulest area of the Tunnels—as far from the Uppers as a rat could get. "Is there a Mister Scratch here, please?"

A wriggling pink nose appeared in the nest entrance, sniffing the air. It froze mid-sniff. "Fin?" squeaked a familiar voice. "Can't be." A couple more sniffs.

A white furry head poked out. Scratch's red marble eyes looked like they were going to pop out of his head and roll away. He shrieked, "Fin! Fin is back! Fin is back!" Scratch flew out of the nest and tackled Fin.

Fin rolled him over and pinned Scratch, chomping his ear. Scratch tried to bite him back.

"Ha! Too slow!" said Fin. "Still blind as a naked mole rat!"

The Great & the Small

"Oh! Oh! I can't believe it! I really can't believe it! Fin! You are *alive*! Everyone said you were dead, but Scratch said, 'Nope! Fin is alive, he's alive!' I knew it! I knew it! Ha, ha!"

"Yeah, yeah. Shut up now, okay?" said Fin laughing. He tackled Scratch again, and they cascaded through the burrow opening, rolling down the slope into the nest. At the bottom they whumped to a stop. Fin gasped. Scratch's nest smelled like raw sewage.

Fin tried to keep from wrinkling his nose. "I…I…looked all over for you. Why did you move…here?"

The smile had dropped from Scratch's face. He sniffed. "Maybe I like it here."

"I didn't mean anything by it. No, it's nice here." Fin stepped back from Scratch and looked around. The walls dripped. The dirt floor was freezing and damp.

Scratch's eyes were lowered. "I like it here. I do. The other one was too fancy. I'm a simple rat, and I like simple things…" His voice trailed off.

Red mucous ringed Scratch's nostrils. The fur around his haunch was reddish-brown, stained from grooming himself with a dripping nose. His bony ribs heaved with each breath, and he wheezed and rattled like an ancient one.

"Why are you really here?" asked Fin.

Scratch sniffed and shrugged. "Dunno. You went missing. My cozy nest in the Uppers went missing too. They kicked me out. Once you were gone, Scratch was nobody. I found this abandoned nest, and I've been taking care of myself!"

"But you should have talked to Papa! He would've taken care of you," said Fin. "After all, you're my best friend."

"The Beloved Chairman is too important to worry about Scratch's comings and goings," sniffed Scratch. His red eyes slid to Fin's. "I haven't forgotten what you ordered me to do. No, no, don't worry! I didn't tell…didn't tell a whisker of your precious secret. Not even a whisker!"

Scratch sighed then sneezed loudly. Nose dripping, he scratched behind his ear with a grimy hind foot.

Your precious secret.

Fin had ordered Scratch to warn Zumi, and then Fin had disappeared, leaving his friend to fend for himself. Scratch could have betrayed him to keep his comfortable life, but he didn't. Fin's best friend had suffered because of him, and he hadn't even thought about it until now.

He forced a smile. "Come on, buddy! You're moving in with me! I have my own burrow now. It's near Papa's, so it's nice."

"Really?" squealed Scratch.

"Really!" Nipping at Scratch's rump to get him moving, Fin bustled him up the slope and into the outer Tunnel.

Scratch chattered non-stop. "Oh, I knew you'd come back, Fin, and I knew you wouldn't forget your little buddy Scratch. When everyone else was saying, 'Where's Fin? Where's Fin?' I didn't say a word. I just kept my mouth shut, and I said to myself, 'Scratch, you know old Fin will be back and then he'll make everything right again.'"

Scratch talked so much that Fin laughed out loud. The guilt he felt about abandoning his friend eased a little.

Fin led Scratch to the burrow, and the two friends settled in, each with a fresh heap of rags. Scratch could hardly contain himself. "Oh, it's dry and the air…I can breathe! I can actually breathe! Oh! You can't imagine what I've gone through…the sneezing…the constant

dripping! And that damp, it gets right into your bones." Finally settled into his soft nest and still chattering, Scratch drifted off to sleep mid-sentence.

As the sun rose over the silent market, and as his friend's snores rattled the burrow, Fin slipped out.

The visitor sniffs around the burrow entrance. Yes, the old rat Hobbs is still here. The visitor creeps down the hole, unseen, unannounced.

At first Hobbs is frightened. He has plenty of reason to fear. After all, he has been "visited" before. But as the visitor talks, quickly, urgently, the old rat finally trusts.

After the visitor leaves out the front entrance, Hobbs wriggles through the bolt hole and scurries through the Lower Tunnels, whispering the new plan against the Plague War. In those damp, fear-ridden Tunnels, seeds of hope grow.

The old rat has many burrows to visit, including the one far away by the warehouses along the wharf. The sun travels across the sky and then dips down into the horizon.

The Resistance gathers.

CHAPTER
FIFTY-THREE

"It seems to me as if the end of the world is very near."

Petrarch, 1350

The frost-covered pavement glimmered in the moonlight as Scratch and Fin foraged their way to the market. It was the first moonrise since Fin had returned.

Fin's breath chuffed before him as he and Scratch walked the well-worn path along the alley's walls. The path was as familiar to him as if he'd never left. But something was missing. Yes, there was the old smell of wet stone and dirt, of crushed smoke sticks, of sewer gas steaming up from the manhole covers—there was never any shortage of *those* kinds of smells in the harbour city. But the delectable aromas that had made Fin's whiskers quiver—the smell of sausages, pastries, sticky buns—they were gone, replaced with another. A gut-twisting smell that reminded Fin of the warehouse: the stink of death.

Dead rats littered the alley. They lay on either side, raked into piles. Snow lay on top of the mounds.

The Great & the Small

There was no sign of any two-legs. Fin's paw began to throb.

They reached the market. Once bustling and dangerous, it stood silent. The fishmonger's stall was closed. Only the smell remained.

"Come on!" shouted Scratch. Bounding forward, he skidded on the ice. His paws flew out from under him and he plunged into a snow bank. "Ha, ha!" Popping out his head, he shook off the snow like a tiny white dog, squealing ultrasonically, *"Now who's the mouse? Ha!"*

He charged at Fin in a mock attack. Fin jumped aside, in no mood to play, but stopped himself. Scratch stood in front of him, his cheeks pulled back in a taut grin. His friend looked like a skeleton. His back was hunched, his ribs heaved, and red mucous fringed his nose like a moustache. But there was a fragile gleam of joy in his eyes that hadn't been there before.

In spite of the throb in his paw and the ache in his gut, Fin hollered, "You'd better run!" Even with his limp Fin could have easily caught Scratch. Instead, he nipped at his tail. Then, on purpose, he tripped and rolled over.

"Ha! Now *you* have to run!" yelled Scratch. He nipped at Fin who jumped to his feet and ran. Scampering up and down through the empty stalls, the two of them played, frisking and wrestling down the aisles of the once forbidden market.

"Enough! I give up!" cried Fin.

"Nope! No giving up!" shrieked Scratch. "Not until you admit it. Say you're a mouse!"

"All right!" said Fin. "You're a mouse!"

"Hey…*ha, ha!* No fair! No fair!" But Scratch stopped suddenly, his eyes bulging. He stared at something behind Fin.

Crouched in the shadow of a stall, a mere tail-length away, sat Papa.

CHAPTER FIFTY-FOUR

"The disciples of evil have brought down the temple.
No longer do they tend to the needy and sickly sheep."

Anonymous poem on the plague, fourteenth century

"Papa!" said Fin. "What are you doing here?"

His uncle said nothing.

Scratch looked as if he'd shrunk two sizes. Crouching low, he bobbed his head over and over. "Oh! Oh! Such an honour! It is *such* an honour to see you again, sir! Oh! I'm sure you don't remember me, after all why should you? I'm just a nobody! But I want to say, Beloved Chairman, how much I admire you and how much—"

Papa interrupted him. "Of course I remember you. My nephew's loyal friend."

Head still bobbing, Scratch chattered, "Ha, ha! That's right! That's right!" The tip of his nose dripped, and his paws were purple with cold, but Scratch blinked up at Papa with a big grin on his face. He wiped his nose on his paw, still blinking happily.

"Go to your nest," said Papa. "I wish to walk with my nephew."

Scratch blinked back and forth between uncle and nephew as he backed away. "Of course! Of course, sir! Absolutely!" He disappeared, nodding and bobbing, around the corner.

Fin turned to his uncle. "What are you doing here?"

"I wanted to see you," said Papa. "To give you something. Will you walk with me?" Without waiting for an answer, Papa started down the aisle. An icy draft whistled through the empty halls, making a low moaning sound, as uncle and nephew walked side by side through the market.

Where plump sausages had once festooned a stall, there was now bare boards. A piece of trash, trapped under the stall leg, flapped in the drafty hall. A crumpled newspaper rolled by.

Papa stood in front of the empty stall, his eyes gleaming. "This is yours. My gift to you, dear Nephew. You have always loved the market, and now no one shall keep you from it."

Fin was stunned. "I…I don't know what to say."

Papa tilted his head. "Don't you like my gift?"

In spite of the cold, sweat prickled along Fin's fur. "Yes, of course! But it's so…different, now. I mean, don't you think we've done enough?"

His uncle stiffened.

Fin laughed quickly. "I mean, we…we sure taught the two-legs a lesson, but don't you think it's…enough? There's no food anymore, and the Lowers…I walked through them, Papa, and there's *nobody*. It's empty, or they're all hiding—"

"Enough."

"Papa, I'm not trying to—"

"Silence!" Papa stepped backwards. "I have waited for my nephew, *begged* the Old Ones for his return. Do not tell me he has returned as a coward!"

The Great & the Small

"No, of course not, but—"

"This is *war*, Fin!" he said. "War to pay back generations of destruction, of *murder*. War is hard on the weak! Does that mean we weep and wail, rip our fur for the ones who will *always* be crushed, will *always* die, whether it's by a cruel two-leg boot or for the Common Good?"

"I don't know, Papa, but when I look around I see—"

"Progress! You see progress! And there is no progress without pain! Without sacrifice! It is the burden of leadership!"

"But, Papa..." Fin's voice trailed off under his uncle's stare. He looked away. "I...I just think it should stop now."

Papa snorted. "We must stop it then. *Council Member Fin* has decided."

Fin's ears burned. "Stop it, Papa."

"*Council* guides the Tunnels, Nephew," said Papa. "*Council* sees our glorious future. Council has the Common Good in mind!"

"And you are Chairman of the Council," said Fin quietly.

"Yes! I am Chairman of the Council! Because *I* know what must be done! And I am not afraid to do it!"

Fin said nothing. He limped a few steps away and gazed out over the empty market. "I've never told you this, but I dream of my mother. I dream of her all the time."

Behind him, his uncle drew in a breath. Fin turned to look at him. "What's wrong?"

"Nothing. I just miss my dear sister." Papa began to groom himself, licking his paws and pulling them over his ears.

Fin nodded. "For the longest time, I couldn't figure out what she was telling me."

Papa paused his grooming and looked at him. "And now you can?"

Fin shrugged. "No. I forget the dream as soon as I wake up." He limped over to stand before his uncle. "Thank you for your present, Papa. I want you to know that I love you. No matter what."

Papa frowned. "No matter what?"

"I appreciate your gift. Really."

They stood in silence for a moment. Papa sighed, and then motioned with his head for Fin to follow. The snow-covered bench was outlined in moonlight as they walked by.

"Nephew," said Papa, "you trusted me in the past to know what was best, and you must trust me again." He stopped and faced Fin. "Will you trust me, Nephew? With one more push we can tip the war in our favour. Then, no more war, no more death, no more ugly two-legs."

Fin chewed his lip.

Papa frowned, searching Fin's eyes. "Don't worry! I forgive you for your moment of doubt. It is gone! Forgotten! My nephew has returned from the dead. It is a sign from the Old Ones. The Tunnels need you." His voice quavered. "*I* need you."

Fin bowed his head. Tears spilled from his eyes and fell on the cobblestones. "Oh, Papa."

"My boy." Papa's voice was thick. "You have no idea what I have suffered in your absence! There are Wreckers everywhere. Everywhere! Thank the Old Ones, you have returned." Nudging up Fin's face with his nose, his uncle stared into his eyes. Tears dampened the Chairman's furry cheeks. "Dear Nephew, tell me. Can I trust you? Will it be 'Papa and Fin' once again?"

Tears streamed from his eyes, but Fin held his uncle's gaze evenly. "Yes, Papa," he said. "I promise."

Papa held Fin to himself. Fin could feel his uncle's heart beating

The Great & the Small

against his own. Then his uncle pulled back. His eyes darted up and down the alley.

"There is no time to lose," Papa whispered. "I received a report before I found you with that albino. There is another Wrecker! Someone close to us! Rebellion is brewing again. Someone is organizing the Lowers! Turning them against us!"

The Chairman's eyes searched the alley as if Wreckers were crouching in the shadows. "I cannot root out this evil without your help. I am too visible—every rat knows the Beloved Chairman!" His eyes bore into Fin's. "Nephew, now is the time to pay me back for all I have done for you. Find the dirty Wrecker."

CHAPTER FIFTY-FIVE

"Where did our friends go? Those ones so dear to us? Did the sky open up and take them? Did the earth open and pull them in?"

Petrarch, 1350

T*he visitor clings to the shadows as he moves silently along the Lowers. He hears another rat coming along the passage. He slips into an empty burrow until it passes.*

When the passage is clear, the visitor continues until he stops at the old rat's burrow, his ears swivelling at every sound. A final glance, a sniff for danger, and he steals down the entrance hole.

"Hobbs!" he whispers. "Are you here?"

A shuffling, and then a pale nose appears in the gloom. "I'm here. You sure about this, young feller?"

"I'm sure. Are you ready?"

Hobbs chuckles. "I was ready the day you first met me. You know that."

The visitor smiles sadly. "Yes."

They speak quickly, urgently, in hushed tones. "Don't forget what I told you," says the visitor.

The Great & the Small

Hobbs moves to the bolt hole and turns. "I won't. May the Old Ones bless you, young feller."

"And you. Go now, friend."

Hobbs nods and ducks out. The visitor slips out the front as Hobbs scurries toward the burrow near the warehouses.

The group hunkers down in the tunnel, waiting. Their eyes flit nervously to each other and to the small female leading the ambush. She meets their eyes and nods. Hobbs had been clear about the ARM squad's route.

Ears quivering, she listens.

They are coming. The ARM members move stealthily, but they are not quiet enough: the hunters are now the hunted.

The female nods again.

As the squad passes, the rebels slip from their hiding nooks and crevices, fanning out, filling the passageway, blocking any hope of escape.

They launch their attack.

In the squealing frenzy of claws and teeth, most of the ARM squad flounders and panics, but a few stand their ground. The squad Captain, a rat named Mink, sees the small female, sees that she is the leader.

Jumping behind her, he sinks his teeth deep into her neck.

CHAPTER
FIFTY-SIX

"Waiting among the dead for death to come, I leave parchment
for continuing this record in case anyone survives this pestilence."

Brother John Clynn, 1349

P apa?" Fin called. "You in there?" He stood outside Papa's burrow with news he knew his uncle would not like: there had
been another ambush on an ARM squad. Fin didn't know the
details—the squad captain hadn't come back yet.

He opened his mouth to call again, when he heard Papa cry out.

"Agh! Nia! Niaaa! Leave me *alooone!*"

"Papa!" Fin plunged into the nest with his teeth bared, expecting
to see someone attacking his uncle. But when he got inside he saw it
was empty. Empty except for Papa. Hunched in a far corner, he sat
transfixed, his eyes bugged out and glassy, staring at the bare floor in
front of him. His teeth chattered.

Fin nosed him. "Papa?"

Gasping, Papa's eyes blinked rapidly, focusing on Fin. "Ah! My
boy!" he panted. "Good to see you! Yes, yes, good to see you!"

The Great & the Small

Fin sniffed his uncle up and down. He reeked of fear. "What is going on?" asked Fin.

Papa looked away. "Ha! Nothing! Nothing! Just an old rat's dreams."

"A dream?" said Fin. "More like a nightmare! And I thought I heard my mother's name."

"Didn't I tell you before?" said Papa. "Dreams are the stuff of nonsense! Let us forget it." He bustled to his cache of food. "Come, eat. They found me cheese yesterday and a tasty biscuit."

The cheese had bitter green mould on it, and the "tasty biscuit" was little more than a crumb. Fin said nothing but took it and chewed, watching his uncle. Papa's large paws shook as he held the cheese to his mouth.

"Tell me about your dream," Fin said softly.

Papa dropped the cheese and turned his face away. "No. We shall not speak of it again." His only movement was the in and out of his ribcage. "What did you want to see me about?"

"There's been another attack."

"I see. Casualties?"

"I'm not sure. When I hear more, I'll tell you."

"Ah." Papa bowed his head. "I am tired, Nephew. Tired of being the only one who still believes. Oh, I'm sorry—I know that you are a good Tunnel Rat. I don't mean you. But the others. Sometimes I lose hope. Yes, even me. I can't tell you how much it means to have you here beside me."

Fin nuzzled his uncle. "Rest. I will take care of everything."

His uncle nodded but then looked at Fin with eyes wide with terror. "But what if I...I dream?"

"Dreams don't mean anything, remember? Forget them and sleep. I'll be right outside." Fin helped Papa settle into his nesting, like a mother tucking in her pup. His uncle looked at him for a moment, uncertainty clouding his face.

Fin nodded. "It's okay. Sleep."

The uncertainty in Papa's eyes changed to trust. He smiled, and his eyes drifted closed. "Thank you, my boy," he murmured. "Thank you."

Fin stationed himself outside the burrow entrance. Cold sunlight cut its way through the twists and turns of the outer tunnel, casting shadows where he stood. An icy draft off the harbour whirled through, picking up dirt from the floor, and riffled through Fin's coat. He hunkered down, ears back, and wrapped his tail around himself.

There was a slight change in the blowing draft. Fin's ears pricked up—someone was coming, and fast. A rat burst around the corner. It was Captain Mink, Fin's former squad mate.

"News!" puffed Mink. "I got news for the Chairman!"

"The Chairman is sleeping," said Fin. "Tell *me* your news."

Mink hesitated. "Well, it's about that ugly Wrecker, Hobbs. It's just for the Beloved Chairman!" He frowned. "But…you *are* the Chairman's nephew."

"That's right, Mink," said Fin. "I am the Chairman's nephew. Any news for the Chairman is news for me. Right?"

The big rat mulled this over, and grunted. "Right! Well, Hobbs is dead." Nodding knowingly, he whispered, "Hobbs was the Wrecker. He was the spy!"

"Are you sure?"

"Sure, I'm sure. After the Wreckers tried to attack us, I found him sneaking back from the docks. The dumb Wrecker made it back to his burrow, but I nabbed him there. One bite! That's all it took!" Mink thrust out his chest.

"Oh?" Fin asked. "*One* bite? That's impressive. I heard about the attack. What happened? Were you ambushed?"

"Yeah, but we got 'em," said Mink. "I bit the leader myself. Once she was down, the rest ran off like mice from a cat."

"*She*? The leader was female?"

"Yeah," said Mink. "A little brown job the size of a mouse. Come to think of it, maybe she *was* a mouse. Ha, ha!"

Fin smiled. "Thank you, Mink. I'll make sure the Chairman hears about this."

The big rat writhed with joy. "Thanks, Fin! And you'll say my name? You'll say Mink did it?"

"Of course."

As Mink bounded away, Fin stared after him.

The dirt in front of the old rat's burrow is black with dried blood. A tuft of fur stands upright in it, glued into place.

"Hobbs!" the visitor whispers. "Hobbs! Are you in there?" But the burrow is silent. So it is true. Hobbs is dead.

CHAPTER FIFTY-SEVEN

"Better that ten innocent people should suffer
than one spy get away. When you chop wood, chips fly."

Nikolai Yetzhov, Commissar-General of State Security, USSR

Fire roars through the girl's veins, burns her lungs with each breath. It consumes every thought, every memory, every bond.

Rising up, rising from bed, from the body stretched out upon it, she regards the figure with curiosity. Its purplish necklace of swollen lumps. Its pale, translucent skin. Is it important to her, this thing lying here? She cannot remember. All she knows is that the pain is gone.

"Ananda!"

Like a nail driven through her, that voice yanks her back. No! She will not go back! Shaking free, she walks to the edge stretched before her.

Only one step farther…

The Great & the Small

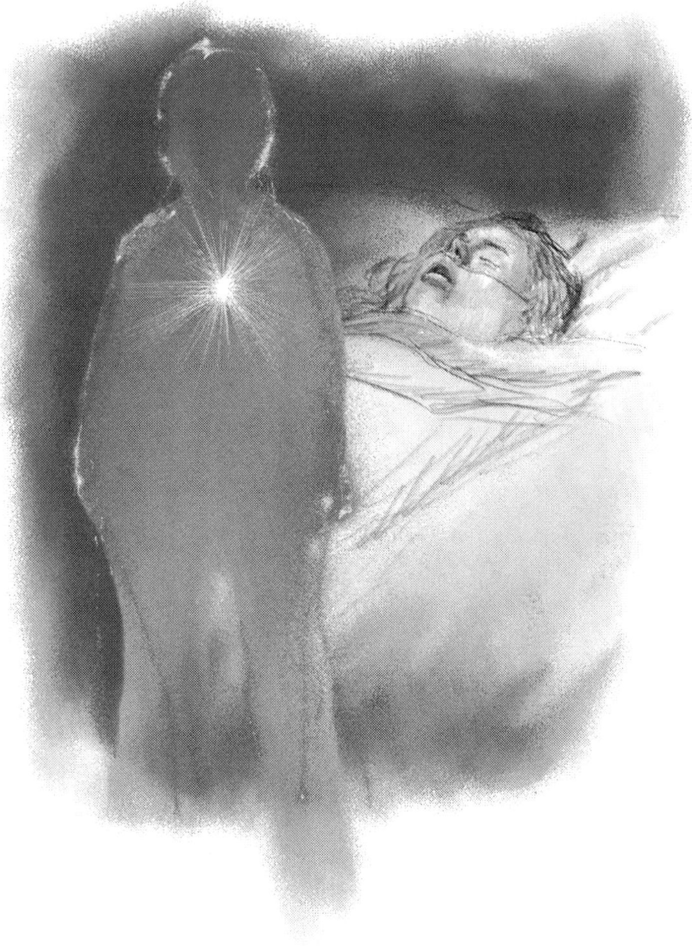

CHAPTER FIFTY-EIGHT

"Go, you who will die…roam the land and sea trying
find riches you can't keep, glory that won't last."

Petrarch, 1350

Hurrying in from the passage, Fin sniffed the air inside his burrow and then sagged with relief. Scratch was here. Thank the Old Ones!

Curled on a nest of rags, Scratch had wound his tail around himself as he slept. His ribs moved raggedly in and out. Except for that, the burrow was still.

"Scratch," whispered Fin. Scratch twitched and drew a paw over one eye before falling still again.

"Scratch!" said Fin again. Grunting, Scratch groped around the rags, then dropped back. Fin shouted in his ear, "SCRATCH!"

Scratch's red eyes flew open. "Aagh! Wh-what's wrong? Oh…Fin! It's just you!" He scowled and, rolling over, tucked his tail back in. "Go away! It's still daylight. I'm sleeping!"

"Get up! I need you," said Fin.

Scratch grumbled, "Okay, okay." He pulled himself up to look at Fin. "Well?"

"Scratch…" Fin said, choking back tears. "Oh, Scratch. Hobbs is dead…they killed him!"

Scratch squinted at Fin. "Who's Hobbs?"

"Hobbs. I…told him…well, he was carrying information to…to the Resistance."

"He was a Wrecker? They got him? The Beloved Chairman must be so happy!" Scratch bobbed his head up and down with glee. "Oh! They got the dirty Wrecker, the dirty Wrecker is dead…"

"Shut *up!*" said Fin, and nipped Scratch's ear.

Scratch squealed and glared at him. "That hurt!"

"I…I'm sorry," said Fin. "But…but I think Zumi may be dead." He started to weep. "I think Zumi's dead, Scratch."

Scratch's eyes narrowed. "Hold on, hold on, hold on! First it's Hobbs, and now it's my sister? You're making no sense, Fin, no sense at all. You wake me up, you bite me, and now you make no sense!"

Fin swallowed hard. "Scratch, I swear I wouldn't ask you this if there was any other way, but I need you to go to Zumi. To see if she's okay. Her burrow is far down the wharf, near the warehouses. *Please,* Scratch!"

"Why? What do you care? And what's my sister got to do with…?" Scratch froze, his mouth open. "You…and Zumi. And *Hobbs.*" He backed away from Fin. "You…but…oh Fin…." He began to whimper softly. "You're a Wrecker."

"It's not what it seems," said Fin. "I'm doing this *for* the Tunnels. I would never do anything to hurt you, or Papa—"

"Papa!" shrieked Scratch. "What's the Beloved Chairman going to say? Oh…oh my!"

"Papa isn't going to find out," said Fin. "At least not until I'm ready. All I need you to do is to go see Zumi. I can't go myself. If I got caught the Resistance would be over, and this war would never end. I just need to make sure she's…" He began to cry.

Scratch said nothing. He stared at Fin with wide red eyes.

"Please," begged Fin. "She's your sister. And I'm your best friend." Scratch turned away. "If you won't do it for me, then do it for Papa!"

Scratch stiffened.

"Do it for Papa, Scratch! Do it because you love *him*! This is for his own good. The war has to stop! It's killing him, like it's killing everything. You've got to believe me, Scratch. I'm doing this for him too."

Scratch looked back at Fin. His eyes had begun to tear up. His lip trembled.

"I…I'm so sorry, Scratch," said Fin. His voice broke, overtaken by sobs. "I never meant to hurt you. I wanted everything to be perfect for you now… That's why I wanted you to move here with me. I wanted you to feel safe after being abandoned. But…but I have no one else I can trust."

A tear dripped down Scratch's nose.

"Please!" sobbed Fin. "I won't ask anything from you again. You'll never have to worry about anything. You can stay in my burrow forever, just—"

"You think I'm so easy?" screamed Scratch. "You think, Scratch will do it! Scratch does what he's told! He's a nobody, but I am Fin! Scratch can't say no to me!"

"Scratch, no! That's not what I meant!"

"Well, let me tell you something. When you had your paw crushed, the Chairman needed me. Me! I was the one who pointed out that ugly fishmonger when you couldn't show him, because you were too scared! And when the ARM collected that ugly outsider rat to leave

The Great & the Small

in the stall, the Chairman let *me* kill it! The Beloved Chairman needed *me*!"

Fin remembered being carried by his scruff to look out over the market. Papa had wanted to find the two-leg who had crushed Fin's paw. He remembered hearing the crash from the fish stall the night he went to visit Scratch so long ago...remembered his friend's odd behaviour. "You killed someone? My uncle *used* you to kill someone?"

"Used? *Used?* Who is *using* who, Mister Fin of the Tunnels?" shrieked Scratch.

Fin began to shake. "I...I am *not* using you!"

"Just a lowly rat," snarled Scratch, "ugly and small! Of course he will go to save his sister, even though she is nothing but trouble, *trouble, TROUBLE*! Of course he will go, because Scratch is so very useful to me."

Fin moved toward him. "Scratch, no! That's not—"

"No! Don't move, Mister Fin of the Council, Mister Chairman's nephew! Stay! Be comfortable! Be comfortable while Scratch goes out into the cruel alley! Be comfortable while Scratch cleans up after Mister Fin! While Scratch cleans up your mess...AGAIN!"

"Scratch, I'm sorry!" Fin called after him as Scratch disappeared into the outer Tunnel. There was no answer.

The wind pounded Scratch like an invisible fist, and the glaring winter sun burned his eyes. He squinted and hunkered behind a brick wall. His fur was still damp from where tears had fallen, and he shivered uncontrollably. Too cold! Too cold!

It was a long way to the docks, a very long way. Once there, he would have to sniff and sniff and sniff to find his Wrecker sister's burrow. Fresh tears welled up in his eyes. He didn't *want* to go to the docks! He was tired of Zumi, tired of Fin.

He stopped. Tired of Fin? Yes! Tired of cheating, of lying, of sneaking.

All for Fin.

Tears tumbled down his cheeks. What to do? What to do?

The face of the Beloved Chairman rose before him…his midnight fur so black, his eyes so sharp, his words so clear. The Chairman had needed Scratch before. It hadn't been the Beloved Chairman's fault that Scratch had been dumped and forgotten like a piece of mouldy cheese. It was Fin's fault. It was all Fin's fault.

Scratch was tired of being used. This time, he would think for himself.

He was going to tell the Chairman.

CHAPTER FIFTY-NINE

"Some victims were covered with boils that were so hard and dry that barely any liquid seeped out. Others had little black pustules that erupted all over their bodies."

Geoffrey le Baker, clerk, 1348, Oxfordshire, England

Fin didn't mean to fall asleep, but as the shadows grew weaker in his burrow and the sun strengthened in the sky, thoughts flew around his head like frenzied moths. Was Zumi alive? Did Scratch get to her in time? What about Papa? What if he found out? It was too soon. Papa couldn't find out yet! Edging between each question flashed pictures of stacked two-legs, mounds of dead rats, silent tunnels, a market that was dead.

Each thought, each worry, weighed him down like heavy stones on his back. His head sank, and he fell into a restless sleep.

Nia stands over him, her eyes fixed on something behind him. Her eyes are wide. She crouches, her haunches tighten, and she springs.

For a moment she seems to fly. She flies over him where he lays curled in the nest, but then he hears her scream.

"Pip! Help me!"

Trembling, he shakes his head. "I can't…" He squeezes his eyes shut.

"The pup is blind!" says a voice.

"Pip!" screams Nia. "Open your eyes!"

"He will never see," says the voice.

And in his sleep, Fin opens one eye. And then the other.

A voice spoke, startling Fin out of his dream. *"Pip, you say?"*

Fin blinked, sniffing the air groggily.

"I should have guessed," said the voice. That voice.

Fin's eyes flew open, but all at once his vivid dream faded. Papa crouched by the nest entrance. "Papa?"

His uncle said nothing. Fin moved towards him. "Papa? What's wrong?"

"Stay where you are."

Fin's blood froze. Papa knew. And he would believe that Fin was a Wrecker. "I didn't betray you!" Fin's voice broke. "I did what was best for the Tunnels. What was best for *you*! If you'd only open your eyes!"

"My sister's son," hissed Papa. "I am betrayed by the pup I have *loved*, I have *cared* for, I have *cried* for…"

"But Papa—"

"SILENCE!" In one leap Papa was at Fin's throat, his teeth seizing his neck. He lifted Fin from the ground. Fin's paws pedalled the air. His body burned for air, and darkness seeped into his mind.

Fin went limp. With a cry, Papa kicked him away with his back legs and launched him into the air. Fin slammed against the wall and slid to the floor. Pain shot up his leg. He groaned. "I love you, Papa. No matter what."

A sob escaped Papa. He began to pace in the centre of the burrow. "Love is a dangerous thing. The *most* dangerous thing. I should have killed you, too." He stopped to look at Fin. "In my weakness, I could not. There was something in you that drew me. All the others, even Nia, yes. But I could not bring myself to kill *you*. And now, still I cannot!"

Fin's head swam. The smell of blood filled his nose. "What? You... you said my *father* killed my mother!"

Papa paced in front of Fin, weeping. "What am I to do? Do I kill you? Do I kill my boy?" Bursting into a fresh round of tears, he shouted, "Nia! You got what you wanted. And now he must die because of *you*. This is *your* fault!"

"Papa," said Fin, "I—"

"SILENCE!" roared Papa. He lunged at Fin's face, forcing Fin to dodge to one side. Papa stood over him. "Disloyalty means death, dear Nephew. I cannot tolerate betrayal. That's why the little ugly one had to die. *Telling* on you, as if you were a common Tunnel Rat and not my nephew. I asked the ugly rat what virtue I valued most, and it didn't know." Papa's eyes glittered with tears. "You know, though. Don't you, Nephew."

Fin didn't answer. The smell of blood was so strong. Not his blood, someone else's. Something pale lay in the dirt by the tunnel opening. "Where...where is Scratch?" asked Fin.

"Nephew! The most important attribute! Tell me!"

Fin stared at the mound. "Papa. *What is that?*"

"Forgotten, eh? Or you never knew it? Like your mother? She didn't listen to me, either. It's loyalty, Fin. Or shall I call you Pip?"

Pip. Memories flooded Fin, rushing at him, pushing him under. He gasped. *"Pip!"*

"LOYALTY!" shouted Papa. "You're just like *him*. Nia knew better than to bring trash into the Tunnels!" Papa spoke as if to himself while he paced. "An escaped two-leg *pet?* Pah! He still had two-leg stink on him!"

"My father…?" The stories Papa had fed him, the history of his father, all lies. The truth had always been there, hidden in dreams… it had been Papa.

Papa. The walls of the burrow swirled around Fin.

Papa stopped pacing and looked down at Fin. "They broke Tunnel Law, and the penalty was death. And you will follow them."

Papa lunged and seized Fin's crippled paw between his jaws, drove his teeth to the bone, just as he had done so long ago.

Squealing, Fin jerked back his paw, but Papa did not let go. With his good leg he thrashed against his uncle's muzzle. "No, no, NO! *Aagh!*"

Papa opened his jaws, dropping the paw. He stared at Fin, panting. "Why is it so hard to kill you?" Fin lay on the ground, his ribs heaving.

"You were the last," said Papa. "It should have been easy! But as I pulled you from your nest, you struggled and fought, like me. I gambled that you would be my own. I gambled and lost."

Fin lay at the entrance and felt his life ebbing. The smell of blood was everywhere. His own, and…and…

The Great & the Small

His eyes flew open. The pale mound was beside him.

The bite was clean, neat. Two red crescents on the snow-white fur. The red eyes were slightly open, as if Scratch were only sleeping.

"Oh, Scratch," choked Fin. He pulled himself off the ground. He turned to Papa. Almost as one they charged. Over and over they rolled. Papa's claws ripped into Fin, rending his back into bloody strips. Fin screamed.

Tears streamed onto him from his uncle, mixing with his own.

Long teeth were drawn at the back of Fin's head. But as the thrusting teeth plunged toward their mark, Fin slipped under his uncle's chin and sank his teeth into the soft, delicate flesh.

"ANANDA!"

Ananda. That was her name. Meaningless now. She is free…she drifts to the edge that opens before her. One step farther …

"ANANDA! NO!"

She turns to the waiting dark, but too late…the name knits itself to her, entangling her, claiming her.

Then, like an ember that smokes, then blazes, pain erupts through her limbs. Over the sound of her own cries, she hears her name, Ananda, said over and over. Ananda…Ananda…Ananda…

CHAPTER SIXTY

"For those who still live, pray for the world so that God can be merciful to us all."

Simon Islip, Archbishop of Canterbury, 1349

Fin stood outside the drainpipe, unable to bring himself to go in. Finally, he forced his feet forward. His claws echoed on metal. Entering the small burrow, he saw that Zumi's careful pile of rags was blown around. The air was so cold that his nostrils stuck together as he breathed in. A stalactite of ice clung to a frozen pipe that ran across the top of the den.

Why had he come? He'd known it was too late.

A whisper of scent stopped him. He sniffed the air, side to side, whiskers trembling. In one bound Fin leaped to a scattering of rags and leaves. Gently, his heart fluttering, he pulled the rags away with his teeth.

She was there. Her fur was still crusted with dried blood, and her ribs heaved. But she was there, and she was alive.

Zumi.

Days followed nights. Each moonrise Fin foraged, bringing back whatever food he could find. As Zumi ate, he tended her wound and groomed her, licking his own wounds while she slept.

She had cried when he'd told her about Scratch. Had cried for Fin when he told her about Papa. But as day followed day her coat became glossy, her eyes once again bright.

"You came back," she'd say.

"Of course I did," he'd answer.

But there was still one thing left undone.

"I've got to go," Fin said to Zumi. "But I'll be back. I promise."

He remembered the way.

Under a shrub outside the little two-leg's tall nest, Fin crouched. His eyes swam with tears, but now he knew, as Balthazar had known, that it was right to cry for someone you love. For one who is dead.

Forgive me, Little One, he thought.

A flicker at the window caught his eye. There, looking out at him, was a familiar face. She leaned close, her pale hand pressed against the glass.

Straining, up on his haunches, Fin tried to see, scanning his nose back and forth. Could it be? Brown eyes found his. Joy flooded his chest. Yes.

Ananda sat up in bed, drawing. She'd been home for a week. The face that looked out from the paper was her own. The thinner cheeks. The eyes that seemed too big for her face. The lingering bruises around her neck. But it was her own.

The plague pandemic had finally released its grip. For months, lab researchers had toiled to find an antibiotic that would work against the "superbug" strain of plague. The trials had saved lives, including Ananda's. But that was only part of the story.

She had been so close to death that no one could quite explain why she was still here. Her parents looked at her with wonder, like she was Lazarus out of the Bible, risen from the dead. They had taken turns sitting with her for the first few days, holding her hand, stroking her hair. Ananda had lain in their arms, as safe and snug as when she was little. Her mother would cup Ananda's cheek in her hand. "My sweet girl," she'd say. Her father found another copy of the book on Stalin, and as he read it to her, the three of them would talk about things that seemed even more important, now.

Ananda had insisted, weak as she still was, on writing a letter to George, and to George's mother. To finally tell the truth about what happened. She had lied. Now her parents knew. And now George would be believed.

Her father's lab was temporarily closed and research suspended. All of the rats had died, and to Ananda's shock, her father was broken up about it. It was odd to see a glimpse of the real man behind her father—the man who struggled just like she did.

Ananda set the charcoal down. She was still so tired.

Through half-closed eyes she gazed out her window. Simple things seemed miraculous to her now. Soft snow piled like whipped cream. Tender green shoots that peeked through the drifts. A cobalt blue sky.

A car puttered down the road. One of several she'd seen just today. There had been a slow return to life in the city, just as a seed awakens after the long winter.

Something flickered below her window. Squinting, Ananda leaned forward, her hand on the glass. Near the road sat an evergreen. The snow around it was pristine, except for a small trough that had been plowed through it. A small, rat-sized trough.

The Great & the Small

A flick of grey and white. A flash of pink tail. Too fast for her to clearly see.

Carefully, Ananda climbed to her knees, trembling from the strain. She leaned on the windowsill.

Could it be? There…it was him! Tommy.

He sat up in the snow on his haunches, swaying his nose back and forth as if looking for something.

Her breath fogged the window. She rubbed at the glass, and his black eyes darted toward the movement. She was crazy, almost certainly crazy, but she could swear he looked straight into her eyes.

CHAPTER SIXTY-ONE

*"The dead shall live, and those who were killed shall rise again.
Awake! Give praise, all who live on earth."*

Friar Johann von Winterthur, quoting Isaiah, Germany, 1348

When Fin arrived back at the burrow, Zumi was sitting, grooming herself. She looked up. "Everything okay?" she asked.

"Yes," he said. "Everything is fine now."

"Good," she said. "I'm glad."

They left the burrow and travelled toward the market. There was a shift in the air. Though it was still cold, the buds on the trees seemed plumper, and anticipation clung to every seed.

About the Author

A.T.Balsara lives in Ontario, Canada, with her husband. She is the proud mom of two adult daughters, two dogs, two cats, and two hives of bees. She writes and illustrates for children and young adults.

To learn more about her, visit:

www.torreybalsara.com,

https://facebook.com/
AndreaTorreyBalsaraAuthorIllustrator

https://www.twitter.com/torreybalsara/

About the Artwork

The illustrations in this story were done digitally by the author, using Corel Painter on a Wacom tablet. All the illustrations are original, with the exception of the following:

Page 105: *Dance of Death*, found in the *Nuremberg Chronicle*, 1493.

Page 118: *The Plague*, by Marcantonio Raimonda, c. 1515-6 (with rats added by the author).

Page 192: "Death Taking a Child" from the Dancing Death series by Hans Holbein the Younger, engraved by Hans Lutzelburger, c. 1526-8.

Acknowledgements

First and foremost, I want to thank my husband. Nav, you believed in me before I believed in myself. I could not have done this without your patient, loving support. You are a constant example to me of what it means to be a truly successful human being. I am the luckiest of women to be married to my best friend.

To my daughters, Katie and Mehra. Katie, your faith in me and enthusiasm for all things mom continues to humble me. So generous with your editing advice and writing expertise, you astonish me with your resilience, depth, and zest for life. Mehra, your patience and support through this has been invaluable. You posed for me without complaint—stooping over pairs of socks that were stand-in's for Fin, laying on the ground while pretending to be attacked by plague-ridden rats—as I snapped reference photos from fifty different angles. And thank you for sharing my joy when I was finally done, buying me a book of cartoons (Gary Larson!) and a celebratory coffee.

To my parents, who taught me to search for truth, and who took me and my siblings through the Dachau concentration camp museum, where the seed of this book was planted. Thank you for teaching me that although there is darkness, there is also light.

To my sister Michele, who was the first to see that I had a story to tell. Thank you for encouraging me to write, and for your mentorship and love over the years.

To Marianne Ward, my first editor who helped me get this story to a publishable state. Thank you for your enthusiasm and belief in this story. Without your help it would still be languishing in a drawer.

To Ellie Sipila at Common Deer Press, a gifted book publisher, designer and editor, who also happens to be an awesome (and funny!) human being. Only Ellie knows who Gary really is. Thank you for loving this book as much as I do and for joining me in the weirdly wonderful world of rats. Your creative insight, vision, and expertise has caused this story to be raised to a higher level than I could ever have done on my own.

The Black Death, translated and edited by Rosemary Horrox, published by Manchester University Press, had a huge impact on this book. The eyewitness accounts of the 1300's scourge of the Black Death were both harrowing and heartbreaking.

Stalin: The Court of the Red Tsar, by Simon Sebag Montefiore, published by Alfred A. Knopf, provided me with the insider view of what it was like to be in close proximity to a charismatic, mercurial, insecure man who had the power of life and death over millions.

And finally, to Frodo, my little rattie. You were never supposed to come home with me that day at the pet shop. I was only doing research, after all. But when you snuggled into my palm and fell asleep, what could I do? I was helpless against your sweetness. With my car bursting with rat supplies, a huge cage, and you, my four-legged guide into this new world, I was ready to write.

91200553R00161

Made in the USA
Columbia, SC
18 March 2018